Totally

Darkest

Sure Mastery
Unsure
Sure Thing
Surefire

Re-Awakening

What's Her Secret?

THE THREE Rs

ASHE BARKER

The Three Rs
ISBN # 978-1-78184-682-7
©Copyright Ashe Barker 2014
Cover Art by Posh Gosh ©Copyright 2014
Interior text design by Claire Siemaszkiewicz
Totally Bound Publishing

This is a work of fiction. All characters, places and events are from the author's imagination and should not be confused with fact. Any resemblance to persons, living or dead, events or places is purely coincidental.

All rights reserved. No part of this publication may be reproduced in any material form, whether by printing, photocopying, scanning or otherwise without the written permission of the publisher, Totally Bound Publishing.

Applications should be addressed in the first instance, in writing, to Totally Bound Publishing. Unauthorised or restricted acts in relation to this publication may result in civil proceedings and/or criminal prosecution.

The author and illustrator have asserted their respective rights under the Copyright Designs and Patents Acts 1988 (as amended) to be identified as the author of this book and illustrator of the artwork.

Published in 2014 by Totally Bound Publishing, Newland House, The Point, Weaver Road, Lincoln, LN6 3QN, United Kingdom.

No part of this book may be reproduced, scanned, or distributed in any printed or electronic form without permission. Please do not participate in or encourage piracy of copyrighted materials in violation of the authors' rights. Purchase only authorised copies.

Totally Bound Publishing is an imprint of Total-E-Ntwined Limited.

If you purchased this book without a cover you should be aware that this book is stolen property. It was reported as "unsold and destroyed" to the publisher and neither the author nor the publisher has received any payment for this "stripped book".

THE THREE Rs

Dedication

This book is dedicated to John, and to Hannah, and to the triumph of optimism over experience

Chapter One

It looks official.

White envelope. It's made of heavy paper, expensive looking. My name and address on the front, and some other words in large, bold letters. I recognize some of the letters. A word starting with 'P' and with a 'v' in it. Probably 'Private'. Not so sure about the other word, that's just a jumble. As if someone simply grabbed a handful of the alphabet and dropped it onto the paper.

But the letter is definitely for me. I do recognize my name, my address. Maybe I should open it, try to decipher whatever's inside.

I put the envelope, still unopened, back on my table. It leans against the cereal packet as I take a sip of my coffee and contemplate it grumpily. It's been two days since the imposing looking white envelope plopped onto my doormat, and I'm no closer now to knowing what the contents might mean than I was when it first arrived. It could just be junk mail. Some organizations deliberately make their rubbish letters look real and important just to trap unwary or gullible people. I like to think I'm neither of those things, but the fact remains I have a letter propped against my cornflakes box which may or may not be important—it certainly looks the part—and it's spent the last two days occupying pride of place on my fireplace taking the piss out of me. It's likely to continue taking the piss for another week, until my friend Wendy who lives upstairs comes back from visiting her sister in the Cotswolds. Wendy does my reading for me when it can't be avoided. Because I can't.

Can't read, don't read. Never really learnt. And now it's too late. Probably.

Childhood leukaemia effectively wiped out the first two years of my schooling. I was nearly eight before a bone marrow transplant finally did the trick and I was eventually pronounced cancer free, but by then the other children in my year were miles ahead of me. They all seemed to be able to read, and I still couldn't. My school did try. They sent work home for me, and a teacher came to see me quite regularly. I was often too ill to listen to her though, and I didn't feel like concentrating. In that cunning, manipulative way that children have sometimes, I soon realized that all I had to do was lie back and close my eyes, look a bit helpless, feeble, pained, and they'd back off immediately.

"Oh, she's tired. Let her rest." My mother was sick with worry about me, and fiercely protective. I milked that relentlessly, idle little slug that I was. Being ill was crap most of the time, but it had its up-side. No one hassled me, and if I didn't want to bother with school stuff, no one would make me. My health was the only thing that mattered—I just had to concentrate on getting better.

And when I was better, school tried again. I had a special reading recovery tutor, they put me on accelerated reading programs, spent a fortune no doubt on my remedial education, but none of it made much impression. I learnt the alphabet, learnt to recognize my own name then to write it. I can string together short words, simple words, and I'm sort of okay at guessing how to fill in the gaps. I've had a lot of practice at that over the years. But it's an unreliable system, I make a lot of mistakes and I completely miss the meaning of most things. I never read newspapers, not even the red tops which I understand are written for people with a reading age of about seven. They're too hard for me. I struggle to understand cooking instructions on food packets, but these days most are done with symbols so that's easier. I can recognize a picture of a microwave, and single numbers are okay. Even double numbers at a pinch, but beyond that I get hopelessly lost. So I'm pretty much unable to read or write anything. Functionally illiterate, is the label they give to people like me, or so I understand.

I'm perhaps slightly better with numbers. I can add up in my head. Adding, subtracting, multiplication—I'm very good at all that mental arithmetic. It's just that I struggle to untangle the lines of numbers when they're written down.

My mother was just so relieved that I was alive, she was prepared to overlook my slow learning. Did I say slow? Of course, I mean I went at the speed of a dead snail. My mother insisted I'd catch up, but she thought I was delicate, and they needed to make allowances. It's true that I had to continue to go back to the hospital on a regular basis for years after I was pronounced clear, for blood tests to make sure there was no recurrence. There never was, and in truth I felt fine.

School wasn't all bad. I loved sports despite my mother's anxiety that I might get over-tired, and I played in the netball team. I was the goal-shooter and pretty good. Nothing wrong with my hand-eye co-ordination. I could draw too, really well, actually. I quite enjoyed the practical aspects of art lessons. I did some nice work, but my art folder was a mess. I recall a lot of red pen in it — the teacher's attempts to set me on the right path, obviously wasted on me.

Overall, my education was limited almost to the point of non-existence. And my initial disadvantages of poor health and laziness turned into embarrassment. The years went by and I made no progress — at least none that I could see — and others in my class moved on to read more and more adventurous books. I saw the Narnia films on the television or at the cinema, I loved Harry Potter and later Twilight, but while everyone else could read the books I could only enjoy the films. While others could use the Internet to find out the information they needed to do their homework, my homework just didn't get done. I was moved into 'special' learning groups, and my school continued to make an effort. But it was half-hearted — I was a hopeless case. I certainly thought so, and I suppose that just clinched it. The best school in the land can't do much with a student who doesn't believe they can learn. By the time I was fourteen or so, they'd given up and so had I. I marked time with netball and art when I could dodge the zeal of the art teacher. She never quite relinquished the task. I left school at sixteen, with no qualifications and all the job prospects of a lettuce.

So now here I am — a twenty-two-year-old cleaner. Ironically, the place I now work, the only place I could manage to get a job at all, is my old primary school. I heard they were looking for temporary cleaners and it seemed better than staying on the dole, so I called in. Luckily the caretaker, Mr Cartwright, remembered me from when I was a gangly ten-year-old with a mop of ginger hair, and was prepared to give me a chance. I daresay all the staff and pupils at my primary school still remember me—I was 'the poorly kid', the one they had to be careful around, the one they had to avoid infecting with any nasty germs. Especially chickenpox.

Mr Cartwright's leap of faith was four years ago, and I've worked hard ever since. I mopped and scrubbed and polished like a maniac, and when my temporary contract was up Mr Cartwright—Dave—was sufficiently impressed to keep me on permanently. So I have regular work, if low paid. And it's enough—just about—to keep me in a small flat as long as I don't eat too much or insist on having the place too warm in the winter.

It's just me these days. For all her frantic worrying about me, my mother herself succumbed to cancer when I was nineteen. It was a shock, she was just fifty years old. I was stunned, I couldn't believe what had happened. And so quickly. It seemed that one day she was fine, just had a bit of a cough. A persistent cough. She went to see her GP and was referred to a consultant. Within days she had a diagnosis of throat cancer, and it advanced so quickly, neither one of us had any chance to adjust. To come to terms. Not that we could have achieved that, no matter how long her illness had dragged on for. Looking back, perhaps, things were mercifully swift, though it didn't feel like that at the time. It just felt horrendous. A mad, headlong dash toward the inevitable end. My mother was admitted to the intensive care oncology ward, and she died within six weeks of being diagnosed.

I got over it. Eventually. Or so I like to tell myself. In reality I had no choice. The Council wanted their three bedroomed family house back—can't really blame them—but they offered me a one bedroom flat on the seventh floor in a tower block. It's not bad, I have brilliant views over the rooftops of north Bradford and on a clear day I can just make out York Minster. Well, I think it's York Minster—Wendy says it is.

So life is relatively untroubled, to the point of boring probably. But I'm safe, secure. I get by.

Then that bloody letter arrives to rock my calm little boat.

And instinctively I know, in my gut I know, that my boat is about to be seriously rocked. What I don't know is how, why and by how much. I can't wait for Wendy—I need to find out. Now. Today. I shove the envelope into my bag to take to work with me later. I'm quite good friends with Sally—Miss Moore to her year five charges. Sally's a classroom assistant these days, but she was in my form at secondary school and also played netball. We got on okay. She knows I can't read and has offered on many occasions to spend some time with me to help with that. She might even be able to do it—she's done extra training as a literacy specialist and works with other children who struggle like I did. Sally's lovely, and if she'd been there to help when I was at primary school, well, who knows? But like I said, it's too late now.

But Sally *will* be able to read my letter and at least then I'll know if it's junk or not.

* * * *

Sally's busy stacking books and sorting crayons as I tap on the open classroom door. The children have just left, and she usually hangs around to tidy up ready for the next day. Gina Simmonds, the Year five teacher, is also there, at her desk, plowing her way through a pile of exercise books. Both heads turn as I hover in the doorway.

"Do you need us out of here?" Gina makes to pick up her stack of blue exercise books, no doubt intending to decamp and head for the staff room to make way for the serious business of wiping down windowsills.

I shake my head and gesture for her to stay. "No, really, I don't want to disturb you. I'll be back later to mop. I just wanted a quick word with Sally. If that's alright." I turn to my friend. "Do you have a minute? Not now, I can see you're busy, but later? Before you get off?"

She smiles at me before turning her attention back to the crayons. "Sure. I'll be about ten minutes. I'll come and find you."

"Cheers. I'll be in the hall probably."

She nods and waves. I smile apologetically at Gina as I back out of the room and close the door behind me. I can't help thinking as I make my way to the school hall, dragging my mop and bucket with me, that Gina, Sally and me have a lot in common. We're around the same age, give or take five years, and we all work together in a manner of speaking, and we're all in the business of helping to educate the next generation. But even so, we're a world apart. This is one of those moments when I bitterly regret my lost opportunities. Maybe I should give some serious thought to Sally's offer.

The lady in question appears as I'm about a quarter of the way through mopping the floor in the school hall. I need to get it ready for tomorrow's influx of little feet, all considerately wearing their regulation indoor black pumps, but nevertheless managing to leave an intricate pattern of scuff and skid marks all over the polished wood.

"Right, what's this about then that you couldn't say in front of Gina?" She settles herself at the end of the hall I haven't got to yet, dumping her bag on the floor before sitting, her back propped against the wall and her long legs stretched out in front of her.

Sally has the longest legs I think I've ever seen. She was always about a foot taller than me, which was useful in netball. I could still out-shoot her though, on a good day. I grab my own battered holdall from one of the benches at the edge of the hall then go to join her. I settle myself alongside her before reaching to rummage in my bag. I pull out the envelope—now slightly less pristine after it's been bumped around in my bag all afternoon—and pass it to her.

She frowns at me, puzzled, turning it in her hands. "You haven't even opened it."

I shrug. "No point." Then, in a sudden and unexpected rush of self-awareness and honesty, I tell her the truth, "And I was scared."

Sally chuckles. "Scared? Why? What have you been up to? In any case, it doesn't look like a summons to me. I take it you want me to open it now?"

I nod. "Yes, please. Put me out of my misery."

Her expression is scornful, but still friendly as she shoves the end of her right index finger under the flap and tears it along the top of the envelope. I wince, it seems somehow like an act of vandalism to ruin that white perfection, and I kept it so safe for two whole days. But the damage is done now, and Sally is extracting the contents. I see two sheets of paper, also expensive looking, and catch sight of a flowing signature on one of the sheets. The writer clearly intended to make an impression — the ink is bright and blue and contrasts sharply with the neat black typed writing covering both pages. She flattens the sheets and starts reading.

"It's from a solicitor. In Leeds."

Right. Probably not junk mail then. I sit quietly, watching her read. A few seconds later she glances at me, clearly surprised, but says nothing. Her eyes back on the letter, she continues to study the solicitor's words, and looks to be concentrating hard. She places the first sheet face down on her knee and moves onto the second page. I lean forward, peering up to watch her eyes moving from side to side as she scans the words. That action, the subtle proof of reading, proper reading as opposed to the pretend looking at the page that I do, has always fascinated me. I don't interrupt.

Sally places the second page on top of the first, and turns to look at me.

"Who's James Parrish?"

I stare at her, perplexed. *James Parrish?* I've never heard of a James Parrish. I shrug. "I've no idea. Why?"

Sally taps the letter with her index finger. "Well, he must know you. He's left you half his business in his will."

I can only blink, totally baffled. This I absolutely did not expect. I'm not sure what exactly I did have in mind, what I did think might be lurking in that posh envelope, but an inheritance from a mystery benefactor? No. No way.

I must have made that last observation out loud, because Sally answers me, "Yes way. And actually, it's more than half. She picks up the first sheet again to double check. "Yes, it says here. '*A two thirds controlling interest*'. Looks like you're someone's boss." She smiles now—her grin broad. She's clearly happy for me. "Hey, get you."

I shake my head in absolute disbelief. "That can't be right. I've never even heard of this James... James what?"

"Parrish," Sally puts in helpfully. "The late James Parrish to be more accurate, who owned Parrish Construction. Sounds like a building firm. Anyway, they're based in Berwick-upon-Tweed. In Northumberland. And this solicitor, Mr"—she turns back to the second sheet to check the signature—"Mr Stephenson, he wants you to make contact with him so he can put you in touch with the executor of Mr Parrish's will. Apparently that's a Mr Cain Parrish. Are you sure you've never heard of this lot? Some long-lost, distant relatives or something?"

For reasons I'm not entirely sure of and not about to analyze now, I'm starting to panic. This is just so bizarre. I shouldn't take it out on Sally, but there's no one else handy right now.

"No, I fucking haven't heard of them. It must be some sort of a hoax, a sick joke. Perfect strangers don't leave their businesses to other bloody strangers in their wills. It's fucking ridiculous. Give it here."

Unfazed by my outburst, Sally hands me back my letter, and I tear both sheets right down the middle. I'm about to go for it again, but Sally's hands are on mine, stopping me.

"Honey, I don't think this is a hoax. And if it isn't, it won't just go away because you tore up the letter. At least try the phone number. We can find out if the solicitor is genuine easily enough."

My hands are shaking, and she easily extricates what's left of the letter. She stuffs the four pieces of paper back into the envelope and pushes herself to her feet. She extends her hand down to me as I sit still slumped against the wall of the school hall. I'm dazed, confused and entirely out of my depth.

"Come on. Head's office should be empty by now. We'll call this lawyer chap from there, more private. Then we can have another think."

Unresisting, I take her hand and scramble to my feet. Sally keeps a tight, protective hold on the envelope as we both pick up our bags and make our way along the corridor to the head teacher's office. I shuffle along behind Sally. I'm still reeling as the possible implications start to cascade around my head, crashing into each other. What if it's true? Will I have to do things? Difficult, complicated, papery things? Will I have to tell people what to do? Can I just refuse to take my inheritance? Surely no one can make me…

As Sally predicted, the room is empty. She shoves me into Mrs Boothroyd's vacant chair behind the desk. "Do you have your phone?"

I nod then dig in my bag for it.

"Right." Sally pulls the tattered sheets from the envelope and lays them out carefully on the desk. She grabs a yellow highlighter pen from Mrs Boothroyd's desk tidy container and uses it to color in a row of numbers at the top of the right hand portion of the first sheet. "That's the phone number. It says it's a direct line, so this Mr Stephenson might answer. Or maybe his secretary. Get dialing."

I shake my head. I don't think I can do this.

"You *can* do it." I must have been thinking aloud again, or maybe it was my expression doing the talking for me. In any case, Sally's having none of it.

She uses her best teacher voice and sternest expression to spur me into action.

"Just dial, and when someone answers say you want to talk to Mr Stephenson. And when you get him on the line, just say who you are, and that you've got his letter. And that you're puzzled about why this Mr Parrish left anything to you in his will. That's the truth, isn't it?"

"Yes, but…"

"Yes. So do it. When we've heard what he has to say, we'll think again."

"It's a mistake, got to be…"

"Abigail! Dial the bloody number." Sally has her teacher face on, and voice to match. Feeling not unlike one of her unruly year fives, I give in and obediently start to tap the sequence of numbers into my phone. I have to do it slowly, carefully, but I can manage. After a few seconds, I hear the ringing tone.

At least the number seems genuine.

Barely two rings later the phone is answered, "Good afternoon, Charles Stephenson."

The crisp, male voice sounds very efficient, very — legal. I'm at a loss what to say now, despite Sally's coaching.

"I… I…"

"Can I help you?" Mr Stephenson sounds marginally less official now.

"Hello. Yes, er, I— My name's Abigail Fischer. You wrote to me…" Not terribly articulate. Still, I'm quite relieved to have managed to string a couple of words together.

"Ah, yes, Miss Fischer. Thank you for getting in touch. Yes, you've taken some tracking down, I can tell you."

His tone is becoming chattier by the second. He does indeed sound genuinely pleased to be talking to me. If it weren't for his comment about tracking me down I might even start to relax, just a little. Even so, maybe I can explain—whatever—and all this will be straightened out. Feeling slightly more confident now, I try for assertive, and failing that, I might settle for polite.

"Mr Stephenson, I think you must be mistaken. I don't know Mr Parrish. There's no reason for him to leave me anything in his will. I think you must have got me mixed up with someone else."

Mr Stephenson seems quite unmoved by that prospect. "We don't usually get this sort of thing wrong, Miss Fischer, but I do have some checks I could make with you, if that would reassure you at all?"

"Oh, right. Yes please." *This should settle the matter.*

"Your full name is Abigail Louise Fischer?"

"Yes."

"And you were born in February 1991, the tenth to be exact, at Bradford Royal Infirmary?"

"Yes." My heart's sinking now.

"Your mother's name is—was—Rachel Fischer. I understand she passed away three years ago."

"Yes, that's right."

"My condolences for your loss, Miss Fischer. You previously lived on the Ravenscliffe estate in Bradford?"

"I, yes. We did."

"Then I'm reasonably certain we have the right Abigail Fischer. My client is the executor of the late Mr Parrish's estate, his nephew, Mr Cain Parrish. Mr Parrish—the executor, not the deceased—asked me to invite you to meet with him and myself, at your convenience. Would you be able to come to our offices in Leeds, Miss Fischer?"

Meeting? Executor? Deceased? Offices in Leeds?

Despite Mr Stephenson's amiable tone, I am overwhelmed, seized by a blind panic. I hit the 'end call' button. I drop my phone onto the desk with a clatter and gaze up at Sally who is just putting the finishing touches to piecing the letter together again. She's re-attached the halves of the pages with sticky tape. The result is a bit crumpled, but passable I suppose.

"So, what did he say? Are we in the building trade then?" Her smile is bright, expectant.

Is she entirely mad?

I glare at my grinning, deluded friend, my body bristling with hostility and barely repressed panic. Attack is the best form of defense, I've heard, so I opt for that as a strategy. "No we're bloody not. He wants me to go to Leeds to meet him and some other bloke. The nephew of James Parrish."

"Right. When are you going then?" She's not letting up.

"I'm not." Me neither.

"Why not? What do you have to lose apart from your bus fare? You could go and listen to what they have to say. It might all make more sense then."

I stare at her for a few moments, my sudden rush of angry defensiveness evaporating in the face of the sheer idiotic impossibility of this madness. My elbows propped on the desk in front of me, I cover my face with my hands.

"None of this makes sense, and I can't see how it ever will. I don't know anything about building, or about running a business. And I definitely don't know James Parrish. So no, it stops here."

I glance up at her as Sally opens her mouth to argue again, no doubt to bombard me further with her brand of supreme good sense. I should listen, hear her out. I should take my time, think this through, try to work out why Mr Parrish wanted me to have a share of his business. There has to be an explanation. But if there is, I don't want to hear it. The more cornered I feel, the more stubborn I usually become. It's always been a failing of mine. That and a belief that if I refuse to acknowledge something, tell myself it's not happening, it will eventually go away. It worked with my leukaemia — it'll work on Mr bloody Parrish.

I shove my phone back in my bag and sling it over my shoulder. "Look, I've got to go. Would you mind telling Dave I didn't feel well and had to go home early?"

I don't wait for her answer, but I trust Sally to cover my back at work. I'm out of there, and I deliberately leave the wretched, much abused letter behind on the desk. I want none of it.

Chapter Two

The red light is flashing on my answering machine as I let myself into my flat. Sally most likely. She's already tried to reach me twice on my mobile phone since I dashed out of Mrs Boothroyd's office, but I switched it off. I'm in no mood for more talking, for more sound advice. I ignore the red light and head for my kettle. I need coffee. Good and strong. And sweet.

I drink my coffee while it's still too hot, scalding my tongue in my rush for caffeine.

The phone in my flat rings again as I'm dropping my empty cup into the sink. I let it go to the answering service, expecting to hear Sally's voice telling me to pick up.

"Miss Fischer. This is Cain Parrish. Again. Please return my call. Now. I left my number previously, but here it is again." It's not my friend. This is a male voice, deep, clipped, sounding distinctly irritated.

He reels off a string of numbers, but I'm not listening. No need, I won't be returning his call. I delete the message, and the previous one without even listening to it. So much for Cain Parrish.

He's persistent though. I get—and ignore—seven more calls during the course of the evening. Each time he leaves a message, and each time I delete it. After the second call, I turn my phone to silent, and my mobile stays switched off, just in case.

* * * *

The following morning I get up early as usual. I'm due at school by six-thirty to do my rounds disinfecting the toilets and hoovering the staff room before anyone else arrives and I like to have time for a shower in the morning before I leave. I use the ten minutes or so I spend under the steaming spray to contemplate what to do now, how to extricate myself from this nonsense. Talk about random! None of it makes any sort of sense—the letter, the quiet certainty of that lawyer, the belligerent persistence of Mr Parrish.

I stare at my reflection in the bathroom mirror as I clean my teeth then comb through my long, straight hair. These days, thankfully, the strident color has softened from the carroty redness of my childhood to a more muted blonde with a hint of ginger, which seems more fitting in adult life. Strawberry blonde, I think it's called. My eyes, a nondescript blend of hazel and green stare back at me from the glass. I recognize that look, that expression of apprehension. I see it often enough in my mirror. Today I have good reason. Today I feel cornered, hunted. Tracked down and caught.

With a quick shake of my head, I try to throw off this crushing sense of foreboding. It will get me nowhere. And I really need to get to work, whilst I still have a job. The hours aren't brilliant—six-thirty until nine in the morning, then three o'clock until six-thirty in the afternoon, five days a week, and seven till one on Saturdays. I do have all day free for other things in the week I suppose, so I shouldn't complain. I daresay there must be a queue of people down at the JobCentre who'd happily take my job. They're long days though, and I don't get the school holidays off because that's when most of the heavy maintenance work gets done.

Between nine and three I do my own stuff. I like to draw and paint. Despite the art teacher's copious red pen, I am quite good at it. I spend great chunks of my time at the city art galleries, admiring the exhibitions there and getting inspiration for my own creations. I can draw anything. I only have to see an item or a picture once and I can recreate it from memory. I'd be a great forger, although I'd struggle with the signatures I expect. But I'm not out to fool or con anyone, I just love re-creating wonderful works of art, and I sell my versions at car boot sales over the summer. It helps to boost my income a little, and the customers seem to like my work. Most of what I make gets plowed back to buy canvases, paints and such like—that stuff doesn't come cheap. But my hobby pays for itself with a little to spare so I'm content. Sally keeps suggesting I should be more organized, that I should think about setting myself up as a micro-business. She offered to help me and thinks it would give me a reason to sort out my literacy issues. Somehow I doubt that. Even if I could read and write, there's nothing I'd like less than to do it for a living. I paint for fun, and I mop floors to pay my bills. That's just me, the way I am.

And no mystery legacy from some unknown benefactor is getting in the way of that. My comfort zone might not be to everyone's liking, and Sally clearly thinks I could do better, but if I wanted excitement and challenge, I'd take up bungee jumping. I pour strong coffee down my throat and I'm headed out of the door by just turned six, ready to apologize to Dave for my abrupt departure yesterday.

* * * *

Dave's fine about it, tells me not to worry and hopes my stomach has settled down again now. Not a chance, but I don't burden him with that. I promise to make up the time, and get stuck into the staff toilets.

It's monotonous work, and I can't help turning the recent series of bizarre events over in my head as I pour disinfectant down the U-bends. Whether I like the idea or not, it seems I actually do now own something. And it occurs to me that it might be a something I could sell. I definitely don't see myself in the building trade, but maybe I could raise some funds to enable me to do what I really want with my life. Sally's words have not been entirely wasted on me—I do sort of like the idea of turning my hobby into a business. Perhaps this windfall might offer the route to that. With some money behind me I could hire an admin assistant, get someone else to do the paperwork and place adverts and such like. If I could sell more stuff, maybe on the Internet or by hiring space in other people's shops, I could build my bespoke portrait enterprise—go from being a hobby artist to a professional one. I could do what I love, and maybe make a living out of it. It would be good to try, surely, and now perhaps I have the means

At quarter past nine I'm headed out of the school gate again, my rucksack containing my sketchpad and painting gear slung over one shoulder. I'm still flirting with the tantalizing notion of self-employment and debating with myself where to spend the day. Should I check out the permanent Hockney exhibition at Saltaire? Or perhaps I could head for Cartwright Hall where, according to the promotional video they have running on a loop there, they have mostly British art from the nineteenth and twentieth centuries. They usually have something a bit more contemporary too. Even though I've seen both galleries many, many times, I still love those places. The calm, quiet, contemplative atmosphere is just what I need today to help me think. I finally settle on Cartwright Hall as I head for the bus stop.

"Miss Fischer?"

The deep, male voice startles me. *Did I forget something?* I turn to see who called me, but the school forecourt is deserted. The driver's door of a black van parked just outside the school opens. I'm standing right alongside and instinctively step back to let the emerging driver pass me on the pavement. I'm still looking around to see who called out.

"Miss Fischer, we meet at last. You've been avoiding me."

I lurch around to face the driver of the black van, who is now leaning casually against his vehicle. He's tall, his hair is dark blond and wavy, maybe a little too long. It brushes his collar, and he's very much in need of a shave as well as a haircut. He's dressed in what I suppose my mother would have described as smart casual, expensive-looking black jeans with a thick leather belt, and a gray shirt unbuttoned at the collar. His sleeves are rolled up, and his arms are deeply tanned. His biceps bunch and shift under the fabric of his sleeves as he folds his arms across his chest. He regards me silently, offering nothing further by way of introduction. He has no need to, I know who he is.

Cain Parrish.

I'm the one to move first.

"Excuse me." I make to step around him, but his hand on my elbow stops me.

He's not rough—I couldn't honestly claim he manhandled me. He just touches my elbow with his fingers, but I jerk away as though he's burnt me.

"I don't know you. Leave me alone." My own reaction scares me as much as anything he might be about to do. He's obviously been stalking me, for Christ's sake. Now I'm determined to get away. I turn on my heel and start marching off in the opposite direction to avoid trying to pass him again. I hear the van door slam shut, then he falls into step beside me. He slips his arms through the sleeves of a black leather jacket, which he must have grabbed from his van when he realized we were going walkabout.

"I want to talk to you, Miss Fischer. We can talk here, on the street, or I could drop you off somewhere and we can talk in the van."

"I'm not going anywhere with you. I don't know you."

"Fair enough. We'll talk as we walk then. I'm Cain Parrish. You and I are business partners, Miss Fischer. Or can I call you Abigail?"

"We're not anything. Please, just leave me alone." I pick up the pace in some ridiculous attempt to leave him behind.

He just lengthens his stride. "Where are we going, Abigail?"

I stop, turn to face him. My heart is thumping in my chest, my breath catching in my throat. This man frightens me. He's been nothing but polite, but he terrifies me nonetheless. His size frightens me, as does his obvious strength. He's affluent as evidenced by his casual elegance, even down to the designer stubble on his chin, and that unsettles me. But most unnerving of all is the fact that no matter what I say or do, he's pursued me relentlessly, first through his solicitor, and now in person. He wants something, and he's determined to have it.

"Can I buy you a coffee?" He gestures with his head across the road to a small transport cafe. I've had bacon sandwiches from there occasionally, and they do a decent mug of Nescafe. Seeing no realistic alternative, and preferring the relative safety of a public place since I seem unable to shake him off, I nod. He reaches for my rucksack, still dangling awkwardly from my right shoulder.

"Here, let me help you with that."

And before I know it he's escorting me across the road, his right hand once more on my elbow and my rucksack dangling from his left. He opens the door to the café and stands back to let me go in first. Inside there are only three tables, and two of those are taken by burly workmen enjoying their greasy spoon breakfasts. Mr Parrish motions me toward the one remaining table, and I take my seat. He drops my rucksack onto the chair next to me.

"Coffee?"

I nod.

"How do you like it?"

"Strong please. With milk and three sugars."

His eyebrow quirks at the mention of three sugars, but he makes no comment. He goes to the counter to order our drinks, and I contemplate grabbing my bag and making a run for it. I abandon that thought—I wouldn't get more than a few yards, and I have an uneasy suspicion he'd have no qualms about rugby tackling me to the ground. He seems determined to have his say.

A couple of minutes later, he's draping his jacket over the back of the seat and shifting my bag into the seat opposite. The seat next to me is now free and he eases his long legs under the table, effectively boxing me in. I'd have to climb over him to get out. He shoves my coffee toward me, and I pick up the mug to sip slowly. It's as good a reason as any not to have to talk.

"Well, it's obvious what James saw in you. I'd happily fuck you myself if our circumstances were different. What attracted you to my uncle though? Or are you just a greedy little gold digger?"

My companion is obviously feeling chatty. I already knew that, he's gone to considerable trouble to engineer this conversation with me. Still, his opening line took me by surprise.

Shocked at his crudeness and stunned by the implication of his words, I put my mug down on the Formica table with a splash and a clatter then make to get out of my seat. If he wants to insult—or proposition—someone, he can look elsewhere.

"Sit down, Miss Fischer, you're going nowhere."

"I bloody well am. This conversation's over." I'm on my feet now, and reaching across the table for my bag.

He makes no move to stop me. Indeed, he makes no move at all. He just sips his coffee—black, I notice—and waits for me to get tired of glaring at him from my lofty height of five foot four. We're drawing some puzzled stares from the other tables, but no one seems inclined to intervene. Yet.

"Excuse me, please. I want to get out." I try for a note of firm resolve, a tone that says 'you don't scare me, you can't bully me'.

He's clearly unimpressed. "Sit down, Miss Fischer. People are looking at you."

Faced with a choice of clambering onto his lap or sitting down again, I sink back into my seat. Cain Parrish nonchalantly uses a paper napkin to mop up the spilled coffee on the table in front of me, before handing my mug back to me.

"Right, where were we? Ah yes, I was just asking you how you've managed to con my uncle out of his business. *My* business."

I glare at him, not deigning to answer. He shrugs.

"I have all day, Miss Fischer. And the coffee here's not bad."

Well, that's true at least, worse luck. I pick up my mug and take a couple more sips, ready to wait him out. Eventually though, I'm the one to break the silence.

"I didn't know your uncle. I never met him. I've no idea why he put me in his will. If you think the business should be yours, you're welcome to it. I want nothing to do with you, your solicitor, your building firm. Nothing." *There, that should be clear enough.*

He drains the last of his coffee before replying, "It's not that simple, though, as I think you very well know." He dumps his empty cup on the table then leans to one side to reach into the pocket of his jacket. He pulls out an envelope, this time a thick brown one, and tosses it onto the table in front of me. "I daresay you're familiar enough with the terms of my uncle's will, but just in case you need to refresh your memory…"

Nothing on God's green earth is going to compel me to take that document from the envelope and make a complete fool of myself in front of this infuriating and terrifying stranger. I glare at the offending article then shove it back at him.

"I'm not familiar with the will, and I'm not going to be. I have no interest in any of it. None at all. Now please, let me go. I have things to do even if you don't." Again I reach for my bag, and again he stays in place, blocking my way.

I try again, abandoning all thoughts of using my inheritance as a stepping stone to my own future. "You can have it. I'll sign whatever you need me to. I never asked for anything from your uncle. How could I? I never even met him. It's yours, all of it."

His eyes narrow, and despite the relative safety of being among other customers, I find myself backing away the two inches or so available before my shoulders hit the wall behind me.

"You can't give your share of the business away, and you can't sell it. Except to me. And there's no way I'm paying you a fucking fortune for what's rightfully mine." His tone is hard enough to split rocks as he delivers his salvo.

His icy composure is definitely slipping. And even though he intimidates me, I can't help bristling. Who is he to tell me what I can and can't do?

"Who says I can't give it away? If it's mine like you say it is, I can give it to the bloody cat's home if I want." I'm still unnerved by this whole mad episode, but now he's started to really piss me off as well, and my stubborn streak is emerging. I could get myself into some real bother here, but I'm on a roll and there's no stopping me. "For the last time, I didn't ask for it, I've no idea why your uncle left it to me and I don't want it. If it's rightfully yours, then fine, enjoy it. Now, I really must be going. Either you shift, or I start screaming."

The vile man just smiles at my threat, but the smile is cold and doesn't reach his eyes. He's playing with me, and he's winning because I'm losing my cool now and he's icy calm.

"Do please feel free to scream, Miss Fischer. And when you've finished, I'll still be here, and so will that." He nudges the brown envelope with his finger. "It seems I'm fucking stuck with you, at least for now. So you can stick your fingers in your ears and whistle all you like, you can hang up on my solicitor and you can try to run away from me, but none of this is going away. So the question now is—how am I going to deal with you? And I should make it clear, Miss Fischer, that I'm getting pretty pissed off with your lies. And with your bloody attitude. I want to talk to you, that's all. I've tried polite, so what's next?"

Polite! On what planet would that gold digger remark be considered even vaguely polite?

I stare at him, trying to gather my wits. His thinly veiled threat is not lost on me, although he has yet to elaborate on 'what next'. And whilst I have a temper, I also have a perfectly functional instinct for self-preservation and I know I can't push him much further. I need to end this, persuade him to let me leave so I can think this whole thing through. It's also obvious that there's something I really need to know about in that will, so I'm going to need to take a copy of it to Sally as soon as possible. I take a couple of steadying breaths.

"You've not been polite, Mr Parrish. You're trying to bully and insult me, you've called me a liar, and worse. If that's your idea of 'talking', I'm not impressed so far." I can hear the slight tremor in my voice as I answer him. I wonder if he can, and if so, will he take advantage of my weakness?

He draws in a long breath, lets it out slowly. Then, "You're right, Miss Fischer. I apologize. Would you prefer to talk to my solicitor then—he's very polite?"

I glance at him, not sure if that's another veiled threat, this time of some form of legal action, although what on earth he might want to accuse me of is beyond me. I need to take the heat out of this if I can, get myself some time to think, to understand and to re-group.

"Mr Parrish, I assure you I'm as bewildered as you appear to be. Could I keep this for now"—I pick up the brown envelope—"and read it later? I'll phone you when I've read it, and we can talk again if we need to."

At first I think he's about to refuse. Maybe it's the only copy he has and he thinks I'm going to burn it or something. But then, he nods. "All right. That's your copy in any case. And make no mistake, we *will* need to talk again. You have twenty-four hours, then if I don't hear from you I'll be coming to look for you. You really don't want me to have to do that."

Another threat. I don't care for this habit he's forming and he needs setting straight.

"I said I'll phone you, and I will. You have my word." I lean across the table to shove the envelope into my rucksack, then turn to Mr Parrish, my hand outstretched. "Until tomorrow, then."

At first I think he's not going to shake my hand. He's gazing into my eyes, and I'm struck by the deep dark gray of his as he seems to be assessing, gauging my trustworthiness. I hold my breath. If he refuses to accept my promise and let me leave, I have no way that I can see of finding out what that will says about me. Long moments pass, then suddenly he seems to decide in my favor. He takes my palm in his and squeezes it lightly. His handshake is warm, firm and over far too quickly. He may be overbearing and arrogant, but his touch makes my toes curl. How very odd.

"Tomorrow, Miss Fischer. Now, can I drop you anywhere?"

I stare at him, startled by the abrupt shift. "What?"

"You were headed somewhere before I waylaid you. Can I offer you a lift?"

I shake my head. "No, no thank you. I'm fine. I'll get the bus."

He smiles at me, and this time it does reach his eyes. He's dazzling, and my toes curl again. Cain Parrish can ooze charm when he decides to turn it on.

"Please, it's no trouble. Where would you like to go?"

Well, since he's offering so nicely now, and perhaps because the moisture gathering in my pussy is addling my brain, I agree, "I was going to Cartwright Hall, actually. It's an art gallery. In Lister Park. And yes, a lift would be nice. Thank you."

His eyebrows rise slightly at the mention of an art gallery, but he makes no comment. Instead he reaches for my bag and stands up, once more stepping back and gesturing for me to precede him. He does have good manners, when he chooses to show them off. And the most gorgeous eyes.

The short drive to the park gates is passed in companionable silence. Mr Parrish pulls up and reaches behind my seat for my bag. He hands it to me as I open the door. He starts to unfasten his seatbelt, and apparently intends to come around and help me out. I quickly assure him I'm fine and scramble down onto the pavement.

"My number's on your answering machine." He glances at his watch. "Twenty-four hours then. I expect to hear from you by ten o'clock tomorrow morning."

I nod and thank him for the lift. His tail lights are just disappearing around a bend in the road as I remember I deleted all his messages. I don't have his phone number.

Chapter Three

I think it's fair to say the calming effect of Cartwright Hall was entirely lost on me today. I wandered the familiar hallways, admiring my usual favourites then ate my lunch as I so often do perched on one of the padded couches arranged down the center of the long gallery. My mind was a blank. Or maybe it was a swirling mass of disjointed impressions and half-formed questions. An image of flexing biceps and glittering slate-gray eyes kept flashing across my consciousness, and all the while I knew that tomorrow would bring an angry Cain Parrish back to my door.

I promised, and now I might not be able to keep my promise. I don't have his number so I can't phone him. I can't look his number up. I do know the name of the building firm he owns. We own. But no contact details unless those are mentioned in the will. If not, maybe Sally could find him from the phone book for me. But not all numbers are listed, I know that. *Shit!*

By two thirty I'm on the bus heading back to work, though my thoughts are a long way from polish and disinfectant. By five to three I'm stationed outside the year five classroom, every bit as eager for the bell to go as any of the children laboring over their Ancient Egypt topic work. At three o'clock, even before the buzzer stops, they're filing happily past me, pharaohs forgotten as they head for the cloakrooms. I absently fall in alongside Sally as we escort her noisy charges there, and see them safely into their coats. These are ten-year-olds, so don't need help buttoning and zipping, but there's always the chaos of lost shoes and missing book bags to sort out. But five frantic minutes see the cloak room emptied, and we sit down together on one of the tiny benches under the coat hooks.

"I'm sorry I ran out on you yesterday."

Sally looks at me, her expression impatient.

"And I'm sorry I didn't answer your calls."

Again, that look.

"I should have listened to you…"

She's had enough. "For fuck's sake, Abbie, what happened? I can tell by your face something's been going on, so quit all the grovelling and tell me."

"He came. Here. Mr Parrish. Cain, the nephew. He was waiting outside when I finished work this morning."

Sally's face is incredulous. "Shit! Here? What happened? What did he have to say?"

"Well, I think it's fair to say he's not best pleased with how things stand. He seems to think I've somehow managed to con his uncle into leaving his business to me. I told him I'd never even met the old guy, but he's having none of that. Pretty much called me a liar."

"Bloody hell, the prat."

I stop, flatten my lips thoughtfully. 'Prat' would not be my description of Cain Parrish, but I can see where she's coming from. I continue, "Yes, well, I told him he could keep his business, I wanted nothing to do with it. And this is where it gets really weird. He said I couldn't give it away, and I could only sell it to him. But he won't buy it because it's rightfully his anyway. Apparently it's all in his uncle's will. He was convinced I knew all about the will, what it said."

"And of course you don't. How can we find out then?"

"Ah, well, that's easy. I have a copy of the will. It's here." I dig into my rucksack and pull out the brown envelope. I hand it, still unopened, to Sally. I was hoping you'd have time to look at it and tell me…"

Sally grabs the envelope, her eyes gleaming with curiosity now. Mine too, I daresay. However unwelcome all this might be, it's certainly intriguing.

"Too bloody right I will. Not here though." She glances around the empty cloakroom, as if expecting to spot some dawdling year five still tying his laces and eavesdropping on us. "No, for this we need wine. And pizza. And probably Ben and Jerry's ice cream too. What time do you finish?"

"Six. I'll be home by half past."

"Right. I've got some stuff to finish off back in my classroom, but I'll be at yours by half-six then, with all the supplies."

I smile. I might well have slipped into some parallel universe where dead builders leave their property to perfect strangers, but in my experience there are few things that can't be put right by a generous helping of Ben and Jerry's. Six-thirty it is then.

* * * *

It's only twenty-five past, but already Sally's ringing the buzzer on my door entry system. I buzz her into the building and leave my own door off the latch for her to come straight in.

"Right, cheese, mushroom and pepperoni, two bottles of Chianti and a tub of Ben and Jerry's fish food. How's that? Will two bottles be enough?" She dumps the lot on my tiny kitchen table and levers open the lid of the pizza box. The delicious aroma wafts out, and we both forget about wills and building firms and sexy builders for a few moments as we help ourselves.

Sexy? Where did that come from? I turn that thought over in my head as I munch on my pizza. Sally's busy opening cupboards looking for wine glasses, but I only have one. I insist she has it, and I'll use a plastic cup. As soon as we're both supplied with the essentials, she launches in.

"Right, I had a quick look through while I was waiting for the pizza. I'm no expert, you know that, but as far as I can make out, there's no question this old Mr Parrish, the uncle, meant you. No mistaken identity. The will gets your name right, even down to the dodgy spelling of Fischer. He knew your mother's name, where you lived as a child, your age. So, my love, you definitely own a sixty-six percent stake in Parrish Construction, based in Berwick-upon-Tweed, Northumberland. And if I remember my geography, that's near enough on the Scottish border."

Parrish Construction. Northumberland. Scottish border. Could this get any more bizarre?

"Does the will give the address, or the phone number?"

"Why? Are you thinking of popping round to check out your property?"

"No, don't be silly. It's bloody miles away and that suits me. I'm staying as far away from it as I can. But I promised I'd phone Cain Parrish tomorrow. When I've read the will and decided what to do. He left his number on my answering machine, but I deleted it."

"Ah, right. Well, I don't think there are any phone numbers on there, but old Mr Parrish's address is, and so is the address of Parrish Construction so we'll be able to look them up in Yellow Pages. Do you want me to do that now, or shall I tell you what else this will says?"

"The will, please."

By mutual but unspoken consent we clear a space on the table and Sally produces the envelope from her handbag. She extracts the heavy paper, several sheets of it, and lays the will flat on the table. She flicks over the first two pages.

"All that early stuff is about old Mr Parrish being of sound mind, and about the executor—who is your Mr Cain Parrish, by the way. You and he are the only beneficiaries. He gets the old guy's house, any money, stocks and shares, his gold Rolex watch and thirty-four percent of the business. And you get the other sixty-six percent. There are conditions though." She turns over another sheet, and her eyes flick back to mine.

Here it comes. I sit back, my eyes on hers, and wait.

"You're not allowed to dispose of the business, whether for consideration or not…"

"For what?"

"Money. Consideration means money here. Your Mr Parrish was right, you're not allowed to sell, and you're not allowed to let someone have it for free…"

"He's not *my* Mr Parrish."

"Whatever. For the next five years, the only person you *are* allowed to sell to is him, and then he would have to pay you the full market value of your two thirds share, as assessed by an independent valuer."

"I see. No wonder he's pissed off. He must have expected to be the outright owner, and suddenly he's saddled with me. Five years did you say?"

She nods, glancing back at the will for confirmation.

Suddenly an idea occurs to me. "He could buy my share, and I could just give him his money straight back, surely?"

"Nope. Uncle James thought of that too. You're specifically required not to make any gift or donation to any individual or organization in excess of one hundred pounds for a period of five years from the date of his death. And you can't forgo your entitlement to two thirds of any income generated by the business. Unless he buys you out, he has to pay you twice as much as he pays himself from any profits. Obviously his lawyers thought of everything and wrapped this up pretty tight." She tilts her head thoughtfully. "It looks to me as though you and your Cain are a jolly little twosome, at least for the next five years. No wonder he's grumpy."

"He's not..."

"Not your Cain, I know. But still. Five years." She leans back and reaches for another slice of pizza.

Me, I need some wine.

* * * *

Half an hour later, we've finished the pizza and most of the ice cream. We're contemplating opening the second bottle. Sally has consulted the online BT phone directory on her smart phone and come up with a phone number to match the address in the will, so at least I'll be able to get in touch with Mr Parrish in the morning. Though I have no idea at all what I want to say. I'd apologize, but none of this is my doing. There seems to be no way I can simply back off and leave him with his property intact.

I say as much to Sally, but she has a different take on it.

"His property? Not any longer. Actually, I don't suppose it ever was. It belonged to his uncle, who decided to leave a big chunk of it to you. So it's yours."

"He thinks it's rightfully his. He said so."

"Well, as I see it, he's wrong. His uncle was entitled to leave his property to whoever he chose, surely, and for reasons none of us know, he chose you. So your two thirds is rightfully yours."

"And what about morally?"

"I don't know, and anyway, that's not the point. Legally you own two thirds. It's clear the old guy expected you to hand it back if you could, or maybe he thought Cain would browbeat you, so he made that impossible. He knew what he was doing, and he meant it. When you talk to this Cain Parrish again, you need to tough it out. It's *your* inheritance, so don't let him tell you it isn't."

I flinch inwardly at the thought of 'not letting' Cain Parrish do anything, but she obviously catches my expression. "If you've any concerns, Abbie, get a solicitor. Deal with him through lawyers if you have to."

I nod, but I know I have no intention of dealing with Cain Parrish through an intermediary. He might be imposing, intimidating, but once I'd agreed to look at the will and had promised to return his call, he was charming and pleasant to me this morning. I liked him. I think. And now I need to convince him that I haven't somehow wheedled my way into his life. Because for reasons I can't fathom at all, I badly want him to like me too.

* * * *

The ring tone manages just two trills before I hear Cain Parrish's low voice on the other end of the line.

"Miss Fischer. Abigail. How nice to hear from you. And so prompt too. I take it you've had ample opportunity to study my uncle's will now?"

"I— Yes. Yes I have. His terms seem rather..." I hesitate, not sure how to describe the bizarre situation we now find ourselves in. Cain Parrish has no such difficulty.

"His terms are fucking ridiculous. I don't know how you ever got him to make that will, but if you think I'm handing you the thick end of half a million pounds for doing fuck all, you're wrong. I take it you're still denying that you ever met him?"

Half a million pounds!

"What? How much?"

"I had the business independently valued. It came out at seven hundred thousand, including premises, vehicles, tools and equipment, existing contracts, etc. I can let you have the full valuation report, naturally..."

Naturally. Not that it would make a scrap of sense to me.

"That won't be necessary."

"No? Well, that means your two thirds is worth about four hundred and seventy thousand by my reckoning. Not that I've any intention of going into hock to raise the money and buy you out, much as I'd love to see the back of you. So unless you can come up with some smart idea, it looks as though we're stuck with each other for the next five fucking years. Nice work, Miss Fischer."

I bristle. I'm not about to take all that same shit he handed me yesterday. "Please don't swear at me, Mr Parrish. And in answer to your earlier question—no, I never did meet your uncle. I never even heard of him before yest..." I was about to say 'before yesterday', but of course I received his solicitor's letter several days ago now. "The first I knew of your uncle was what I learnt from Mr Stephenson's letter. If you're about to accuse me of lying again, then I'm going to hang up now."

There's a silence at the other end, then, "Very well, Miss Fischer. We'll call a temporary truce until this is resolved. I don't think either of us believes this is random, my uncle had some reason for including you in his will, but for now I'll accept that you're as much in the dark as I am. But Miss Fischer, if I later find out that you did know more than you're saying now, you have my absolute promise that I'll put you over my knee and spank your arse. Your bare arse. Hard. Is that clear and understood? Are we proceeding on that basis?"

Now the silence is at my end. I'm stunned, absolutely stunned. Whatever I might have expected him to say, it wasn't that. I'm outraged. But not nearly as outraged as I really ought to be. A bare bottom spanking? He wouldn't. Couldn't. Could he?

And above all, how the hell could he have known? I've never shared my fantasies with anyone. How did he know just what to say to set my toes curling again, and, in my delighted anticipation, cause my knickers to moisten. No one has ever spanked me, my mother would never have countenanced such a thing for her delicate little flower. But as a big girl I've harbored my secret ambitions, though I've never had the courage to seek out a way of fulfilling them. And if I had, I would never have chosen a man like Cain Parrish to spank me. He's too, too...

Too everything I'm afraid of.

"Miss Fischer, are you still there?" His tone is hard.

It occurs to me again that he could shatter concrete with that voice. I shiver, but not from the cold.

"Yes. I'm here. I was just..."

"Are my terms clear so far?"

I hesitate, but only for a few seconds. "Yes. Yes, they are clear. We can proceed on that basis." I almost add 'Sir', but manage to stop myself.

"Good. Let me continue to explain how our—association—will work then."

Is that a hint of relief in his voice now? And does he have more to say to me about spanking?

"I'm not buying you out, and you know by now that you can't sell to anyone else. Under the terms of my uncle's will I'm obliged to pay you a proportionate share of the profits, but I expect you to work for that. Parrish Construction does not carry passengers. Everyone here pulls their weight, and you'll be no exception. I expect you to work here at our offices in Berwick, full time, and more than that when we're busy. Which is most of the time. Is that clear?"

"But I can't. I have a job. I already work full time."

"Resign. You're needed here."

"But—what would I do? I mean, I can't..." I break off. The list of things I can't do is endless.

"We'll find a use for you." He seems to have more confidence in my abilities than I do.

Yeah. I could clean the offices.

I'm still wriggling around on his hook, desperately trying to think of some way to put him off this mad notion.

"Do you have any trade skills?" He seems unconcerned, ignores the deafening silence from my end.

"I... What do you mean?"

"Electrical? Joinery? Plastering? Decorating? Plumbing? Can you do any of those?"

"No, of course not."

"Why 'of course'? One of my best subbie plumbers is a woman. She likes the work, she's a lone parent and can fit it around school hours."

I shouldn't ask. I know I shouldn't ask but my mouth has developed a mind of its own. "Subbie? What's a subbie?"

"Well, in this context it's a sub-contractor."

In for a penny, my mouth on a solo mission once more, I ask the obvious question, "And in other contexts?"

"Well, Miss Fischer, that's a whole different conversation. One for another time. Please concentrate on the matter in hand." His tone is low, rich and sexy as he responds.

I find myself mumbling an apology. And the struggle not to call him 'Sir' is intensifying.

"Right. What about in the office then?"

Now my heart sinks entirely. I can do practical things, I might even have been able to manage some basic plumbing, work as an apprentice to subbie super-woman perhaps, but work in the office? I've as much chance of flapping my arms and flying from here to Berwick. I'd be an unmitigated disaster.

"No, not in the office. I've never worked in an office. I'd be no good at that."

"You're my business partner now, Miss Fischer, which means you don't pick and choose. Neither do I, we both get on and do what needs doing. I need someone to take charge of the admin side, get our accounts in some sort of order, invoicing sorted, chasing overdue accounts, bank reconciliation. If you're new to all that I don't mind talking you through it at first."

"No, Mr Parrish, this is just out of the question. I have a home here, in Bradford. A job I like. I can't just up and move to Berwick on a whim. I don't mind pulling my weight, helping out if need be occasionally, but there must be something else I can do? I don't see myself behind a desk."

"And I didn't see myself standing quietly by while most of my fucking business was whipped out from under me and handed to some bloody stranger. It seems we all have to adapt, Miss Fischer. How much notice do you need to give at the school?" His tone has hardened again, his words clipped and cold.

"What? And stop swearing at me."

He ignores my complaint. "How much notice do you need to give? I want you starting here as soon as possible."

"But I can't. I've already told you that. I have a flat here, in Bradford. Berwick is miles away."

"About two hundred miles, I'd say. Too far to commute, I agree. Especially as I gather you don't have a car."

Naturally not. How would I ever manage to pass my driving test? I'd never get past the written bit.

He continues, neatly re-arranging my whole life as though I have no say in any of this, "You'll need to move to Berwick. I'll sort out some accommodation for you. You need to talk to your boss at the school and then get back to me with your start-date here. Is that clear?"

"I-I... Yes." I feel as though I've been hit by a steamroller, all my objections crushed. My answer was whispered, as my head now whirls with all the awesome potential for disaster. A strange town, strange bus routes, knowing no one. No Sally or Wendy to ask when I need help. It's going to be a nightmare.

And, just possibly, this could be the most wonderfully exciting, life transforming thing to ever happen to me since my bone marrow transplant. And I know I'm going to Berwick.

"Good. Talk soon then, Miss Fischer." And with a sharp click the line goes dead. He's gone.

Chapter Four

A week's notice. That's all the school is entitled to. They pleaded with me to stay longer, until the half-term break perhaps which was only three weeks away. I could have told Cain I couldn't up sticks and move to Berwick until the school holidays, insisted I was contractually committed or something, but I don't feel comfortable lying to him. He was quite explicit regarding his actions if he were ever to find out I'd been untruthful regarding my prior knowledge of his uncle's intentions, so I don't expect he'll be any more tolerant over this. I explained to Dave, apologetically but firmly, that I could only work until the end of the following the week. So now, just ten days after first meeting Cain Parrish, I'm at my flat, watching out of my living room window as I wait for his van to pull up outside.

I phoned him later that day, after I'd spoken to the school, and told him I could start work a week on Monday. I said I'd come to Berwick the day before, on the Sunday. I intended getting there by train, but he insisted on coming to pick me up, and said he'd drive down to Bradford on the Saturday to help me pack up any stuff I insisted on bringing with me. It seems there's a small flat over the firm's office. It's furnished and Cain says I can have the use of it until I decide where I want to live longer term. I'm assuming I'll be coming back to Bradford eventually, so I'm reluctant to give up my tenancy here, but I may need to. There's no point, after all, paying rent for an empty flat. And it could be as much as five years, unless I can find a way out of this.

I spot the van driving up the central avenue toward my block right at the top. I recognize the red and gold lettering on the side, though I can't actually make out what it says. The firm's name, no doubt, but there looks to be more than that. I feel a biting frustration that I can't read it for myself, a frustration that's been growing and eating at me for the last several days with a ferocity I've never been particularly aware of before now. I simply accepted my 'problem' and worked around it. Now I resent it, and I resent the limits it places on me. And most of all I resent the humiliation I know is in store when Cain Parrish eventually rumbles me. I'm good at concealing my illiteracy, I've developed a raft of excellent coping and concealing mechanisms, but up until now, I've never been transplanted away from all that's familiar and expected to take charge of a busy office. For Christ's sake…

The van pulls up in a parking bay at the foot of the steps leading from the front entrance. Cain drops down to the tarmac from the driver's seat and stands for a moment looking up at the block. I watch him surreptitiously for a few moments, admiring his sexy black jeans and white T-shirt, perfectly filled out by a lean, chiseled torso and slim hips. He really is a very attractive man when he's not being rude. Well, there's rude and there's rude, I suppose. I don't like him to call me a liar or a gold-digger, but he can offer to spank me any time he likes.

He knows I live on the seventh floor, and I see him counting the rows of windows. On impulse I open my living room window and wave to him. He waves back, and I think he may have smiled, though it's impossible to be sure from this distance. He points to the door, so I nod and duck back inside to buzz him in.

A couple of minutes later there's a knock at the door of my flat, so I call out for him to come in.

As soon as he enters, it's as though the all the air has been sucked out of the room. My flat is small, but he totally fills it in a way I never have. He dominates the space merely by standing in it. He looks around him, evaluating and assessing. I stand in the entrance to my kitchenette, my kettle in my hand, trying to suck enough moisture into my mouth to be able to offer him a cup of tea.

There's a pile of boxes in the middle of my living room. One or two contain the few clothes, CDs and other bits and pieces I want to keep with me. Most of the boxes, though, contain my extensive collection of paints, brushes, spare canvases and several works in progress. I also have an impressive collection of completed canvases which I'm thinking might appeal to a new crop of car boot sale enthusiasts in Northumberland. Cain's gaze falls on these, his brow creasing as he cranes his neck to see the contents. He crouches alongside one and starts to flick through the canvases.

"These are nice." He glances up at me, waiting for some sort of explanation, more information about the artwork I seem intent on carting off to Berwick with me.

"Thank you. I like to paint. I'm not really very good, but…"

"Oh, I don't know. They look great to me. Are they all your work?"

"Yes. I sell some, when I can. At car boot sales mostly."

"You might not have much time for painting, at least not for a while."

There he goes, not five minutes in my company and he's telling me what I will and won't do. I stiffen immediately, and set my shoulders stubbornly. "I'll make time."

He grins at me, and I get the worrying sense he's actually enjoying my defiance. Deliberately provoking it even. Still smiling at some private joke he seems disinclined to share, he stands up and hoists the biggest of my boxes into his arms.

"Yes, I think you probably will. I'll start loading your stuff while you do whatever you have in mind for that kettle. Black coffee for me, no sugar."

* * * *

The journey to Berwick passes pleasantly enough, given the distance. It's a shortish drive up the M62 to join the A1, then the route is all motorway until we get north of Newcastle. The A1 becomes a normal road beyond that, but still our progress is brisk. Our conversation is amiable, and I get the impression Mr Parrish has decided to play nicely today. I'm relieved. Having given up my job, I'm short on alternative options now, so I don't want to argue with my new business partner if I can help it. And if he goads me, I know I won't be able to stop myself reacting.

Cain pulls into some services at Durham and we both need the loo. He's waiting for me as I emerge from the ladies. "Fancy a coffee? Or something to eat?"

I thank him, and we head for the Costa section of the concourse. Cain gets us both a coffee and some sticky chocolaty concoction to share. He hands me a spoon. "Dig in. We've a way to go yet."

It's heavy and decadent and absolutely delicious. We clear the plate between us. When he's not being rude and confrontational, Cain Parrish can be very, very nice. If he continues to bribe me with chocolate, I could really get to like him.

He offers me the choice of music to listen to on the drive so I rummage in the glove box and shove something by The Killers into the CD player. I recognize the picture of Brandon Flowers on the CD case, so that seems a safe bet. Still playing nicely, Cain nods his approval. We both have a sweet tooth and we share the same taste in music. It's something to work with.

I catch sight of the imposing Angel of the North — that awesome piece of outdoor art towering over the Tyne and Wear landscape — long before we actually get to it. From a distance the haunting outline of the Angel, arms or wings outstretched, is intriguing. Up close it's simply stunning. I love art, in any form. This is the first time I've actually seen this particular masterpiece, I don't want to just sail past.

"Could we stop? I mean do we have time?"

"Of course. We've made good time so far. And we're in no hurry anyway." Cain signals to pull off the motorway and follows the signs to a small parking area. The huge statue is in front of us, just rising up and up from the grassy mound alongside the road, almost as if it's been planted in a field. There's a path leading to it, and a gaggle of people strolling around. I grab my bag and open the van door. Cain says nothing, but there is a thud from his door closing so I know he's coming too.

Up close, the metalwork seems rusty, but I know this is what the artist intended. The real impact of this piece is gained from looking up at it. The ground slopes away downwards so I make my way to the foot of the hill, and turn to look back at the Angel. Moments later my sketchpad is out, and I'm seated on the ground, my pencil moving swiftly across the sheet as I draw the shape of the Angel silhouetted against the bright blue of the sky.

"Most people would take a photograph." His tone has no hint of impatience in it. Instead, he sits down beside me and slightly back so he can watch me drawing.

"Not me. I like to draw."

"I can see that. You're good at it."

"Thanks."

We sit in companionable silence while I finish my sketch. It's a simple enough image, which is probably why it is so beautiful. It doesn't take long. When I finish I pass the sketchpad to Cain for him to look at my picture.

"Mmm, it's good. Better than a photograph."

"It's just different, that's all. I prefer drawings. Later, I might copy it in watercolours."

"That'd be nice too."

I turn to grin at him. "Now you're just being polite. You want to get off, don't you?"

He shrugs, smiling as he hands the sketchpad back to me. "When you're ready. No rush."

Even so, I get to my feet and turn to him. He extends his hand, an invitation that I should pull him up too. I grin, admiring his cheek. And his optimism. I take his hand, and with some effort haul him to his feet. Laughing, we make our way back to the van.

* * * *

I don't know Berwick at all so I've no idea where we should be headed. Still, I'm surprised when Cain maneuvers the van between the pillars of a large gateway and along a gravelled drive lined with thick shrubbery. He parks in front of an imposing double-fronted house.

"This doesn't look like a builder's yard. Why are we here? I thought you were going to drop me off at my new flat." I turn to him, puzzled, but strangely I'm not alarmed by this unexpected turn of events. Cain might be intimidating, and on occasions rather too forceful for my liking, but I feel safe with him.

"There's a problem with the flat. The boiler's broken. I've got a new one on order and I can fit it for you next week. For now though, you'll be in my spare room. Unless you prefer a hotel, of course. There are a couple of nice places in the town center. I can book you in somewhere and you can leave your stuff here for the time being...?"

A hotel? I can't drum up even the slightest enthusiasm for spending hours alone in a strange town, stranded in an impersonal hotel room. A few days as Cain Parrish's guest might be unexpected, but the house looks nice. And more importantly, it looks big enough to allow me to have some privacy if I need it.

"I see. No, no hotel, thank you. This is fine. I'd prefer to stay with you, if you're sure I won't be in your way."

"I'll let you know soon enough if you are. Come on, I'll show you round. If you're still insisting you never met my uncle, then I have to assume you've never been here before." He opens his door and leaps to the ground before strolling round the front of the van to help me down.

I take the hand he offers and glare at him, making no attempt to conceal my irritation at his continued mistrust. "Of course I haven't. This was his house then?" I step down onto the driveway and study the stately frontage of the house, unconsciously imagining it reproduced in charcoal. It would make a nice picture, and I might well spend tomorrow creating it, as it sounds as though I won't be able to do anything about getting settled into my flat.

"Yep. I inherited it when he died. Moved in here myself only about a month ago so the place is still a bit old-fashioned. Needs redecorating, a modern kitchen, that sort of thing. Nothing I can't handle, it's just a case of getting round to it." He's opening the rear doors of the van as he explains, and he leans in to grab the largest of my boxes.

I step forward, intending to help carry my stuff, but he's having none of that. He pulls a key from his pocket.

"This is yours, for while you're here. Could you open the front door please?"

I nod and turn to do as he's asked. I unlock the door then push it open wide for him to carry the first of my boxes through. He strides along the hallway and up the stairs, me following in his wake. At the top of the stairs he turns left along the landing then stops by a door.

"This is the spare room. I think you'll be comfortable enough in here. Could you...?"

I reach around him to open the door, and he marches in. He deposits my box at the foot of a double bed before crossing the room to open the curtains. I stand inside the doorway, looking around at my new — if temporary — home.

It's nice. Very nice in fact. Old fashioned, certainly, but comfortable. Clean, light and airy. Cheerful. This is a happy place, I can feel it. James must have been a very nice man, in spite of his odd habit of writing strangers into his will. My bed is a double, the frame made of solid wood. Oak perhaps. There's a matching wardrobe and dressing table, and a small vanity unit in one corner. It's just a wash basin, with a mirror over it, but it's somewhere to do my make-up.

The room even has a tiny fireplace, but I don't think it's used often. The central heating seems perfectly efficient. The walls are papered in a tasteful pale yellow, and the carpet is gray and yellow, and feels very thick, the pile deep and soft under my feet. I'm tempted to slip my pumps off and sink my toes in, but I suspect that might seem a little over-familiar given I'm only to be here a few days.

"Will this be all right?" He looks at me expectantly, hopefully even.

I nod my agreement. "It's lovely. Thank you. It's very kind of you to put me up like this. I mean, in the circumstances..."

He smiles now, and it's another of those genuine smiles, the sort that lights up his gorgeous face and actually reaches his eyes. "Ah, Miss Fischer, I might not want you in my business, but I've no objection at all to having you in my house. Or anywhere else. Make yourself comfortable while I bring up the rest of your stuff."

He leaves me to consider the exact meaning of his remark as he heads back down to the van. My pussy is dampening, encouraged no doubt by his sensual innuendo. I note this fact, not without irritation. How come he keeps on doing this? I don't fancy him. I don't even like him, well — unless he has chocolate.

Ten minutes later, and all my boxes are neatly stacked at the foot of my bed. Six trips up and down the stairs, and he's not even out of breath. He turns to me, his smile warm still, welcoming. "If you prefer to keep your room clear, there's another spare room across the hallway that you can use for storage if you like. It's the door opposite. My room is two doors down. Bathroom's in between. Now, I'll leave you to get unpacked. Obviously you're welcome to use the kitchen, the lounge, just come down when you're ready. I'll cook tonight, but I expect you to take your turn."

"Yes, of course. Thank you again. And — I don't mind doing the cleaning while I'm here. Sort of pay my way…"

He's half out of the door, but turns to answer me, "No need for that, I have a cleaner who comes in a couple of times a week. Just do your share of the cooking and I'll be happy. And don't worry, Miss Fischer, you'll definitely earn your keep. Till later then." He offers me a brief nod, and he's gone.

* * * *

An hour later, my clothes are hanging in the wardrobe, my few other belongings are neatly placed in the drawers and my boxes of art paraphernalia are stacked in the room across the hall. I might not be staying long, but I don't intend to live out of a suitcase. My bedroom looks out over the garden, which seems to mainly consist of an expanse of grass surrounded by trees and shrubbery. Very leafy. When I open the window, I can hear the faint hum of traffic, but the house is private and has a secluded feel to it despite being close to a main road. It's a nice place, and I can easily understand why Cain chose to live here rather than put the place on the market following his uncle's death. From his remarks when we arrived I get the impression he intends to stay here and make it his over time.

I've always lived in rented property, and that's what I expected would remain the case for me. I never considered any alternative. Now, perhaps, I could contemplate buying my own home. Not somewhere as large as this, of course, but still nice. If I get to like Northumberland I might look around for somewhere here. Or I could go back to Bradford. Either way, I suspect I'll be giving up my tenancy on the seventh floor in a tower block before much longer.

On that thought I decide to explore the rest of this house, or at least the bits of it that concern me. I've already found the bathroom and toilet, made use of those facilities, but now it's time to branch out. Cain said he'd be downstairs, so I head in that direction. At the foot of the stairs, the low drone of a television somewhere is the only clue to Cain's whereabouts, so I try to locate that. I try a door on my right and find it leads to a large lounge. The mismatched sofas look very traditional, over stuffed but comfortable, and I'm sure these are another legacy from James. The huge wall-mounted flat screen television, however, is pure Cain Parrish. The jury's out on the drinks fridge beneath the window — for all I know James might have been fond of a beer. I notice the fridge is empty now. If I lived here I'd make sure it was kept well stocked with crisp white wine.

There's no Cain Parrish in here though, so I step back out into the hallway and close the door behind me to continue my quest. On the opposite side of the hallway, I find a light and airy dining room, again furnished in an old-fashioned style. The large dining table is made of some sort of dark wood, and I wonder if it could be mahogany. When I'm not lurking around art galleries I tend to be at home a lot during the day so I watch a fair bit of daytime television — more than is good for me, probably, but I've seen enough antique programs to have some idea what I'm looking at. The table has carved legs with pretty lion-style feet, and eight matching chairs are neatly arranged around it. There's a sideboard, also part of the same set I'd say. This room looks expensive, classy and dignified, the whole lot polished to a high sheen. Cain's twice weekly cleaner knows her job. I don't get the impression this room is used much, the heating is not on in here, and despite the beautiful furniture, the room has a lonely, excluded feel to it. I step back out into the hallway.

The next room I find myself in is the kitchen. Two things strike me immediately. The first, I don't think I've ever been in a kitchen this large — I'm pretty sure the entire floorspace of my own flat would fit easily in here. The room is more or less in two halves, the business end for cooking, and the sociable end for eating. There's a huge oak table, heavy and squat-looking which totally dominates the eating section. There are four solid-looking chairs scattered more or less around it but at untidy angles. This is obviously why the dining room proper looks so under-used, whereas in here the atmosphere is homely, welcoming, much-loved. The other end of the large space is occupied by a full size kitchen range, one of those trendy white enamelled sinks, a monstrously huge double fronted fridge and freezer, and more cupboards than I can easily count, although I expect some of those will have gadgets cunningly concealed within. He must have a washing machine somewhere hidden in here, a dryer maybe, dishwasher, the lot. Cain said it needed modernising, but I'm not convinced I'd agree. It has definite charm as it is.

The second thing that strikes me is the scent, the aroma of something quite delicious cooking. That mysterious kitchen range is harboring some seriously decent food within its interior, no doubt bubbling and simmering, braising nicely. Promising to tantalize my taste buds before much longer. I can cook a little, but I feel totally intimidated by all this professional looking equipment and the mouth-watering scents. If Cain Parrish uses all this kitchen stuff and can conjure up something that smells as good as whatever is inside the oven, then he clearly likes his food. He knows his way around a kitchen, and knows how to eat well. I suspect tomorrow's fare, left to me, may fall short of expectations. Still, he didn't bring me here to be his live-in cook, so my signature chilli and rice will have to rise to the occasion. Or it can try to. If pressed I can even throw together a half-decent chicken curry.

Who am I trying to kid? I sidle back out into the hall, set to continue my quest to find my host. The sound of the television is louder now, but the dialog seems strange. Sort of constant. I realize it's not a television I've been hearing at all, it's a radio. More specifically, a play or some sort of drama on the radio. I follow the sound along the hall, and in any case there is only one door left to try. This time I'm sure he's inside — there's nowhere else he could be, so I knock. It seems polite. Cain replies, telling me to come in.

It's an office. A small, home office, and Cain is at his desk under the window, something open on his laptop. The sound I've been hearing comes from an old, battered looking radio balanced on the window sill, but Cain reaches to turn down the volume as I enter.

"Please, there's no need. I don't want to disturb you." I hover in the doorway, not sure if he has either the time or indeed the inclination to make small talk.

His quick smile dispels that doubt, and he gestures for me to take a seat. Problem is, there's only one spare chair, and it's already occupied. A large, dark-gray cat is fast asleep on the battered armchair set in the corner, his nose buried between his front paws. He's snoring softly and it seems distinctly rude to even contemplate usurping him. I'm a little uneasy around cats, and this particular specimen is huge. No, I'm not looking for bother. He can keep his chair.

Seeing my dilemma, Cain stands up and shoves his own wheeled desk chair in my direction. "You're right, best not to ruffle Oscar. He's a grumpy old sod at the best of times. Here, you have that. Won't be a sec." He strides from the small room, to return moments later with one of the kitchen dining chairs.

He sets that down in front of the desk, plonks himself down on it and briefly returns his attention to the laptop. The screen goes blank, and I realize he must have closed down whatever he was working on.

I *am* disturbing him, obviously. I try to apologize again and stand up, intending to leave.

"Miss Fischer, please sit down." His tone has an unmistakable thread of authority woven through it, the richness of velvet with a steel core.

I obey without ever questioning for a moment why I should.

"Is everything all right for you? The room? Did you find the bathroom and toilet all right?" His tone has softened now, no hint of his commanding presence of just a moment ago. Now he's friendly, genial, the perfect host.

I start to relax, just a little. "Yes, I did. It's all great. Really. Thank you. I'll be very comfortable, until the flat's ready."

He nods. "Good. Make yourself at home. I put a casserole in the oven, should be ready in an hour or so. I was just about to peel some spuds to go with it. Unless you'd prefer rice?"

I shake my head. He's clearly the authority on all matters relating to food and I've no desire to interfere. "I'm easy, whatever you think…"

He grins, and I'm not sure what I said that was so amusing. He turns back to the laptop, still open on his desk, tapping the keys briskly. Yet another basic skill everyone else takes for granted, but I never learnt. "This set up here links to the office at the yard so you can work from here if that suits you. You might like to go into the office though, meet Mrs Benson." He tosses the brief explanation back over his shoulder as he finishes his task.

I frown at him as he turns to face me once more. "Mrs Benson?"

"Mrs Benson, yes. Phyllis. Works for me four mornings a week, and she worked for James before that. Been with us for nearly forty years. I suspect if I ever come to check, I'll find she's mentioned on the title deeds to the property. Phyllis keeps the office ticking over. She'll be able to show you what needs doing."

"But—I thought you said you had no office staff, and that's why I need to do it?" I see a possible glimmer of a reprieve here. And after all, it wouldn't be right to edge Mrs Benson out of her job. Not after forty years.

No such luck. "Phyllis is great, but she keeps threatening to retire. Apparently she's got it into her head she should be spending more time with her husband now that he's given up work. If you ask me, she'd die of boredom within a week, but there's no talking to her once she gets something in her head. So, I need a long-term solution, and that's you."

"But, surely it'd make more sense to get her an assistant, someone she could teach the ropes to. Then when she retires you'd have someone already trained. Someone who's good at office work..."

Someone who can read.

He smiles at me, another of those 'lips-and-teeth-only' smiles that don't come close to reaching his eyes. "Phyllis *is* getting an assistant. You."

"But I thought you said I'm a partner. The senior partner..."

"So you are, according to dear old Uncle James, God rest him. But that doesn't mean you've the first inkling how to run a construction company. Does it?" He hesitates, as if waiting for me to argue with him.

I'm bristling at his off-hand, dismissive manner and I more than half-wish I'd stayed in my room. But he has a point, and I manage not to argue. Well, not this time.

With a satisfied—and in my view somewhat arrogant—nod, he continues, "So, no matter how big your majority shareholding, you, Miss Fischer, are the junior partner round here in every other way. You'll do as you're told, learn how things work, learn how to make yourself useful, and you'll earn your bloody salary like everyone else."

He may be right about my lack of knowledge, but I deeply resent the implication that I may not do my share of the work. I was lazy at school and look where it got me. Now, I'm a grafter. Despite my good intentions, I can't keep my mouth shut, it seems, when he starts in this vein and I'm straight back on the offensive, "Thank you, Mr Parrish, but I do think I've heard enough now. I'm fed up of you talking to me as though I'm some sort of free loader. I didn't ask to be here. I don't mind working hard, I'll do my share. But I'm telling you now, I'll be rubbish in the office. Mrs Benson'll probably sack me before the first tea break."

His steel gray gaze catches and holds mine, and despite my sudden rush of bravado a moment ago, I feel my resolve shrinking under his stare. He waits a few moments before he replies, "One. If you want tea breaks, join a bloody union. And two, you get on the wrong side of Mrs Benson, and you and I will be discussing spanking again. More than just discussing it in fact. Are you understanding me here?"

I catch my breath and just stare at him. His words were toe-curling enough when he threatened to spank me from two hundred miles away at the end of a telephone, but here, in the same room, sitting just two feet away from me... My knickers are dampening yet again whilst my mouth goes bone dry. Speechless, I grapple with my conflicting responses. I should be insulted, outraged. I should be telling him to treat me in a professional manner. I should be ranting about sexual harassment and threatening him with God knows what dire consequences the law makes available to heap retribution on abusive employers. But I say and do none of that. And he watches me, his lip quirking in an amused half-smile, knowing exactly the effect he's having on me.

Sure enough, "Well, Miss Fischer, I'm guessing from your expression that the prospect of a spanking is not entirely terrifying. I thought maybe not when you didn't protest unduly the first time I suggested it. And we've already established I can't dock your wages. Maybe I'll need to come up with something else."

Still I don't answer, but I'm shifting in my seat, my knees pressed defensively together as I clench my buttocks.

He glances down at my legs, clearly sees my stiff posture, my awkwardness, and his smile broadens. "Panties wet just thinking about it? Oh, Miss Fischer, what am I going to do with you?"

It seems to me perfectly obvious what he's going to do with me—to me—the first chance he gets. The question is, will he get that chance?

And yes, on reflection, I think he probably will.

Chapter Five

We peel the potatoes together, side by side at the huge sink, watched closely by Oscar who has followed us into the kitchen and is now sitting hopefully beside his food bowl. Cain takes the hint and tips some dried food into it. He tops up the drinking water too. The cat crouches over his dinner and starts to chomp noisily as we get on with preparing our own meal.

"I wouldn't have imagined you as a cat lover…" I offer this observation by way of making conversation.

"I'm not, not really. I inherited Oscar. He was James' cat and he's lived here for the last ten years. He's old and bad-tempered, but he mostly minds his own business and we rub along fine by ignoring each other. The deal is I feed him, and he stays out of my way."

"I wouldn't say he's keeping his end of the bargain. He follows you around everywhere."

Cain turns to me, frowning. "No he doesn't…"

I just nod. "He does. He sleeps in your office while you're there and when you came in here, he came too."

"Only because he was hungry."

I shrug. "Well, he's not hungry now."

We both turn to watch the huge old cat pad silently across the kitchen toward a battered old lone fireside chair in the corner. He hops up and makes himself comfortable on the rather flattened cushion there. He regards us solemnly from his vantage point and, apparently satisfied we're not about to get up to any mischief, he shoves his nose back between his paws and closes his eyes. I shoot my best 'I told you so' look in Cain's direction, and return to the potatoes. I wouldn't mind betting the old moggy sleeps on the cushion I spotted on the landing earlier, just outside Cain's bedroom.

"What makes you say he's bad-tempered?" In fairness, although I'm no authority on cats, Oscar hasn't struck me so far as being anything other than mild-mannered.

"He hisses at me. When I stand on him."

"Well, I'd hiss at you if you trampled all over me as well. So how come you manage to stand on him? He's big enough to see."

"He trips me up. All the time. I just seem to turn round, and he's there. Getting under my feet and bloody hissing. What's so funny, and why the fuck are you so interested in a grumpy old cat anyway?"

I shrug, trying not to laugh. *'Stays out of my way'* indeed. That cat follows him around everywhere. I find myself developing a soft spot for old Oscar.

"Just asking… And Oscar's not grumpy. He's just loyal. And he likes you. I can't imagine why."

Cain grabs a vegetable knife and starts to chop the peeled potatoes into smaller cubes. "What do you mean? I'm perfectly likable."

"Sometimes. When you're not threatening to spank me."

Now it's his turn to chuckle. "Threatening, or offering?"

I consider that while I dump water into a pan and place it carefully on top of the stove. He has to give me directions for lighting the gas ring, but soon our potatoes are simmering happily. Cain checks the beef casserole in the oven, gives it a stir then grabs a couple of wine glasses from a cupboard above his head.

"Red or white?"

I seem to remember hearing somewhere that it should be red wine to go with red meat, but I prefer white and say so. He selects a bottle from the bottom of the monster fridge, the sort with a proper, old fashioned cork not a screw top, and deftly twists the corkscrew into it. He pulls the cork out with a lively *pop* then pours us both a glass before sitting down at the table opposite me. He takes a sip, waits for me to do likewise, then goes for the jugular again.

"All this talk of spanking has drawn my attention to what a perfectly gorgeous bum you have there, Miss Fischer. So, will you be tempted to let me leave some hand prints on it, then?"

My second sip of wine narrowly misses going down the wrong way. As it is I'm coughing as I replace my glass, and find myself once more staring at him. Cain Parrish leans back in his chair, perfectly composed as he waits for me to right myself. I make a decent attempt, trying to inject a note of sternness into my voice.

"Don't be ridiculous. I hardly know you."

"Ah, I see. You only let men you know well spank you, is that it?"

"No, I don't... I mean..." Another fortifying sip of wine, but still, with just a few casually suggestive words from Cain Parrish, my composure has fled, never to return, I suspect. This time though, Cain takes pity. He puts his glass down, leans across the table and reaches for my hand. I try to pull away, but his hold is firm. He turns my palm up, and with his middle finger caresses the sensitive heart of my hand.

"Would it be your first time then? Being spanked, I mean. Or maybe you're a virgin...?"

I can only stare, shaking my head briefly. No one has ever spoken to me like this before, or asked me such personal, such totally outrageous questions.

He doesn't press me to answer, but he holds my gaze. I feel like a rabbit caught in headlamps, I couldn't tear my eyes from his if I wanted to. And in this moment I'm not at all sure what I want.

"No? So you *have* enjoyed a nice, erotic spanking before now?" His tone is soft now, seductive.

At last I manage a response. "What? No! Of course not."

"Ah. But you want to."

"I... How...?" I'm stammering, not certain what I want to say. Do I tell him the truth, that no, I've never been spanked but I've wanted to be. But I've never dared ask. And that I'm not a virgin, very nearly but not quite. A few sweaty episodes of clumsy fumbling, however enthusiastic, in my late teens is hardly an adequate apprenticeship for this. I desperately wish I could come up with some witty, sophisticated line that would make me seem more worldly, more interesting and less the gauche girl who last got laid over two years ago and is now dampening her knickers with her own juices just because a handsome man is stroking her hand. But none of that happens. Instead, I just whisper, "Yes, I've thought about it. Fantasized. And no, I'm not a virgin."

He smiles at me, a sweet and gentle smile, absolutely compelling, drawing me in. He continues to caress my hand. I've stopped trying to tug it away.

"This sounds interesting. Delightful, in fact. Have you any other fantasies you'd like to share with me?" His tone is soft, beguiling and very sexy.

I shake my head. "No, not just now."

"Pity. Maybe later then. So, what are we going to do about your yearning to be spanked? I'd love to oblige you. And I think I ought to tell you, I'd really, really love to fuck you afterwards, though I'm not going to insist on that. I'm offering you a free, no-strings erotic spanking, with an optional fuck-fest to follow. Would you like that?"

There's silence, and he waits. The last word here has to be mine. He knows it, I know it.

Is that me? Is that really my voice saying yes? And am I really thanking him for his kind and generous offer. And telling him I'd really like to try the fuck-fest too? I suppose I must be, because he's smiling broadly now, his sexy grin taking on a hint of the distinctly wicked. And my knickers are soaked.

He lifts my hand, drops a kiss in my palm before folding my fingers into a fist. He stands.

"Potatoes are ready. We'll eat, enjoy our wine then get an early night. My room, I think."

Cain makes no further reference to our plans for later in the evening as he serves the meal. He places my plate in front of me.

"Enjoy." His smile is deceptively bland as he takes his seat and picks up his fork. I reach for my utensils, conscious that my hand is shaking and hoping that Cain won't notice. If he does, he's too polite, or wise, to comment. I start to eat, determined to achieve some passing resemblance to cool. As if agreeing to let a man I hardly know spank my bare bottom is a perfectly normal thing to do on a Saturday evening in Berwick.

Half an hour later we're seated at the table, our empty plates evidence of Cain's culinary skills. The meal was delicious, as I knew it would be, but I didn't do it justice. I'm acutely conscious of the gorgeous man who shared the food with me, offering me extra helpings, refilling my wine glass. And when we finished, insisted I remain seated while he cleared the table and made coffee.

Now, he's going to spank me. Really. Truly. And, I suspect, beautifully. Will he use his hand? Will it be across my bare bottom? The skin on my buttocks and the backs of my thighs is tingling in anticipation. He knows it, he must know. Every time he's smiled at me, clinked his glass against mine, every time his fingers have brushed my hand as he's passed me the potatoes or the sugar bowl, he must have felt the heat between us. My imagination may be over-active—God knows I've run this particular fantasy through in my head a time or two, but I'm not dreaming this. Am I?

In the circumstances I feel justified in studying Cain Parrish carefully. After all, we're soon to become much more intimately acquainted. His dark blond hair is swept back from his face, and his teeth are white and very straight. His smile is absolutely stunning, and he's turning the full force of it on me now. His white T-shirt hugs his torso seductively, and his jeans look to me to be bulging ever so slightly behind the zip. Maybe. I hope so.

I wonder if he'll take his clothes off when he spanks me. That would be nice—maybe I could ask him to...

Surely he'll be naked for the fuck-fest. Yes, definitely something to look forward to, among all the other somethings.

As we each cradle our mugs of coffee, his black as usual, mine very sweet and rich from the cream he offered me, he lifts one eyebrow. I'm coming to recognize this as a signal he's about to speak. I wait, expectantly. There's only one place this conversation is headed.

"I promised you my bed, Miss Fischer, but I'm thinking we might start in here. The table would do nicely."

I take a deep breath, then reply in the same matter-of-fact manner, "You mean for spanking me? You want me to lean over this table for you?" I somehow don't think my version is quite so convincing, but I'll lose no points for effort.

He nods, his grin gleaming. Wolfish. "If you would be so kind, Miss Fischer. For me, yes, but for you too. You *do* still want this?"

I nod, but my fragile nonchalance is wrecked by the deep blush I can feel scorching my cheeks. I know he can see it too, maybe he's realizing, a little belatedly, what a naïve fool he's saddled himself with as a house guest-come-fuck-fest partner

Apparently not, as he leans across the table again, this time to cup my heated cheek in his palm.

"Feeling a little shy, Miss Fischer? The first time is exciting, but never easy. Let me help you?"

Help me? I glance up at him, surprised. Under all his brash, tough demeanor, I never expected that. 'Drop your pants, bend over, let's get on with this', now that wouldn't have surprised me. But the tender, sweet way he's caressing my cheek, holding my chin up when I would have dropped my eyes? His own expression is more caring than lustful just now, though his eyes have certainly darkened in the last few minutes. I open my mouth, intending to speak, but I have absolutely no idea what I want to say. What I want to ask him to do is to help me.

He knows though. He releases my face, leans back on his chair. "Come here, Miss Fischer." He beckons me with the tips of his fingers. I get to my feet immediately and walk around the table to stand beside him. He takes my hand and pulls me forward, turning me to sit in his lap.

"Kiss me, Miss Fischer."

To the best of my recollection, I've never initiated a kiss before. And definitely never with such a beautiful man. Are men beautiful? This one certainly is. And enticing. I place my hands on his face, my palms covering his cheeks. The ever-present designer stubble slightly abrades my skin, and it feels sensual, intimate. I flex my fingers, and he smiles at me again, that eyebrow lifting slightly as he waits. I drop my face forward, slowly, and place my mouth ever so carefully across his.

His hands are at my waist, and he makes no attempt to pull me in or deepen the kiss. For now, this is my show, and he lets me set the pace. I'm grateful, it gives me the space to think, to adjust, to melt into the mood. I open my lips slightly, feathering them across his mouth. He holds still, letting me explore, letting me take my time. I have no idea what constitutes 'good' kissing, but instinctively I open my mouth a little wider and use the tip of my tongue to stroke the seam of his lips. He responds to that signal, and I find I can slip my tongue between his lips. He tastes quite, quite wonderful, of coffee and wine, and sweet lust.

I can't claim, genuinely, to have tasted lust previously, but I'm pretty certain this is it. I dip my tongue farther into his mouth, exploring his teeth, tangling with his tongue, loving the way his lips have opened and are now sweeping sensuously across mine as he joins in the kiss. I'm combing my fingers through the soft waves of his hair, and suddenly I'm turning toward him, standing briefly, then straddling him as I'm gripped by a desire to get closer. My loose fitting calf-length skirt is bunched around my knees now, and as I shift forward I can plainly feel his erection under me. He's as aroused as I am, it seems. He drops his hands from my waist, but only to grasp the soft woollen fabric of my skirt and tug it backwards from under me, gathering it at the back of my waist. Now, only my underwear and his jeans separate us, and my pussy is rubbing against his solid length. I'm rocking against him, loving the friction and desperate for more. I want him to...what?

Touch me? Yes. Undress me? Yes, that too. Fuck me? Oh, please...

"Ready now, love?"

He's pulled his lips fractionally back from mine, just enough to be able to murmur the words. I can only groan and nod, before laying my forehead against his. In a few moments I've gone from a blushing, more-or-less innocent girl to a voracious sex kitten. And he's hardly laid a hand on me yet, nor anything else.

"Does the skirt stay?" He asks the question softly.

I lift my head, and he raises his hands to now frame my face. I shrug, not sure what the protocol here might be.

He smiles again, a smile of reassurance and approval, and I feel a serious urge to kiss him all over again. "I'll want you to lose the underwear, but if you prefer, you can just lean over the table and lift your skirt for me. For now. It all comes off later, but by then you'll be feeling a lot less inhibited. I promise."

"I-I think I'll keep the skirt, if that's all right. For now."

"Perfect. And so sexy when you lift it up to bare your gorgeous bottom for me. Am I drooling?"

I smile back, his mix of sensuality and humor just what I need. "No, not drooling. But I can tell you're pleased to see me."

I wriggle on his lap, and he closes his eyes in mock pain. "Have a care, sweetheart. You really don't want me to lose my train of thought here."

He stands, effortlessly lifting me to my feet too. His hand is outstretched, waiting for something. I'm puzzled, but he soon sets me straight.

"Your knickers, please."

"Ah, right. Of course." I quickly reach under my skirt and tug them down, before stepping out of them. I place them in his hand, pleased that I had the foresight to wear a pretty, lacy pair today. And my bra matches—how's that for planning? Or dumb luck?

He nods his approval—whether at my choice of underwear or my ready compliance I'm not entirely sure—and crumples my panties before shoving them into his jeans pocket. "Ask me for them later. If you remember. Or maybe you'll let me keep them, as a souvenir?"

In this moment I think I'd have agreed to let him keep my entire wardrobe, such as it is. He gestures with his head toward the table behind him, moving to one side to allow me to step forward.

"Bend over, lean on the table. If it's more comfortable, you can fold your arms and lay your head on them. Or you can reach across and grip the opposite side. Just whatever feels best for you. And when you're happy, I'd like you to reach down and lift your skirt up around your waist, please."

I feel my courage start to desert me as the moment of truth looms. It's now then. Or never. He sees my hesitation.

"Take your time, love. Or if you don't want to do this, that's fine too. But you've got as far as letting me have your panties, seems a shame to stop now…"

I shove any remaining doubts aside — not that I have any of real significance — along with my modesty, and I lean over the table. Christ, I've been waiting for this as long as I can remember and there's no way I'm backing out. Even so, it's harder than I imagined it might be to reach down and take the hem of my skirt, raising it up to tuck all of the fabric under my stomach. I feel the cool swish as my pale buttocks are exposed and I have to concentrate on remaining still.

His eyes are on me, caressing me. I know it. I'm conscious that he's behind me, not two feet away, and my bottom is bared for him to slap. *Oh. My. God.*

He speaks at last. "Very pretty. And very pale. I think we can make your bottom go a very sweet shade of pink, Miss Fischer. First though…"

He steps forward, and now he's directly behind me. I flinch as he caresses my bottom briefly, but still I don't move from my position. He leans over me, his hands on the table, on either side of my shoulders. My head is turned to one side, and I can feel his breath, warm on my upturned cheek. He leans in to nuzzle my ear, clearly in no hurry to get started. Unlike me.

"If you develop a real fondness for this sort of activity, Miss Fischer, then we'll need to have a proper discussion about safe words. On this occasion though, when you've had enough, you need only say so. Just say 'enough' or 'stop', and that'll be it. I'm going to keep it light, at least at first, but if it's too much you just tell me."

"And what if I want you to hit me harder?"

He chuckles. "Well then, Miss Fischer, you tell me that too. Are you ready?"

I nod and close my eyes. He stands, and my bottom clenches in anticipation. Something tells me this is going to be good.

"You can stop this with a word, whenever you want to. But as an extra failsafe, I want you to count. After each spank, you say the number. When you stop counting, I stop spanking. And if I think you've had enough, I'll stop anyway, whatever you might say or not say. Fair enough?"

Cain's tone is deep, sensuous, and he's stroking my bottom as he explains the 'rules' to me. I'm trying to concentrate, but he's very skilled at distracting my attention. I don't answer him, and it seems that's not good enough.

"Miss Fischer, are you listening to me?" The hand caressing my bottom stills, and he's somehow managed to make sure his fingers have slipped into the furrow between my buttocks. I shift, not sure what I actually want him to do now, at this moment. I want the spanking, but my pussy is almost throbbing with anticipation. Maybe if he were to just touch me…

"Miss Fischer. I want you to count. Okay?" He taps my left buttock lightly with his fingertips, but it's enough to focus my attention, bring me back to the matter in hand, so to speak.

"I, yes. Yes, I'll count."

"Excellent."

He straightens, and I relax, expecting him to resume his massage. Then I scream as the first slap lands, sharp and hard on my right buttock. There's a resounding *slap* as the blow falls, and instinctively I start to stand up. His hand is on the small of my back, not forcing me down but reminding me I should stay in place.

He murmurs in my ear once more. "You're doing so well, and now you know what to expect. You *will* love this, I promise, and I'll make it good for you. Just trust me and let yourself relax into it. Was that too hard, love?"

I gasp, catch my breath, then, "No, no it was fine. Really nice, in fact. It was just—the sound, I suppose…"

"Nice? That's what we like to hear. So, that's number one, then? Shall I continue?"

"Yes. Yes, please." And, trusting him completely, I settle in to enjoy my first experience of erotic spanking.

"Two."

Slap. "Three."

Slap. "Four."

Slap. "Five."

I'm breathing in deeply between each blow, and out as each slap lands. Cain is painting a pattern across my buttocks, alternating between each side and placing each spank just below the one before it. Knowing where each slap is to land makes it easier, although my buttocks are still clenching sharply with each new stroke. I'm not making any other sound apart from counting out loud. Not yet anyway. This is painful, as I expected it would be, the discomfort radiating sharply with each slap. But the sensation is incredibly good too, and the pain is nowhere near enough to make me want to stop. I imagine I could lie like this for ever, just absorbing the tingling, stinging blows, drowning in sensation. It's sort of liberating, something forbidden, but I'm doing it anyway. And absolutely loving it as this man—a man I hardly know—leaves his palm prints all over my bottom. And very soon, he'll fuck me. I hope.

"Nine."

Slap. "Ten."

Slap. I pause, needing to think, to focus, then, "Eleven."

My hesitation was only slight, but it's enough to alert Cain.

"How's it going, Abbie?" He pauses, slap number twelve suspended for a moment.

I mutter my response into my hair, now tangled across my face. "I'm fine. Really. Please, I want more. Don't stop."

"You sure? Open your eyes and look at me, Abbie."

He sweeps my hair away from my face. I nod sharply, but my eyes remain tight shut.

"Abbie, open your eyes. Now."

The tone is gentle, but unrelenting. He means me to obey him, and until I do nothing else is happening. Grumbling to myself, I force my eyelids to part. His face is close, his expression one of care, concern. He's still combing his fingers lightly through my hair, and his touch is absolutely wonderful. I could drown in it.

"How many's that, Abbie?"

I let my eyelids drift closed again, but with his free hand he shakes my shoulder firmly. "I said look at me. How many slaps is that now?"

I open my eyes again, and I'm struggling to focus. My memory seems hazy. I'm not a particularly big drinker, but this feels almost as though I might be a little bit drunk. How much wine did I have with our meal? I shake my head now, trying to clear it.

He asks me again, "How many?"

"I-I don't know. Was it eight? Nine?"

He smiles, his lop-sided grin so sexy that my pussy is clenching. I so want him to fuck me, and soon. I'm not entirely sure what I need, but I wouldn't mind betting he has a good idea. He doesn't disappoint me.

"When you lose count, sweetheart, that's a sure sign it's time to stop. Bedtime?"

I just about manage a slight smile, but he takes that as the agreement it's intended to be.

"Stand up, love." With his hands on my shoulders he gently eases me back into a standing position.

I sway, and he slips his arm around my waist, then suddenly he picks me up in his arms. The fabric of my skirt tightens across my tender bottom and I draw in my breath sharply.

"Is that sore?"

"Not really..." I turn my face into his chest, burying my nose in his T-shirt in a sudden surge of probably belated embarrassment. He tightens his arms around me.

"Liar," he murmurs into my ear. "Your bottom's a lovely deep shade of pink. It's got to smart. Did it feel good though?"

I nod, firmly quashing any pangs of guilt at the naughty brand of pleasure he's so generously given me. "Yes. It was fabulous. It still is."

He heads out into the hallway, and there's no further conversation as he carries me upstairs. He shoulders open the door to his bedroom, and I cling onto his neck when he tries to place me on the bed. He takes the hint and lies down alongside me, responding to my need to cuddle, to just be held right now. I tighten my arms, loving the feel of his palm circling between my shoulder blades, massaging me firmly, soothing, reassuring.

I'm surprised at my reaction. I expected to feel sore probably, embarrassed definitely though I'm managing that pretty well. And maybe a little scared. I've been all of those in the last few minutes, but this intense emotional response, this clinginess, has taken me completely unawares. I'm hanging onto Cain as though he's my lifeline, my anchor, my rock of sanity in a world that just now seems confused and chaotic. And he's in no hurry to let me go. His soft voice is comforting me, though I'm in no sense distressed. He's stable and certain and reliable. I need him, I trust him, I'm depending on him and I'm not letting him go.

Chapter Six

"Steadier now?" Cain's husky voice penetrates my foggy consciousness and I realize I've been drifting in and out of sleep. I lift my head, looking around for a clock, but that takes too much energy and I flop back down again. I did see enough to know that I'm in a strange room, one that I've not seen before on my tour of the house. I remember that Cain said we'd be in his room later. This must be it. I'm lying in his huge double bed, by the look of things, and using his chest for a pillow. He seems not to have any objection though, as he strokes my hair back out of my eyes.

"How long...?" I mumble my question, it seems to me to have been ages since we were downstairs, in the kitchen, my bottom bared for him to obligingly spank. Wow, did I really do that? Did he?

"Half an hour."

I screw up my eyes, still struggling to concentrate and make sense of where I am, and what's been going on. "What happened to me? I remember you carried me upstairs. Have we..."

He laughs. "Hell, no! I like my women to be conscious, and better still—awake—when I fuck them. You were out of it for a while, that's all. You needed a power nap. Feeling more lively now?"

I push myself into a sitting position, noting the pleasant soreness in my bottom. I didn't dream this then, he really did spank me. And by the sound of it, I fell asleep straight after. I turn to him, puzzled.

"But, I never sleep during the day. And how could I just drop off when we were in the middle of…well, you know."

"You mean when I was about to peel off your clothes and fuck you until you scream? Or pass out again?"

I stare at him. Is he serious? Can he really do all that?

He grins broadly, wickedly. "You look to me as though you may be requiring a demonstration, Miss Fischer." He rolls away from me, his feet planting firmly on the carpet as he gets off the bed. He strolls across the room to the window where the curtains are still open even though it's now dark outside. He closes them, and turns to face me.

"If you've quite finished snoring, I'd rather like you naked. Now."

My clothes are exactly as they were downstairs, namely I'm fully dressed except for my knickers, which I suppose are still tucked up in Cain's jeans pocket. I have no serious objection to undressing, especially as my head is clearing fast now. And I distinctly recall he made me some delightful promises which he has yet to deliver on. But I resent the accusation that I snore. On this matter, he will get an argument out of me.

"I do *not* snore!" I fold my arms across my chest as I kneel in the center of the bed, glaring at him defiantly.

He ignores my protests, and his grin is fading now. His expression has become more sensual, more purposeful than playful. The time for small talk is apparently at an end. "Naked. Now. Unless you think we should backtrack to more spanking…"

Maybe not. Not yet anyway. I'd definitely repeat the spanking if he offers, but the prospect of that fuck-fest is much more attractive just at this moment.

Which is another surprise for me. I'm not ordinarily given to bouts of uninhibited sexual expression. In fact, I'm probably the least sexually active person I know. And I'm about as far from a sex object as you can get. Without doubt, Cain Parrish could do a whole lot better than me. But me is what he's got, at least for now, so why shouldn't I take advantage of what's on offer? Still, I can't resist one last parting shot of defiance.

"You undress too. I want to see you naked as well."

His smile now is pure sensuality as he strolls back toward the bed. "Of course, Miss Fischer. My pleasure."

He removes his T-shirt first, and I can only stare. Cain Parrish is absolutely beautiful, quite magnificent. I wouldn't normally ogle a man's pecs, but I have to make an exception for Cain. Years of hard physical work have evidently honed his body, firmed and sculpted it. He is, in my view, quite, quite perfect. His shoulders are wide, and his muscles flex as he reaches for the button on his jeans. He has a sprinkling of chest hair, which narrows to a delectable trail leading past his waistband. His nipples are small and flat, and I experience an unfamiliar urge to lean forward and flick one with my tongue. *I wonder if he'd mind?*

Before I have an opportunity to talk myself out of it I'm shuffling on my knees to the edge of the bed and reaching for him. The zip on his jeans is open now. I place my hands on his waist. He stands still as I lean in toward him, and is commendably stoical when I trail the tip of my tongue across his nipples, first the left, then the right. My lips still on him, I raise my eyes to meet his, only to find his eyelids are closed. I take that as a good sign and continue to taste and tease.

"Mmm, that feels good, Abbie. My turn now. And you do still seem over-dressed..."

I peer up at him again, to find he's watching me now. His expression is amused but determined, and this time he takes my chin in his hand and holds my face still while he leans down to kiss me. This is the first time he's actually kissed me. Downstairs he asked me to kiss him, and although he reciprocated, I was definitely the initiator. Not now. Now he is all control, all dominance as he places his knees on the bed and presses me backwards. He eases me onto my back, his weight on his elbows, and deepens the kiss. My lips part, his tongue slides between them curling around mine. It feels wonderful, sensual and very, very intimate. I take his tongue tentatively between my teeth, and his low growl suggests I release him immediately. He is definitely not wanting me to take the initiative this time. Not in this. I'm happy to let him lead, and lie still while he continues to explore my mouth.

I lift my body helpfully as he tugs my knitted top over my head. He breaks the kiss to glance down at my bra, possibly matches it in his head to my knickers still secreted in his pocket, and slides his hand behind my back to unsnap the clasp. Moments later he's admiring my naked breasts.

Well, I hope he's admiring them. He does seem to be if the growing bulge inside his jeans is any indication. His erection is nudging my stomach, and I suspect he may be feeling rather constricted by now. My helpful mood extends to this matter, and I reach down to push his jeans and boxers aside to release his cock. This is one initiative he seems to not mind from me as I close my hand around the shaft. I try a couple of experimental strokes, sliding my fist down to the bottom then right to the top. His sigh seems to be one of appreciation, so I repeat the gesture, this time pausing to swipe the pad of my thumb across the smooth head. There's moisture there, his juices ready to mingle with mine.

Or not. I'm sure I had something drilled into me about not mixing body fluids in my sex education lessons at school. This is yet another occasion when I wish I was able to read—I'd have much more idea about how this all works if I'd been able to do some dummy runs through reading those erotic books they stock in supermarkets now. There's only so much you can glean from suggestive covers.

I shove that problem from my mind for now, sure that Cain will be up to speed, as it were. I continue to pump his cock as he trails his lips across my shoulder then down to my left breast. He takes my nipple between his lips, rather as I did to him a few moments ago, but there the similarity ends.

I definitely did not draw my tongue over his nipple like this, nor did I bite it so gently it almost hurt. And it never would have occurred to me to suck on that flat little nub. Cain does all those things to me, and I arch under him. He caresses the lower curve of my breast with his hand, squeezing and lifting. My grip on his cock relaxes as my attention is focused on the fabulous sensations he is creating. It feels as though some electric current is flowing through me, connecting my nipple directly to my pussy. He seems to be increasing the pressure, and now he's grazing the sensitive tip with his teeth. I experience a moment of unease as I realize he could hurt me, but I know he won't—at least, not in a bad way. I've learnt a lot already about pain and pleasure, and I'm struggling to separate them entirely now.

He shifts his attention to my right breast. Soon that nipple, too, is quivering and swelling, hardening to a pebble. I'm writhing on the bed, his body still covering mine but not restricting my movement at all. My skirt is now a hindrance and I reach for the button at the side. I unfasten it, unzip it and lift my hips as Cain pulls it down. I kick it away and roll to my side. Cain rolls too, allowing me to shift our positions as he reaches to caress my bottom. The soreness is still there, but only just, reminding me of the erotic prelude to all this.

Cain shifts again, and I'm on my back. This time his knee is between my legs. He releases my nipple briefly as he rolls to his back to finish removing his jeans and boxer shorts. He dumps them on the carpet beside the bed where no doubt the rest of my stuff already is. Then he's kneeling above me. He runs his eyes all over my body. I'm self-conscious, it's been a while since I last rolled around naked in a man's bed—indeed, I'm struggling to recall another time I ever did—but this feels right to me. I like Cain, when he's not being rude to me, and I know I like the way he's making me feel just now. So I smile, content to let him look.

"You're a pretty little thing, under all those prim skirts and old lady tops. I should have undressed you earlier."

I'm not sure if he's being rude or not. His remark leaves me vaguely uncomfortable though I'm not sure just why. I decide to let it pass and settle for a stab at humor.

"Who are you calling little?" I jiggle my breasts at him suggestively.

His answering grin is pure lust. *Result!*

"Christ, Abbie, you're fucking gorgeous. So hot." He takes my nipple in his mouth again, briefly, but this time he's on a journey south. He nibbles a trail across my stomach, dipping his tongue into my belly button before setting off again. His hands are under my knees as he reaches my mound. I know what happens next, he's telegraphed his intentions clearly enough. I don't resist as he gently lifts my knees and spreads my legs. I remain still, open, on display, feeling his eyes on me as he looks his fill again.

"So fucking beautiful. Hot and wet, and very nearly ready."

I groan, now thrashing my head from side to side. I want him to touch me. I need him to touch me. Now! And the moment he does, I just know I'll detonate. Most of my orgasms to date have been self-induced, and I strongly suspect he'll be rather more skilled than I am at all this. His approach so far has seemed practiced enough, certainly.

But he doesn't touch me. I want his hand, his fingers, his tongue, his cock, anything. On me. In me. But still he waits, and looks. I open my eyes, to find his gaze is on me. The slate gray of his eyes is almost gone, they are dark now, with arousal. Mine too, surely. And still he waits. I shift my hips, hoping he'll take the hint. He smiles.

"Do you want something, Miss Fischer?"

I mouth my reply, *"Please."*

"Please what? What would you like me to do?"

Annoying man! I shift my hips again.

"I want you to ask me. Tell me. I want to hear the words."

I narrow my eyes at him. "Are you always this chatty?"

"Mmm, mostly. So, what would you like me to do to you now?"

"Anything. Just—do it. And quickly before I fall asleep again."

The exasperation in my tone doesn't seem to faze him, but he clearly doesn't take too kindly to the words. "Do I need to teach you some good bedroom manners? Miss Fischer? I could. I really could, and it would be such a pleasure…though perhaps not for you."

I gaze at him, and his expression is unwavering. He's different now, but it's very subtle. Not the playful, gentle lover in this moment. Now he's dominant, commanding, maybe very slightly dangerous. Certainly stern. He means what he says, maybe. I wonder if he would—what? I experience a thrill of anticipation, and his lip quirks in response. He knows what I'm thinking, and he might just…

"Touch me. Please." I say the words quickly, eager to break the silence. And afraid of what might lie under it. What more might he be able to beguile me into doing?

He smiles at me, a smile of triumph, a smile from a man who knows he's calling the shots here. "Of course. Where? And what with?"

"There. Please." I'm whispering now, not wanting to provoke him but finding this hard.

"Where, love. Say it for me." His voice gentles, his expression softens.

"My pussy."

"Not your clit, then?"

"Yes. Yes please. There too. Especially there. Please, Cain..." My whisper dies away. I'm mortified with embarrassment, and so desperate with need I'll do or say anything as long as he'll just relieve this clenching emptiness. I'm keenly aware of my wetness, my pussy must be positively dripping, glowing with arousal. And if he doesn't stop looking and start doing within the next millisecond, I'm going to burst into flames. Without a shadow of doubt.

"Right. Clit *and* pussy. What would you like me to touch you with?"

I'm past messing now, past defiance or evasion. My eyes are closed, but I can still see that uncompromising gaze. It might as well be tattooed onto the backs of my eyelids. I grind out the words. "Your fingers. Your tongue. I want your cock inside me."

"Like this?" His tone is positively liquid now.

I jerk violently as he rubs my clit. My eyes fly open—he repeats the action. He draws the pad of his thumb along the sensitive, greedy little nub, and all my nerve endings are apparently now directly connected to it. I scream. I actually scream, it feels so good. He continues to caress me. I start to come. One more stroke, and I plunge past the point of no return. And I'm not quiet about it. I scream again, thrusting my hips wildly as he increases the pressure, wringing the whole of my response from me. Nothing, no self-administered orgasm in the privacy of my little bathroom or bedroom back in Bradford could have prepared me for this. This is sheer, mind-numbing pleasure. If it were possible to die of pleasure, this would do the trick. Absolutely. Totally.

My body is shaking, vibrating with sensation as he relentlessly presses the matter. The waves of pleasure seem to be endless, washing through me. I feel as though I'm floating, weightless, drifting. Then, as suddenly as it started, my orgasm subsides. My pussy is clenching, I want him inside me. I'm lying still, content, satisfied for now, but so very ready for him.

Unfortunately my view is not shared by Cain Parrish, and in this he's the one setting the pace.

"Mmm, very impressive, Miss Fischer. Now let's see if you can manage a repeat performance."

Not in this lifetime.

Cain has other ideas though. He stretches out, face down on the bed, his shoulders between my thighs. He gently slides his fingers through my folds—wet and so ultra-sensitive—parting the lips of my pussy. He touches his tongue to my clit, making me shiver. He licks it, and I thrust up at him. He wraps his tongue around it and sucks. Moaning now, I feel the pull of orgasm. *Christ!*

He slips one long finger deep inside me. Now I'm screaming again. I squeeze the muscles inside my pussy around his finger, seeking more friction. He slips another finger inside, and a third. Now he's twisting and spreading them inside me, pressing against the walls of my pussy. He withdraws them, right to the fingertips, then plunges deep once more. Another scream from me, and he shifts up a gear. He's finger-fucking me hard, still flicking my clit with his tongue. I come for a second time within moments.

My climax is not so explosive this time, more a slow unfurling of warm pleasure which seems to drift on and on. Cain's in no hurry, continuing his sensual assault on my pussy and clit until he's sure every last tremor and shiver have vibrated from me, every last wave and pulse of sensation have flowed out through my fingertips. Then and only then does he lift his head and start to lick his way back up to my breasts. He stops briefly to re-acquaint himself with my nipples before taking my mouth again in another deep, drugging kiss. I'm furrowing my fingers through his thick, wavy hair as I respond, plunging my tongue into his mouth as he rolls to his back, pulling me on top of him. I spend a few brief moments as the aggressor, kissing him deeply, fiercely, before he reverses our positions. This time he's positioned his hips between my thighs, and his cock is nudging my pussy. I expect him to plunge deep and fast inside me, but he doesn't. Instead he reaches over me to grab his jeans from the floor, and pulls a small foil sachet from the back pocket.

Ah right, body fluids. Good thinking. As long as he's quick.

He *is* quick, and in moments he's unrolled the condom along his cock, and he's ready for action. I am too, and I close my eyes, holding my breath as I wait for him to fill me. He's large, I can tell that, and I expect this will be a tight fit.

"Abbie, open your eyes. Please." His tone is soft now, achingly gentle. Gone is the hard, dominant, commanding presence of a few minutes ago.

I obey, this time because he's asking me so nicely and I want to please him.

"Are you okay with this?" His expression is slightly uncertain, though I have no idea why.

"Okay? What do you mean?"

"I came on pretty strong for a while, back there. I need to be sure that you're okay with this. You can say no, you do understand that, don't you?"

What is he talking about? Why the hell would I say no? I want this more, probably, than I want my next breath. I need to make him understand and get on with it. Fast.

"Yes. I do know that. And yes, I'm okay. Now, please…"

He smiles. "Just checking, Abbie." And in the next instant he surges forward, burying his cock balls-deep inside me.

My mouth opens, my eyes widen, I gasp. He's big, and it's tight. Incredibly tight. He holds still for a few moments and I'm intensely aware of the impossible fullness. I'm scared to move.

"You still okay?" His voice is tender, he sounds concerned.

I manage a small nod, though in that moment I'm not entirely convinced.

"Be still for a moment, relax if you can, I *will* make this good. I promise." His tone is low and sexy, and totally assured.

Again I nod, and incredibly I am starting to relax. He's not hurting me, it was just—more—somehow. More intense, more sudden, more—everything. I'm adjusting fast though, and after a few seconds, I shift under him, instinctively wanting the friction, the movement. I want him to thrust.

"Please, Cain, could you…?"

"On it, sweetheart." And he slowly slides his cock back, almost withdrawing from me, before plunging back in again. His movements are smooth, unhurried, and very, very deliberate. He's holding my gaze, my eyes fixed on his, and he withdraws and thrusts a second time. And a third. He picks up the pace a little, still gentle, achingly careful. It's what I need, and I arch under him. His next thrust is firmer still, and I gasp again. He pauses, one eyebrow raised as he silently seeks confirmation that I'm still with him. I am, I most definitely am. I manage a slight smile before my eyelids flutter down and I start to thrust back.

That's Cain's signal to make it good, to deliver on his promise. He does. He quickly sets up a rhythm, angling his thrusts to hit my G-spot each time. I clench my pussy franticly around him. I'm gripping him, seeking more. And he responds, he delivers. I grasp his shoulders, my body shuddering with desire and something akin to desperation. I want him harder, faster, deeper. My wordless moans and frantic clutching at his body are all I have to convey my need, but he knows it, understands it. And he responds, pumping his long, thick cock into my pussy like a piston. It feels glorious, absolutely wonderful, and I lift my legs higher, hooking my ankles together behind his waist to pull him deeper into me. His weight is taken mostly on his elbows, but my body is firmly pinned underneath his and I feel delightfully dominated, deliciously vulnerable and totally safe. Cain Parrish knows exactly what he's doing. I'm in very, very good hands.

Leaning on just one elbow, he angles back slightly to reach down between us. His fingertip connects again with my clit, and he rubs hard. With a small squeal and a powerful ripple of pure friction along the entire length of my pussy. I climax powerfully. The previous orgasms have been nice, better than nice, absolutely stunning, but they really were just the warm up act, the prelude to this. Now the sensation just keeps on coming, as I do. Cain's thrusts are deep and hard, his cock a solid presence totally filling me, to my absolute limits and just possibly beyond. Even as I feel my orgasm start to build again, quickly passing the point where I could exert any level of control, I'm aware that he's tensing, his whole body rigid. His cock if anything is even firmer, more relentless, and he continues to fuck me hard. Harder. Then I'm there, soaring weightlessly, spinning, my body spasming wildly. And Cain's there too, with me, his breathing short and rasping as he buries himself one last time, the head of his cock nudging my cervix as he comes. The condom fills, and I feel the warmth of his semen inside the protective layer. I tighten my legs around him, my heels pressing on his buttocks to silently urge him to stay where he is, deep inside me. Forever.

But forever's a long time, and eventually Cain rolls to his side and withdraws from me. He quickly slips the condom off and disposes of it, wrapped in a tissue from a box beside his bed. He rolls back to face me.

"That was quite a ride, Abbie. And you were very tight. Hot and wet and fucking lovely, in fact. Did I hurt you?"

I shake my head. "No. Well, maybe slightly, at first. I'm not used to, well… It'd been a while."

He lightly caresses my cheek with his knuckle, the gesture both tender and reassuring. "It won't be a while until you're doing it again. At least, not if I get my way."

I smile. "No. I don't think it will." I pause for a moment, then, "And, what about spanking?" I need to ask, need to know how much he's offering me, and what exactly. He doesn't seem fazed by the question.

"What about spanking?"

"Will…will there be more of that soon as well?"

Now he chuckles, his laugh a little bit wicked and more than slightly sexy. "I daresay I can oblige you. If you insist. Are you likely to insist, do you think?"

Now it's my turn to grin. "Yes, Mr Parrish, I believe I will. Especially if you can follow it up like that every time." I hesitate for a moment, then, "You're really turning out to be quite talented."

He laughs out loud at that. "And you're turning out to be a very demanding house guest, Miss Fischer. But I'll do my best to accommodate you. But not straight away. You've tired me out, for now at least. Do you need the loo or anything before I turn out the light?"

More serious now, I make to sit up, feeling I've perhaps outstayed my welcome. Cain snakes his arm around me and he pulls me back toward him.

"Make it quick in the loo, Abbie. On second thoughts I'm beginning to think that perhaps I've not quite finished with you just yet."

I turn my head, glance down at him, propped up seductively on his pillows. It would be nice to stay.

"I thought, maybe, you know, that I should go back to my own room now…?"

He gazes up at me, his expression considering. At first he doesn't answer, and I think it must indeed be time I made myself scarce.

Then, "Is that what you want?"

I shake my head. I see no point in playing hard to get. Not now. But there are things I need to say, things not quite squared between us, however beautifully he might be able to fuck me. Or spank me.

"It's kind of you to let me stay here, in your house, but I don't expect to share your bed. I mean, you don't even like me."

His expression is inscrutable. And more to the point, he's not arguing with me. He just regards me seriously, the moments slipping past. But still he doesn't release his hold around my waist, and I feel it would be rude to pull out of his arms.

At last, he responds, "I don't, as a rule, fuck women I don't like. It's a theoretical possibility, and there's no biological problem with it as far as I know, but still, I tend not to. And I'd be very cautious about spanking one." He stops to consider that prospect further, and nods slowly. "Yes, that could get really awkward."

His reasoning sounds very nice, very wholesome in fact, but there's no getting around the circumstances that brought me here, and his furious reaction to finding himself saddled with an unwanted business partner.

I try to explain my concerns. "We fancy each other, but that's just sex. Great sex, well, I thought so. Although I'm no expert, not really…" My voice trails away, and I notice his expression darkening. This isn't going too well. Anxious to get it over with I just blurt out the rest of what I have to say, "You want me gone, I know that. Maybe not now, at this moment, from your bed, but definitely from your business. You think I've somehow schemed and cheated to get my hands on what's yours. You don't trust me…"

He silences me, just one upturned palm sufficient to halt my flow of not especially well chosen words.

"Hold it, before you dig yourself in any deeper. You're right, I did think that, or something along those lines, at first. But you've told me you had nothing to do with my uncle's decision to write that will, that you never even met him. I've no reason not to believe you, so you'll get the benefit of the doubt. And I *do* trust you. I don't blame you for the situation we're in—that's entirely James' doing, though I don't have the first idea why he did it. And I believe you when you tell me that you don't either. And I definitely don't dislike you." His serious expression becomes mischievous as he continues, "And finally, just for the record, sweetheart, you are entirely welcome to put your hands on what's mine. And I've every intention of reciprocating."

I stare at him, just one phrase from his answer leaping out at me. "You believe me?"

He nods, serious again. "Yes, I do. We're in this together, as I see it. For reasons of his own, my uncle seems to have locked us up with each other for the next five years. I see no reason to take that out on you, and every reason to make the best of it. Don't misunderstand me, my solicitor—Mr Stephenson, you hung up on him, remember, when he tried to set up our first meeting?"

I nod slowly, feeling I may have treated Mr Stephenson less than courteously, on reflection.

Cain continues, "Right, well he has his instructions which are to keep on looking for a way of overturning the will. If he can find a legal loophole I'll take it and extricate both of us from this, this…"

"Mess?" I put in helpfully.

He glances at me, and I suspect that's not the word he might have chosen left to himself. "Situation," he corrects me firmly. "If that happens, well, we can rethink our options. But for now it's just you, me, our business, a mutual enthusiasm for spanking, my throbbing cock and your incredibly tight pussy—which I'm thinking, hoping, might need some more attention quite soon. I can live with that if you can."

I stare at him, not sure how a perfectly serious discussion about his uncle's last will and testament became transformed into something much more promising. And intimate. But it does sound like a reasonable approach to me.

"I think I can live with that. Should we shake hands on it?"

"If you insist. I'd much prefer it if you were to suck my cock though."

I manage to keep a stern expression on my face. "I could do that. But what about my tight pussy?"

His eyebrows quirk, and his lip twitches. My poker face is winning this round. But he'll have his way. He's already shifting his position to kneel over me, his once more fully erect cock delightfully close to my lips. "You really must learn to wait your turn, Miss Fischer. Now please, open wide."

Chapter Seven

I wake up alone, still curled up snug and warm in Cain Parrish's bed. Of him there's no sign beyond his discarded clothes from yesterday still strewn around the room. Actually, that's not strictly true. As I shift and stretch I can feel his unmistakable, lingering presence. I ache everywhere. In places I'd no idea I even had. A sure sign of his being in me, on me, all over me. I'm entertaining some hope I may have left him with a twinge or two, but nothing on this scale.

Cain is generous as a lover, I really have no idea how many times he made me come in the hours we spent rolling around in his bed. And when I wasn't actually coming, I was hovering on the brink of it more or less constantly. He has an uncanny knack for knowing just when to hold back, how to make me wait until I'm literally begging him to finish the job. And his finishing touches are quite, quite exquisite. Remembering, re-living, I roll onto my back, gazing up at the ceiling and tingling still at the recollection.

And I become aware of another sensation, one even more insistent just now than my aching muscles and interestingly tender places. I'm hungry. Starving in fact. I need the loo first then food and hot, sweet coffee, and I need those things now. I ease my legs out from under the duvet and curl my toes in the deep pile of the bedroom carpet. I sit on the edge of the bed, and note that my bottom is no longer sore. Pity really, but more than made up for by the bone-deep aching in my thighs and the pleasant soreness in my pussy. I peep into the small waste bin beside the bed where there look to be at least five used condoms. Proof positive that Cain had a good time too. So, he made love to me at least five times in one night. A whole lifetime's worth in my limited experience, all at once. No wonder I'm feeling the strain. And needing nourishment.

My clothes are in the room along the hall, so I opt to borrow something of Cain's for now. There are a few shirts neatly ironed and stacked on an oak blanket chest under the window, so I take the top one and shake it out. It's a black and red check, made of soft cotton. It's quite thick, a work shirt, I expect. He probably won't mind me borrowing it. I slip my arms into the sleeves and fasten the buttons. It hangs past my thighs, and is very loose on me. I glance in the mirror on my way to leave in search of Cain and food.

Is that me? I look—different. Sort of sexier, more alluring. It's an image of myself I don't recognize, but there I am. Large as life and twice as rumpled. My strawberry-blonde hair all mussed and tangled around my face and neck, my mouth still red and swollen from his kisses. The shirt looks seductive, inviting, as though I'm begging for someone to just slip the buttons open and unwrap me.

I'm not bad looking, but this sexy stranger in the mirror actually looks quite beautiful. I'm glowing, my eyes, normally a presentable enough blend of hazel and green, are now shining. My skin is flushed, still warm from the bed, but it's more. It's more an anticipation, a sense of something sweet and soft and intriguing just waiting to happen. Christ, even I'd fuck me at this moment. Is this the Abigail Fischer that Cain Parrish sees? How come I've never met her before now?

I gaze at my reflection for a few more moments, before my stomach growls loudly, pulling me back to the here and now. My immediate needs are gathering urgency. I leave the room and head for the bathroom before making my way downstairs.

I find Cain in the kitchen, several newspapers spread out on the table. He smiles at me when I appear in the doorway.

"Morning, Miss Fischer. Did you sleep well?" His morning tone is husky and low. And sexy.

I nod, and head for the worktop behind him, where the kettle is. "Yes. Eventually. Do you want more coffee? And aren't we on first name terms by now?"

He closes his newspaper and stands. "Yes please. And 'Miss Fischer' suits you when you've got that just-fucked, sexy look about you. Toast or croissants?"

My stomach growls again in response, and my pussy clenches in joyful expectation. I wince, intensely aware of his recent presence inside me. But no matter how delightful the prospect of a repeat performance is, my need for other sustenance is acute, and I'm not convinced toast and croissants will quite do the trick.

He obviously hears my bodily functions issuing their protest, and his grin broadens. "Right, toast to start with, then you get dressed and we'll go find some proper food. There's a pub down the road where they do a mean Sunday lunch."

I glance at the clock on the kitchen wall. It's quarter to twelve. I never sleep this late. Ever. I'm astonished that I'm only just getting up and it's already lunchtime. I could get into some really slovenly habits around Cain Parrish. He, on the other hand, got even less sleep than I did last night, I'm sure of that, but he looks to have been up for hours. He's all fresh and showered, neat and tidy, while I look just-fucked and messy. I never even picked up a hairbrush before trotting down here. My mother would be turning in her grave if she could see me now. And I daresay she'd be spinning like a top if she'd seen me last night!

Still, we're here now. And life's pretty good from where I'm standing as I pour hot water into two mugs. I watch Cain drop bread into the toaster and press the lever. He grabs a tub of butter from the fridge and turns to me as he waits for the toast to pop. His smile is stunning, dripping with pure lust. He rakes his eyes up and down my body, as though noticing only now that I'm wearing his shirt. I tug at the hem self-consciously.

"It looks good on you. You can keep it. I want you to wear it often, and every time it'll remind me of how gloriously sexy and utterly fuckable you look right now. If I do extra toast, do you think you could last another hour or so?"

I glance down, and his erection is unmistakable, straining the front of his black denim jeans. Even in my new-found state of sexual allure I never anticipated having such a profound and immediate effect, and especially not on a man with the experience and skill of Cain Parrish. He's no doubt had breakfast with countless sexily rumpled bedmates in his time, but still seems to appreciate me. And his appreciation is now seeking more direct expression.

I'm even more conscious of my aches and pains as I contemplate a re-run of last night's exertions, and I'm honestly not sure, no matter how willing the spirit, whether my flesh is going to be up to it. I grimace subconsciously, but he catches the fleeting expression.

"Feeling a little sore this morning?"

I nod, blushing now. Surely he's not going to ask for details.

He is.

"Where? Did I hurt you?"

"Not 'hurt', exactly. But we were rather — energetic. And I'm out of practice."

"Well, you were energetic, certainly. And I'd suggest you're not out of practice any more, though there's no harm in working on your technique. I'd be happy to help…"

"Did I do something wrong?"

His tone was light, teasing, but my perpetual self-doubt is never far below the surface, coiled and ready to spring at the slightest whiff of criticism. My newly-discovered status as a sex siren is under scrutiny and seemingly found wanting.

He grabs the toast and drops it onto a plate before coming around to me and dropping a kiss on my mouth. "Not a thing, sweetheart. I'm joking. You were fucking wonderful." He cups my chin with his hand, his expression thoughtful, and perhaps a little concerned. "You *are* okay?"

I nod quickly, and on impulse wrap my arms around his back and hug him. He returns the hug, nuzzling my hair with his lips as he reaches down to caress my bottom.

"So, a little tender just now, but you could do justice to a roast dinner with all the trimmings? Yes?"

I nod. "Yes. If that's okay with you?"

"It sounds a like an excellent plan. And you'll keep for later. You and your tight but slightly sore little pussy. So, eat your toast and then get ready. We'll be out of here in half an hour."

* * * *

In fact it took us less than twenty minutes, but now we're comfortably ensconced in a quiet corner of the Fox and Goose, the remains of two monstrous carvery lunches strewn on the table in front of us. We're sipping yet more coffee—we both seem to be caffeine addicts—and Cain's reeling off ideas for how to spend the afternoon. Incredibly, hot and sweaty sex back at his house doesn't seem to be on his immediate agenda.

"I could take you and show you the office and yard if you like, while no one else is around. But that'll save till Monday either. Or we could go for a walk, maybe a bit of shopping if that's what you want to do? We'd have to go to Newcastle though—Berwick is dead at a weekend."

I wouldn't mind a walk, but I'm not fond of shopping. Especially not with someone else who doesn't know me that well. And that's an odd thought—surely now Cain Parrish knows me better than pretty much anyone else. At least, he knows my body very well indeed. But almost nothing else about me.

I generally find shops a bit of a trial, if I'm honest, full of special offer posters and complicated buy one get one free price tickets. I can manage to make sense of all that, given time, but it's all just a bit hectic and immediate for my liking. I usually go shopping with Sally, and that's a nice girlie day out, but this seems different. So no, not shopping. Far too much danger of being rumbled for the illiterate dunce I am.

"I like walking. Maybe we could find a nice park or something?"

Cain shakes his head. "We can do better than that. Who needs a park when you've got the Northumberland coastline. Come on." He leads the way back out to the car park where we scramble into his van. A few minutes later, he takes a sharp left turn and we're trundling down a long drive between grassy sand dunes to a small clearing overlooking the sea. Several other cars are parked there. He's right, it really is a beautiful place. I reach for my sketchbook, and he smiles wryly as he props his feet on the dashboard to wait for me. There are seabirds circling in the air and floating serenely among the gentle ripples. I do my best to capture their swooping motion as well as their calm companionship on the water.

"Fancy an ice cream?" His voice interrupts me, perhaps fifteen minutes later.

I glance toward the jolly little ice cream van parked close to the car park entrance. Our shared sweet tooth is asserting itself again. I nod and thank him.

"Just vanilla, please. With a flake."

His sardonic grin is lost on me at first, the meaning of his muttered "hardly vanilla" not dawning on me until he's halfway to the van. There's a queue, he'll be a few minutes, so I re-apply myself to my drawing.

I don't see or hear him returning until he plonks himself down alongside me again, my ice cream just starting to melt on the cornet. I set the sketchpad down on my other side and turn my attention to the serious business of licking the dribbles away.

"You're good at that. I still think a little more practice though, later on..."

"What?" I glance up at him, to catch his wicked grin. "Ah, right. You have a very dirty mind, Mr Parrish."

"I did say I'd help you with your technique. And my dick's so hard I could crack rocks with it, just watching you sucking on that ice cream…"

"Well, since it seems to be a health and safety issue."

"Your concern does you credit, Miss Fischer. Maybe I could express my gratitude on your bare bottom later. Though your interest in spanking does somewhat suggest your tastes are not entirely vanilla."

I shrug and can't help shifting in my seat at the mention of another erotic spanking later. My buttocks clench happily as he continues.

"Yes, Miss Fischer, who'd have thought, under that unassuming exterior, you had such a kinky nature to go with your diligent attention to my welfare? You're turning out to be an interesting asset to Parrish Construction. Who knows what your range of duties might eventually encompass?"

Who indeed? He's yet to see my woeful attempts at running the Parrish Construction office. I suspect my duties there might soon be severely curtailed, unless I can find a suitable niche for myself. A long way from any of the paperwork he seems so hell-bent on shoving my way. I know it will be a disaster, but he just won't listen. I'm not sure I entirely like the mention of my 'unassuming exterior' either, but I'd prefer to leave that stone undisturbed for now. I know my clothes are a little on the drab side, plain, ordinary. And above all, cheap. I don't have a lot of spare cash to spend on good quality stuff. Actually, any spare cash I get goes on paints or canvases, and I'm happy with that. I don't want to draw too much attention, I'm happy just getting along with my life. Or I was.

Now, these things seem to matter. Before yesterday, I didn't much care what Cain or anyone else thought of me. I'm here only because he insisted on it, or at least I was initially. But that's changed. Now, I find I'm starting to want to stay. With Cain.

I'd like to find some way to...to what? To make this work? I really can't see how though. I'm in no way qualified or suited to the role he seems to have envisaged for me, and apart from a mutual interest in pleasantly kinky sex, what else do we have in common?

"Hey, Abbie? What's wrong?"

His concerned voice breaks into my thoughts, and I quickly lap at the large dollop of ice cream sliding down my fingers.

"Nothing. Really, I was just thinking."

"You can think tomorrow. Today we're having a day off. Let's go walking."

I turn to reach for my notepad. Cain's ahead of me though and picks it up from the seat. He glances at me, one eyebrow raised in query, asking my permission before he looks. I see no reason why not, I've only been sketching the coastline and seabirds, so I shrug and gesture to him to go ahead. He looks at the picture I was just working on then glances at me, cocking his head to ask if he can look at more. I nod, and he slowly turns over the pages, studying my sketches and drawings. Some I took time over, most are just quick working sketches, things I saw and captured with a view to maybe using later.

He glances briefly at yesterday's rendition of the Angel of the North then turns over more pages. He pauses over one particular drawing, and I lean around to see what it is. It's him, a sketch I made the day I first met him, after he dropped me off at the art gallery. I forgot I'd done it. His face is clearly recognizable, though I'd certainly draw him differently now. In this picture his face is sharp, forbidding, uncompromising. He looks dangerous, angry, quite dark and brooding. If I drew him today he'd be laughing, definitely. Sexy, probably. Much more gentle, approachable. Likeable. Lovable.

He raises his eyes from the page to look at me. "Is this how you see me?"

There's warmth in his gaze, his expression one of concern.

I shake my head. "At first, maybe. Not now. I drew that just after I met you. You—intimidated me back then. I think you did it on purpose."

He glances at me sharply. "Yes, maybe I did. And now?"

"Not now. Especially not now. Not after..."

"Not after last night?" He smiles at my slight nod. "That's a relief. A little healthy trepidation works fine, adds some spice to a spanking, but for what I have in mind for you, it really wouldn't do if you were seriously afraid of me."

My chin lifts. "I see. And what do you have in mind?"

"Later, Miss Fischer. Now, I'm still looking at your etchings. These really are good, you know. You've a serious talent here."

"Thanks. I like drawing, painting. I wish..." I drop my gaze, wondering how much of my secret ambitions I can share. I can hardly tell him that my first thought, on learning I'd come into possession of over half his business, was that I might sell it to raise money I could use to set myself up as an independent artist and illustrator.

"What is it you wish, Abbie?" He reaches for me, cups my chin and tilts my face up to look at him. He holds my gaze, and waits.

Eventually, I give in. Partly.

"I'd like to be a professional artist. Maybe illustrate children's books." Especially very young children's books as I can just about read those.

"So, why the job as a cleaner? Why aren't you working as an artist then? Or going to college at least?"

Why indeed? I shrug. "It's just a dream, that's all. I like cleaning too."

I hold out my hand for my sketchpad, and he gives it to me. His expression suggests though that this conversation may not be over. As far as I'm concerned it is, so I shove my pad quickly into my rucksack and sling it over my shoulder.

"What about that walk?" I open the van door and scramble down to the ground. I start to walk away in the direction of some rough steps leading down to the beach, and he quickly falls in alongside me. I'm reminded sharply of our first meeting. He pursued me then, and I suspect he'll continue to do so, until he prises all my secrets from me. Or until the determined Mr Stephenson finally hits on an exit route for us all. I'm not sure which I'd prefer. Meanwhile though, I make no comment as he reaches for my hand and we make our way slowly along the sharp, damp sand, parallel with the lapping waves of the North Sea, our fingers loosely entwined.

* * * *

We're both stuffed from the massive lunch. Even our exertions plodding along miles of rough beach have done little to re-kindle our appetites. We arrive back at Cain's house late in the afternoon, and apart from our habitual coffee, we're not in the mood for much else. Well, not food, certainly.

"I have some emails to catch up with, and a tender to make a start on. Will you be all right for an hour or two? Unless you feel like helping me, that is?"

I feel guilty as I shake my head. I've nothing better to do, that's for sure. He'll think I'm just refusing to pull my weight, and I know his opinion on that already. He made it plain enough when he was insisting I come to Berwick and work for Parrish Construction. I think fast to come up with something resembling a good reason for ducking out of the paperwork.

"I have a bit of a headache. Maybe I'll just go and lie down for a while…"

At once he's all concern. "Of course. I thought you were rather quiet this afternoon. Can I get you anything? I must have some Anadin around here somewhere."

"No. No, thank you. Just a lie down will be fine. I'll use my room."

"No, use mine. Ours. If you don't mind, that is…?"

Now I do feel guilty. Not only am I lying to him, but I'm taking advantage of his kindness and concern. I slope off upstairs before he offers me anything else, any other evidence of his decency and compassion that I'll find myself obliged to ungraciously refuse.

Once in Cain's room, the curtains closed to lend an aura of authenticity, just in case he comes up to check how I am, I have plenty of time to think about my predicament. Later this evening I have no doubt he'll be amenable to another torrid session of spanking, fucking and all points in-between. That's rather my hope as well, but I'll have to fake a miraculous recovery first.

And tomorrow? Tomorrow my promising career as a fraud really goes up a gear or two as I'll have to try to convince not only Cain but also his efficient and loyal office manager, that I'm not entirely incompetent. I've yet to meet Phyllis Benson, but I've no reason to suspect she's anything less than sharp. As is Cain. My deception won't last long. Then what?

I'd be of limited use, even as some sort of labourer or apprentice. But in any case, Cain's made it clear he has no need of that. No. I'm to learn the ropes as Mrs Benson's assistant with a view to taking over her duties when she retires. I mull over the sorts of tasks that are likely to come my way, but I've only the vaguest idea what they might be. Filing? Possibly opening the mail? Cain mentioned finance, invoices, accounts. Apart from in the broadest terms, I've pretty much no notion what any of those things are, and certainly no idea what I'd need to do to make myself useful around the office. I could perhaps staple bits of paper together, or work a shredder, but that about sums it up.

Or I could come clean. I could explain why I'm so not cut out for this. Cain seemed fierce at first, not a man I'd choose to confide in, certainly not about something so personal. But now? Could I? I know him better now. I've discovered that he's kind, gentle, fun, a tender lover and a pleasant companion. And I've also found out how absolutely serious he is about Parrish Construction, how completely driven he is as far as his business is concerned. If he knew I couldn't read and write even as well as the average eight-year-old, he'd certainly not want me around his paperwork, messing with his admin, his financial records. The question is—would he want me anywhere at all?

He wouldn't insist on me working for him, I'm pretty sure of that. In fact, he probably wouldn't be able to get me out of there fast enough. He'd have no use for me. He'd be incredulous, stunned, as everyone is. Because everyone can read and write. Well, everyone I know, except me. There's no excuse for illiteracy, no earthly reason for someone to get to my advanced age of twenty-two, unable to string more than a few letters together. It's not as though I don't have a decent vocabulary, I just can't recognize the words when they're written down. I like to think I'm not stupid. I can get by, pretty well, relying on my excellent memory and using other clues to fill in gaps. I recognize company logos, memorize them religiously, my mental arithmetic is really very good indeed. I've had to compensate, and although lots of things are hard for me, or just plain impossible, I do get by. Always have, and I always will.

Maybe, one day, if I get time, and if I manage to convince myself that I could stand the mortification of having to go to 'special' tuition classes, I might do something about it. I could read, probably, if I bothered. I could learn. I just—haven't. And now, tomorrow, my chickens will be home to roost.

Chapter Eight

"How's the head?" Cain's voice is low, soft, as he crouches beside me in the semi-darkness. I must have fallen asleep, I never heard him come in. I struggle to sit up, and he reaches to help me, arranging a pillow behind my shoulders.

"Feeling better?" he asks me again, sounding concerned.

I nod, smiling at him apologetically and feeling like a total fraud. "I'm fine. Much better. Did you finish your work?"

"Enough for now. I was wondering how you were, and if you might be hungry yet?"

"A little. Not much. What about you? Maybe I could fix us a snack. We did agree I'd cook today…"

"No need. I've sent out for pizza. Are you coming down, or are we having a picnic in bed?"

A bed picnic? My mother used to let me do that when I was little and ill. Really ill, obviously, not pretending like I am now. Back then, before the transplant, I was often too weak to come down for my meals. I imagine Cain's version could be very different.

Not on this occasion, however. My just deserts for claiming to be ill are that he flatly refuses to contemplate even the mildest spanking on the grounds that there's no such thing. He'll do it right or not at all, and in his view, my currently delicate frame is not up to such exertions. And his view is the one that counts in this matter. Instead, he convinces me to get undressed—nightie optional—and to stay in bed while he sorts out food. Earlier I simply lay down fully dressed on the top of his duvet, not intending to stay here for very long. But now I do as he's suggested, choosing to slip a loose T-shirt over my otherwise naked body and snuggle under the quilt to wait for my meal. Cain brings the pizza up on a tray, with a complementary two liter bottle of cola, a couple of tubs of coleslaw and some potato wedges. The whole thing is delicious. I'd have preferred the spanking, but this is a close second.

Also, it's quite nice to feel cared about. Cain pampers and fusses over me almost as much as my mother used to, urging me to eat more, pouring my drinks for me, plumping up my pillows. He's a regular Florence Nightingale, and I feel absolutely wretched that I'm lying to him. I'm taking advantage of his kindness and consideration. And this won't be the last time. I'm going to be heaping lie upon lie in the days and weeks to come in order to conceal my shameful secret.

* * * *

Later, as I lie in bed waiting for sleep which is showing no signs of coming, I turn that prospect over in my head. I loathe the thought of the deception to come. It can only get worse. I'm basically an honest person—this doesn't sit well with me.

After we finished eating Cain went back downstairs to clear up, insisting that I should stay where I was and rest. He was soon back, offering me more painkillers, and expressing the view that we could both do with an early night. It was only ten o'clock, and I was not in the least sleepy after my power nap earlier, but I couldn't find a way to persuade him otherwise. I offered to take myself off to my room, the spare room, but he was having none of that. He supervised my medication then undressed quickly, clearly intending to slide in beside me. I tried not to stare too openly, but he really is extremely good to look at. His body is firm, hard, toned by work and exercise, the muscles flex sensuously as he moves. He seems totally comfortable with nudity, and I had ample chance to admire his rather fine bum as he strolled around the room putting his clothes into the washing basket, plugging his phone into its charger, setting the alarm, turning off lamps and generally sorting things out. He's tidy, efficient in a way I can't come close to, though he doesn't seem inclined to insist I keep to his house rules. I'm not so sure the same tolerance will apply at work.

Now, it's after one in the morning, and I'm wide awake. I'm listening to Cain's gentle, even breathing alongside me and know he's been asleep for hours. His leg is heavy, flung casually across mine, but I don't want to disturb him by moving. And in any case, I rather like it there. His cock is nestling against my bum, bared now as the T-shirt has ridden up. He's not erect, but still an imposing presence and I'm optimistic that the morning will at least bring some interesting developments in that department. As long as he doesn't think I'm still unwell.

Now, that's an idea. I could pretend to be not well, claim some lingering effects of my headache, and surely he'd insist I take the day off. I consider that plan for a few moments but dismiss it quickly. It would only be delaying the inevitable. No, I need to convince him that I can contribute, I need to satisfy his insistence that I shoulder my share of the workload, but just not in the office. The problem is, I've absolutely no idea what to suggest I do instead, Maybe I *am* just plain useless.

My thoughts continue in that vein for the next three hours or so, until I eventually slip into a light doze.

* * * *

I'm awakened, what feels like just moments later by the insistent trilling of Cain's phone. It's the alarm, set for six-fifteen. I'm used to being an early riser—school cleaners don't get to lie in as a rule—but after no more than a couple of hours sleep, I'm wrecked. I groan and try to shove my head under the pillow as Cain rolls over and reaches for the offending article. He silences the din, then turns to me.

"No use hiding under there. I know you're awake. You have been all night."

So much for him being asleep.

I drag my face out into the light. He's switched on the bedside lamp, and there are faint slivers of daylight filtering through the curtains. He's leaning up on one elbow, looking down at me. He really is absolutely beautiful. How can anyone look so—delicious—at quarter past six on a Monday morning? It's all I can do not to lick my lips.

"Do you feel well enough to come to work today?"

I knew it. Now's my chance. "Yes. I'm fine. Just didn't sleep that well. I'll be sound after a few slugs of coffee."

His smile is lazy and sexy and quite irresistible. "Is that a hint you want to kick me out of bed?" He shifts slightly, and his erection presses firmly against my thigh. I doubt even a nun would have kicked him out of bed at that moment.

"No. I mean, do we have time…?"

"Oh yes, we do indeed have time." He lowers his body over mine and kisses me. I did at least manage a quick trip to the bathroom before I scrambled into bed last night so my teeth are clean. Well, cleanish. I consciously put any thoughts of morning breath aside as he deepens the kiss. He has no qualms, why should I? I run my fingers through his tousled bedroom hair, loving the rough silkiness against my skin. I'm soon exploring lower, trailing my palms along his shoulders and down his back to grasp his tight, slim waist. He's not entirely idle himself, and my T-shirt is quickly pulled up to expose my breasts. Not satisfied with that, Cain breaks the kiss to remove my T-shirt altogether. He rolls it into a ball and chucks it across the room. Not always Mr Tidy, after all.

He fastens his mouth on my nipple, and I arch under him. He continues to suck, tugging my nipple and as much of my breast as he can take into his mouth. He increases the pressure, and I cry out. My hands are back in his hair as I clutch at him, holding him close. Closer. He continues to tease me with his mouth as he uses his hand to caress my other breast. He takes the nipple between his finger and thumb, pinches it firmly. I squeal, and he slants a questioning glance at me.

"Too hard?"

I shake my head. "No. Do it again. Please…"

He chuckles. "Okay. And please try not to interrupt, Miss Fischer."

I take the hint and remain still and reasonably quiet, as he treats my breasts to a fine selection from his extensive repertoire—he sucks, flicks, nips, squeezes, scrapes his teeth across my nipples, biting gently. He firms and shapes my not especially ample curves as I fight not to wriggle. My breath is catching in little staccato bursts by the time he eventually transfers his attention to my belly button. I get the impression he doesn't intend to dawdle there for long.

"Open your legs, please."

I'm happy to oblige, bending my knees before allowing them to fall open, exposing me to his gaze. He shifts lower, props himself up on his elbow to get a good look.

"You're looking very shiny and pink, Miss Fischer. Glistening, in fact. Are you wet for me already?"

I'm not sure if I'm supposed to answer, and in any case my arousal is quite, quite plain to see. I just wish he'd stop discussing it and fuck me.

"Miss Fischer?" His tone is hardening slightly, and I sense a warning shudder. I'm not ill anymore, he knows I'm not, and Cain is turning out to be something of a dominant presence in the bedroom. In any room, actually.

But here, now, naked and with my legs spread wide, I want him to devote his attention to pleasuring me rather than enforcing his will.

"Yes. I am. I think." I answer quickly, hoping that perhaps he'll drop this line of questioning and get down to what's important.

"You think? Aren't you sure, Miss Fischer?"

Uh-oh...

"I, yes, I'm sure I am."

"Then why didn't you say so? Are you being coy with me, Miss Fischer?"

"I didn't mean to be. I just wasn't sure... I mean..."

"Either you're sure, or you're not. Which is it?" His tone is stern now, low and insistent. Worse though, he's making no move at all to touch me as I lie still, my thighs opened wide for his inspection.

I'm starting to feel extremely vulnerable, and somehow as though I'm at fault, though, I've no idea how that came about. If I knew what he wanted from me, I'd do it like a shot. I'd say whatever he wants me to say, as long as he puts his hands, his mouth on me soon. Or better still his cock deep inside me.

My pussy clenches at that delightful prospect, and my wetness increases. He must be able to see it dripping from between my folds. I lift my hips in silent invitation.

He smiles at me, his eyes glinting wickedly. He might be giving me a hard time just now, but his eyes promise much, much better to come.

"You know, Miss Fischer, yours is quite the most gorgeous cunt I've ever seen..." His conversational tone is sharply at odds with the intimacy of the moment and his words. And such words! This is praise indeed. I start to relax. Slightly.

"Mmm, an exquisite little tush you have there. What should we do with it, do you think?"

Lick it, fuck it, do anything you damned well like with it. Please just do something, and do it now.

"Miss Fischer, such impatience. We'll get around to all those things."

Oh no, did I say all that out loud? Apparently so. Cain is grinning at me, his expression now one of undiluted lust. "First though, I have a little toy you might like to try. Don't move."

He rolls easily and athletically to his feet then strolls across the room to the blanket chest. I remain where I am, my legs conveniently spread as he lifts the lid and rummages. I take the opportunity to admire his firm buttocks as he crouches by the chest, then the rippling muscles in his thighs as he straightens. He turns, and he has a vibrator in one hand, and what I think must be a tube of lubricant in the other. The silicone vibrator in a delicate shade of pale pink, looks somewhat on the large side. A glance at his swollen, hard cock as he returns to the bed convinces me that, on reflection, the vibrator is less impressive.

Cain comes back to the bed and tosses both items onto the duvet beside me. He sits on the edge, his back to me. He's wholly concerned with my so-called exquisite little tush now as he casually leans forward to trail his index finger around the entrance to my pussy. He dips his fingertip inside, and my whole body lurches. He shoots a sharp glance back at me, over his shoulder.

"I told you earlier to keep still. I don't want to have to tell you again."

He's removed his finger and my empty, abandoned pussy is spasming wildly in desperate protest. I'm ready to plead if that's what it takes. It seems it's not though. He turns back to his task, and now all I can see is his back and shoulders as he bends over me. He uses the fingers of one hand to part my folds, opening up the entrance to my pussy, and with his other hand calmly slips one finger back inside. I get the whole length this time, but his touch seems impersonal. He's just checking, testing. Even so, my juices are flowing freely as he thrusts slowly, adding a second finger for good measure. Moments later he withdraws them again, and I could almost weep with frustration. He glances at me once more.

"What a perfect little slut you are, Miss Fischer. So hot and wet, and possibly ready. Do *you* think you're ready?"

I nod quickly. Emphatically. "Yes. I am. Please…"

"Yeah, I think you'll do." He reaches for the vibrator, and the lubricant. His expression is considering, and he takes the time to slip two fingers back into my pussy to double check the wetness there. "I reckon I could pretty much swim in your cunt, you're so wet now. We may not need the lube, but we'll have a splash I think, just to make sure."

He squirts a liberal amount onto his palm and proceeds to smear it all over the pink silicone, paying particular attention to the head. I should be more grateful for his attention to detail, I suppose, but at this moment I'm some way beyond coherent thought, and my manners have deserted me. I just want him to fill me. With anything. His cock preferably, but I'll settle for battery-operated if that's what's on offer.

Satisfied that both me and the vibrator are prepared to his liking, Cain shifts his position slightly so that now he's facing me, though still with an excellent view of my quivering pussy. He glances down, carefully opening me again with the fingers of his left hand, using his right to position the head of the vibrator inside me. Just the head, and he's so achingly gentle I could scream.

"Tell me if I hurt you."

His tone is soft now, no longer the fierce, uncompromising man and more the tender lover I prefer. Though only sometimes if I'm honest. The harsher version is lovely too, in his way. But for now that man has stepped outside the room, and Cain is all solicitous concern as he eases the slick silicone into my welcoming pussy. I sigh, my eyes closed in sheer ecstasy as the smooth edges slide along my sensitive walls. I grip tightly, seeking more friction, greedy for more sensation. My hips are moving involuntarily, thrusting slowly, then more firmly.

"Not yet, love. Keep still a moment longer."

His voice is seductively reassuring, and I trust him. I lie still, my back arched in anticipation, as the vibrator slides all the way into me. It may not be as wide as Cain's cock, but what it lacks in girth it makes up for in length, and I gasp as it nudges my cervix. Cain stops there, satisfied the toy is in place. He stands, walks to the end of the bed to look at me.

"That color suits you. Matches your pretty pink tush." His grin is almost boyish now as he surveys his handiwork.

He winks at me before he strolls back to the chest, and I have a moment's unease. What now? Surely there can't be more...? He doesn't open the chest though, just picks something up from on top. He turns back to me. I catch a flicker of movement in his right hand, then all sensible thought shatters.

The vibrator bursts into life, sending delicious ripples of quivering sensation the length of my pussy. I scream, actually scream out loud, my body jerking with the potency of it. It feels good, almost too good. Too intense. My instinct is to snatch at the vibrator, try to pull it out, but he's there ahead of me and catches my hands before I can reach it. He pins them lightly at my sides and leans over me.

"If it's too much, tell me."

I gaze at him in dazed but awestruck shock. Too much? Nearly, perhaps. But not quite. Certainly not quite yet. My body relaxes, and my eyelids drift closed as I give myself over to the powerful rhythm pulsating through me. Each throb, each rippling shudder is exquisite. Cain's grip loosens as he realises I'm with him again, and loving this. He lies alongside me, and I roll over to nuzzle his chest. He strokes my hair, his fingers tangling in it as he whispers sweet words in my ear. "Is that good, baby?"

I nod, beyond speech as my body begins to convulse. I'm squeezing down hard on the vibrator, wringing every shred and tingle of sensation from it on my headlong descent into orgasm. It doesn't take long, not long at all before I'm moaning and convulsing in his arms. He tightens his embrace, holding me close while I shatter.

"This is for you, baby, all for you. Enjoy. Take more, take all you want. Squeeze it, grip it, it's yours..." His voice is both soothing me, and urging me on as he murmurs words of encouragement in my ear.

And I do. I take all I want, all I need, as he holds me safe. The vibrator nestled deep inside me is strong and powerful, overwhelming my senses. But it is nothing compared to the raw, unrestrained potency of Cain Parrish as he cradles me gently in his arms and the rest of the world falls away.

And I fall in love.

As the final aftershocks of my climax drop away, Cain rolls me onto my back. He uses the remote control to slow down and eventually stop the throbbing in my pussy then pulls a pillow under my shoulders. Satisfied I'm quite comfortable, he parts my legs and removes the vibrator. He drops it lightly onto the carpet, to be followed by the lube then positions himself between my legs. He has a condom in his hand. I've no idea where he produced it from, but he clearly keeps his supply within easy reach. He snaps the foil and is ready in seconds. Which makes two of us.

"Now, honey, you get me. Okay?"

I can only nod, but in this moment if he asked me for my last kidney, I think I'd give it up to him gladly. He can take absolutely anything, everything. I'm his.

He thrusts forward, filling me instantly. I moan my welcome, lifting my legs to hook my ankles behind his waist. The angle provides better access, and he surges even farther forward, his cock nudging my cervix as the vibrator did earlier. Not satisfied even with this, he loops his arms under my knees and lifts me further, now holding me still and exposed, fully open to him as he starts to thrust in earnest. He quickly finds a rhythm, pumping faster, his balls slapping against the lower curves of my bottom as he picks up speed. He fucks me hard, deep, powerfully, and the muscles in my pussy clamp around him in avid response. My body spasms wildly, any fragile, brief interlude of control scattering as the churn of fast approaching release again seizes me.

He must be aware of my response, seems to be reveling in it as he increases the pace, racks up the pressure. My body is coiling, tightening, my muscles clamping in readiness for the final, explosive climax. I don't hold it back, couldn't if I wanted to. I feel utterly powerless in this moment, my body surging on, completely under his control. I shatter, gloriously, brilliantly, my head a firestorm of dazzling lights as every nerve ending stands to attention then leaps off the cliff with me. And I know Cain is there too, spinning mindlessly as he mutters something singularly obscene in my ear before plunging once more into me, to the root, and holding still as the heat of his semen fills the condom.

Afterwards, as we lie side by side, I'm still panting from the exertion though I'm not at all sure I did any of the work. Cain drops a light kiss on my mouth.

"Well, that killed half an hour. Do you want to start your shower while I get us some coffee? I seem to remember you saying you might benefit from some, though I can't really find anything to complain about so far."

"Idiot." I lightly punch his side then I remember something. From earlier. I stiffen, and he knows immediately.

"What is it, Abbie?" He rolls me onto my back, cupping my chin.

His eyes are on mine, and I can't look away even though I want to. He's going to press me, insist on — what — something. He'll demand I tell him whatever's on my mind, but I'd much rather not. Not yet. I had what I can only describe to myself as a 'moment' back there. As he held me, as the wondrous ripples of pleasure streamed through me, as I lay vulnerable and shaking and totally protected in his arms, I had a moment when I knew I loved him. I love him now. And will, into the future.

But it's no good, it's no use at all. I'm not who, or what, he thinks I am. He imagines he's making love to a business partner, co-owner of his building firm. Maybe even some sort of soulmate. And what am I really? Some functionally illiterate girl who can't even write her own name without counting the letters to make sure she's put enough in there? And still it's touch and go as to whether they're in the right order

For the first time, I'm dissatisfied with my life. Truly, properly dissatisfied, so much so I might even contemplate doing something to rectify matters. Always before I've made excuses, put off seeking help, managed to get by. Now, a future filled with getting by seems less attractive. For once, and maybe for the first time, I have a reason to want to change. For me, for my own reasons, and not because someone else told me I should. But I don't want to share any of this. Not yet. For now I want to hug it inside me, explore and taste it. Get to know this new me, and maybe find a way to let Cain know me too.

"Abbie, tell me…"

I shake my head, my eyes closed as tears prick and inexorably start to leak. He sees, wipes them from my cheeks with his thumb.

"I came on strong just now, I know. I upset you. I'm sorry…"

"No, it wasn't that." And I don't really know what he means—there's no way he upset me.

"No? Then what? Tell me, Abbie."

"It's nothing. Just me."

"We had great sex. Well, I think it was great?" He waits, clearly needing some sort of confirmation.

In fairness, I can do no less. "It *was* great. More than great…"

"So, if the sex was so great, why the tears?"

I try to shrug it off. "It's just me, I get emotional sometimes." Yeah, well that's half-way to being the truth. Not bad, by my standards. 'Emotional' *could* describe my reaction, at a pinch.

"Abbie, promise me this is not because I called you a slut."

"No! Why would I…?" I'm astonished, genuinely.

"I scared you. I know I did…"

I'm staring at him now, more than a little confused. "I'm not sure…"

"Exactly. You weren't sure back then either, when I got heavy about how wet you were…"

Ah, yes.

"So I pressed you on it. Deliberately. Bullied you a little perhaps. I know you were off balance, unnerved. You were meant to be."

I remember it now, more vividly as he talks me back through it, and yes, he did intimidate me. I recall I wanted him to like me, and approve of me, but it seemed I'd done something wrong. Then he called me a slut, and yes, that did sting a bit. But I'll forgive him anything if he can produce orgasms like that for me. I tell him so, and his smile is one of knowing.

"That's how it works, sweetheart. I can touch you in lots of erotic, exciting ways. I can use toys, like today, or my hands, my tongue. My cock, which I'll readily admit is my personal favorite."

Mine too, probably.

"I can suck your nipples, your clit. Finger-fuck you into oblivion. Would you agree so far?"

I nod dumbly, wondering if perhaps I'm a little too easy to please. Cain doesn't seem to be getting at that though, and in any case, I'll take what I can get in life, right? He pauses for a moment, his slate gray eyes intent now.

"But the most erogenous zone on your body isn't between your thighs. It's the one between your ears. What goes on in your head is a far more powerful turn on than anything else, so I worked on your head. A mind-fuck, if you like. I forced you to acknowledge your body, and to be attuned to your responses. I asserted my dominance over you, brought your submissive side to the surface. If you let me have control, if you trust me, I will take care of you. You will have what you need."

"How did you know? That I was scared? I didn't say."

He traces the outline of my lower lip with his fingertip as he watches me, watching him. "Your eyes, sweetheart. I can see your fear there. And your submission. It's heady stuff, and quite, quite beautiful. I can see it now."

"I'm not afraid now."

"Perhaps a little. But it's submission I'm seeing now." His voice has softened to not much above a whisper as he drops his mouth to mine, brushes my lips with his. I open my mouth and his tongue slides inside, as I submit again. Long minutes later, he breaks the kiss, slowly withdrawing his tongue as my head spins madly. I'm trying to take it all in, to make some sense of what's happening here.

Seeing my confusion, perhaps, he's in no hurry yet to leave our bed. "Do you understand what I'm saying to you? What's happening here, between us? And you do know, don't you, that your safe words are your safety net?"

I frown, trying to process everything that's happening. It does make sense, sort of. He is most definitely the dominant partner here, in every way. And I've naturally let him take that role. I've deferred to him, and he's taken good care of me. Excellent care, in fact. If I've been responding instinctively, my instincts have served me well. They usually do. He tuned in almost at once to my secret fantasies and made them come true. I expect that's why he's been so ridiculously easy to fall in love with. I'm head over heels, and it's not even seven o'clock in the morning yet.

I don't say that though. I say nothing about the L word. Instead I smile, and I nod, and I lean up to kiss him back.

Chapter Nine

"Right. You, shower. Me, coffee. I'll be joining you so don't nick all the soap." Cain rolls out of bed and in almost the same motion, he's grabbed his jeans and pulled them on, though he leaves them unfastened. He smiles at me as he leaves the room, headed for the kitchen. I take the hint and hit the shower. A few minutes later, Cain slips in behind me. He very kindly washes my back for me, paying particular attention to the valley between my buttocks, so I feel it's only reasonable to reciprocate. In spite of our sensual ministrations, however, we manage not to end up fucking like bunnies on the shiny white tiles. I'm already totally sated from the glorious interlude when we first woke up, and I get the impression Cain really does want to get to work.

We get dressed, drinking our coffee as we go, then it's a quick bowl of cereal in the kitchen. I never usually want to bother with hairdryers and straighteners and such things in the mornings, and Cain doesn't seem to mind me just brushing my wet hair out and leaving it to dry naturally. He's probably quite relieved really as it's clear now he's itching to be off. By seven-forty-five we're in the van and headed down the road toward the small builders yard and office about a mile away.

"It's an easy enough walk back, if you want to do that. I'm often out on sites until quite late so you don't have to wait for me. It's pretty much a straight road."

I take special note of the route, but he's right, it's straightforward enough. And in just a couple of minutes it seems, we're pulling up in front of the locked gates. Cain hops out and removes the chunky padlock, and we're quickly inside the yard. I clamber down from the passenger side of the van, eying the small stone built office block warily. The building is on two storeys, and I understand my flat is the upper floor. If it *is* still my flat. It does seem to me that our domestic arrangements might have shifted rather in the last forty-eight hours.

"Phyllis usually gets in around quarter-past or half-past eight. I'll show you around, where the coffee is, that sort of thing, until she arrives. She's the best one to give you the guided tour of the spreadsheets and suchlike." Cain unlocks the door to the building and leads the way in. He stops just inside to disable the beeping alarm system, then gestures for me to follow him.

I doubt anyone could teach me around a spreadsheet, but I keep that grim observation to myself as I warily follow Cain into the small but quite tidy office space. No doubt I'll screw up before too long and it'll be obvious enough. I wonder for the umpteenth time as I follow Cain through the door into the nerve center, which is Phyllis Benson's domain, why on earth I don't just come clean.

But I haven't, and I'm not about to, so here I am.

And suddenly, so is the redoubtable Phyllis.

"Morning, morning, sorry I'm a bit late. My Stan just wouldn't let me go this morning, wanting extra cups of tea, his paper, his tablets. It's a madhouse sometimes, round at mine. And the buses are no help. I had to wait nearly twenty minutes. I was hoping to get in before you did, get the kettle on so's Miss, Miss…?" Her torrent of chatter stops as she contemplates what she should call me.

I rush to get my answer in before Cain does. "It's Abigail. Abbie. And I'm delighted to meet you, Mrs Benson." I step forward, my hand outstretched. I want her to like me, and this seems as good a way as any to start.

Mrs Benson takes my hand, shakes it warmly. "Phyllis. Just call me Phyllis, dear. Welcome to Parrish Construction. Have you had the guided tour yet? Not that there's much to see…"

"I was just about to, but now that you're here…." Cain smiles warmly at Phyllis, and is that perhaps a hint of gratitude that now he can leave me in her capable hands? Sure enough, "I could do with getting over to the warehouse site in Rothbury, and if I get off now I should be there by ten. I want to supervise the delivery of that dressed stone if I can. You'll be okay with Phyllis." He turns to me and I'm half-expecting a kiss, but this is his office environment so he just nods politely as he moves toward the door.

His van keys are in his hand, and moments later the engine starts and there's the sound of the vehicle turning around in the yard. With a low growl the van disappears into the morning traffic, and Phyllis and I are left looking at each other across the office.

Phyllis is obviously keen to progress matters. "Right, first things first. I'll show you where the kettle is. Then we'll get you sorted with a desk and a computer." It's not as though I've never actually used a computer before. Of course I have. Everyone has. But I normally just play Candy Crush Saga, Tetris occasionally. What I don't do is log on to business sites, write letters, examine spreadsheets. All of those things that Phyllis is blithely rattling on about as I sit and gaze at the more or less incomprehensible screen in front of me.

Having fortified both of us with cups of tea—for her—and coffee—for me—Phyllis shows me to a spare desk crammed in alongside hers, already set up with a computer, phone, some pens in the top drawer and a pile of notepaper. She leans over me to start the machine up and navigates into what I'm assured is to be my desktop. The various icons flashing happily on the screen will take me to the places I need to be, open up files I'll need to access. Satisfied I'm on course, Phyllis returns to her own desk, leaving me to explore.

Or more accurately, to sit transfixed like a rabbit caught in headlamps.

A few minutes pass, and I manage to shift the mouse around a little, the small arrow jumping about on the screen. I point to one of the symbols, a letter W in a nice bright blue. I know this one, it'll take me into the written stuff. I click the mouse experimentally, and my screen transforms into a list of God knows what. I stare at it, really starting to panic now. None of it, not a thing, makes any sense to me. No matter how long I sit and stare, no matter how hard I concentrate, I just can't understand any of what I'm seeing. None of it is familiar—it's just an incomprehensible jumble of strange words, letters and numbers leaping about in front of my eyes. And I don't know how to make it go away. I want my pretty desktop back—at least I had some idea what that was. I decide to look for it again. I point and click some more. Chunks of dark shading cover some of the words, then they simply disappear.

Christ! I start to panic in earnest now. What did I just do? Where did those words go to? What did they mean? Was it important? Will anyone notice? Can I get them back?

"Everything all right, dear?" Phyllis has turned in her chair and is looking over my shoulder at my screen. "Ah, right, the A.R.T. contract. That's where Cain is now, at the site in Rothbury. Good idea to start with that. You need to get your head round our current projects."

Shit! I just wiped out half his contract.

"I-I..." I'm stammering, knowing I need to say something, ask for help before this gets worse and worse.

"Problem, dear?" Phyllis has turned around properly now and is looking hard at my screen.

"I think I just lost it. Some of it. I don't know how..."

"Let me see." She stands up, leaning over me from behind and reaches around me to tap two keys on my keyboard. Instantly the missing chunk of writing reappears. "There you are, all safe and sound again."

This time. I feel sick. What if she hadn't been here? I didn't even know what it was I'd been messing with, let alone how to repair the damage.

Phyllis is watching me closely now, seems concerned. "Are you feeling all right, love? You look a bit shaky."

I'll say I'm shaky. But I nod and manage to stick something not unlike a smile on my face, and I thank her for helping me. Then I have the presence of mind to ask her to remind me what she did to get the writing back again.

"You just press Control 'Z'. Undoes whatever you just did. Here, like this." She drags the mouse across the screen, covering another huge chunk of the writing in blue, and moments later that's gone as well.

I stare at the screen, and at her.

She just chuckles and reaches for my keyboard again. "Look. Control, and then you press 'Z'. All back."

Sure enough, a couple of magical keystrokes and the contract is once more rescued. Control 'Z' is clearly of the utmost importance to me. I commit it to memory.

"How do I find that first thing again? Where all the pictures are?"

"Pictures?"

"Yes. For the different places…"

"Oh, you mean the icons. That's your desktop, love. You can just hit the back arrow…" She demonstrates and my lovely, plain and more or less comprehensible desktop is restored. "Are you not familiar with Windows then? Did you use a Mac before?"

Now she's lapsed into some obscure dialect of Swahili for all I can make out. I just stare at the screen, and say nothing. What is there to say? I'm completely and totally out of my depth, as I knew I would be. Phyllis is already starting to rumble me and I'm not halfway through my first mug of coffee yet.

Then inspiration strikes. "I've come out without my glasses, that's all. I need them for working." I've never worn glasses in my life, but Phyllis isn't to know that.

"Oh, well don't be straining your eyes, love. What about if you just help me collate these letters for now and get them into envelopes…?"

My excuse seems to convince her. For now. Stuffing envelopes sounds more like my sort of thing. I get to my feet, anxious to be away from the computer as quickly as possible, before I do some damage that can't be so easily dealt with by Control 'Z'.

"Right, no problem. If you just show me what to do, I'll be getting on with that." And I'll somehow find a way to make the job last all day if I have to.

Phyllis leads the way into the room next door, a small space more or less completely filled by the photocopier and a table. There are three stacks of neatly printed documents on the table, some sheets of sticky address labels and a large box of envelopes. Phyllis explains that these are publicity flyers and a covering letter which are to be sent to all contacts on the Parrish Construction mailing list. My task is to take one sheet from each pile, in the correct order, and fold them into thirds before shoving the whole lot into an envelope. Then I'm to stick an address label on the front of the envelope. When all the envelopes are filled, she promises to show me how the franking machine works. That's something to look forward to. Meanwhile, this looks like a task I can spin out nicely to at least fill the rest of the morning.

And I do. Phyllis keeps popping in to see how I'm doing, on one occasion bringing me a fresh cup of coffee, but seems satisfied I'm safe to be let loose on this. And I am. It's not especially interesting, it's repetitive and I'd definitely get very bored if I had to do it all the time. But for today it's just a relief to have a job I can do.

At twelve o'clock Phyllis tells me it's time for her to get off. She needs to get back to 'her Stan', who I gather is her husband who retired a couple of years ago and hasn't been well recently.

"It's his heart..." Phyllis explains, and this is why she's quite keen to give up work herself soon. "Makes you see what your priorities should be," she tells me.

I can see that, and I thank her for her help today.

"What will you do this afternoon, then? You've almost finished the mailing."

I have. There are only a couple of dozen envelopes left to stuff. I need to think fast. "I was wondering about having a look at the flat upstairs. I know the boiler needs fixing, but maybe there's other work too, stuff I could get on with?"

"It think the place is pretty much fine apart from the heating, but by all means go up and have a look around. Make yourself at home. The keys are in the key cupboard, it's the set marked 'flat'."

She fastens her coat ready to leave, so I thank her for all her help today. I'm not sure I'll be able to work out which set of keys is marked 'flat', but if need be I'll try them all. With a final wave, and a cheery 'see you in the morning', she's gone and I'm left to my own devices. It's only as she disappears around the corner I realize I haven't asked her how to turn the computer off.

I finish the remaining envelopes and stack them all nice and neatly in the box, ready for whatever comes next. Franking machine, perhaps? Then I take a stroll around the corner to pick up a cheese salad sandwich from a small bakery I spotted on the way in. I eat that as I gaze balefully at the mysterious computer screen once more — the desktop, I understand — and debate whether I might risk a bit more experimentation. I decide against such foolishness and spend the rest of the day pottering in the flat upstairs. Fortunately for me, there were only three sets of keys to choose from, and only one looked even remotely like keys for a flat. The others were either much too small — desks perhaps, or a cashbox, and the third set looked like they were for a vehicle.

The flat is really rather nice. It's about the same size as my previous home, one bedroom, a living room, kitchen and bathroom. There's direct access from the office up a narrow set of stairs, and also from the outside. It's fully furnished, nice, modern stuff, and the kitchen is well equipped. I could have been very comfortable here, although if Cain invites me to stay I won't be in any hurry to move out of his house. Maybe we could rent this place out?

I decide to clean the place up a little, although it's not especially in need of it. It's what I'm good at though and I actually do enjoy housework. I find everything I need in the cupboard under the sink, and get set to. I apply myself to cleaning, dusting, polishing. The next three or four hours drift past in a pine-smelling haze, until I'm startled by the sound of the door downstairs.

"Abbie? Where are you?" It's Cain's voice.

"Up here." I go to the door at the top of the internal stairs, peeling off my rubber gloves. Cain peers up at me in surprise from the main office below.

"What are you doing up there?"

"Just giving the place a once over. I'll be down in a moment." I hurry to put my cloths and disinfectant back under the sink, and make my way downstairs.

"The new boiler'll probably just mess it all up again." Cain is helping himself to coffee as I re-emerge, and I notice his clothes are dusty and his hands still grimy from whatever he's been doing all day. No office job for Cain Parrish. He's wearing a brightly colored light waistcoat which is flapping open, and his hard hat is dumped on my desk. He shrugs the jacket off too and stuffs it inside the hat then places the pair on top of a filing cabinet before making for the loo. "I'll just wash the dust off, then we'll head for home if you're done here."

I step aside for him to pass me, but he turns to drop a quick kiss on the edge of my mouth. His cheek grazes mine, the ten hours or so of stubble feeling sexily unkempt as it rubs against my skin. He smiles at me, winks and the toilet door swings shut behind him.

This brief respite leaves me a couple of minutes in which to sort out the computer, or more accurately to work out how to turn it off. I consider just unplugging it from the wall, but I know that's not right. Computers are strange beasts, and one thing I do know is that you need to press the start button to stop it. I remember that because it's just so ridiculous—a snippet of information I gathered from somewhere and managed to store in a corner of my brain. Not that it helps me now as I peer into every corner of my desktop for the start button. It used to be at the bottom, on the left—well, that's where it was on the machines I occasionally used to play Candy Crush on at school, if I managed to finish mopping a bit early. Not here though. Here all I can see where my start button should be is a round circle a bit like a globe. Someone must have changed everything around.

Shit, shit, shit! Why didn't I start this earlier? Cain will be back in a few minutes wanting to get off home, and find me still messing about trying to shut down a computer, a task even a three-year-old can do in their sleep. I hear him coming back, and in desperation hit the power switch on the wall behind the monitor. The screen goes blank, and I squelch any misgivings about maybe offending the machine's delicate sensibilities. I'm only just in time as Cain comes back out of the toilet, looking a little cleaner but still probably in need of a shower when we get home. I wonder if perhaps we both might be...

"Ready?" He retrieves his van keys from inside his discarded hard hat, and flashes me his sexiest smile.

My stomach clenches, way down deep, and my pussy starts to moisten. All thoughts of uncooperative computers are instantly dispelled. I smile back, nod and pick up my bag from the back of my chair.

"So, what did you do all day then?" Cain tosses the casual question to me as he re-sets the alarm.

I mutter something about dealing with some letters.

"Right, good start. What else?" He opens the van door for me to clamber in, then makes his way around to the driver's side.

"Not much really. Just, you know, finding out where things are." Yeah, like the kettle. And the Control 'Z' keys.

Still, my vague answers seem to be enough to keep Cain off my scent, at least for now. A few minutes later we pull up in the driveway in front of his house.

"Okay, I need a shower. I've been scrambling around in bloody holes all day checking foundations with the clerk of works. Do you want to dig around in the freezer and see what you can find for us to eat?" He's unlocked the door and ushered me inside, pausing at the bottom of the stairs to give me my instructions.

I have a better idea though. "I could, but I'd rather wash your back for you..."

His eyes narrow, but he nods. "Or there is that approach. Give me a couple of minutes to get the thick off though..." He starts up the stairs, but pauses halfway. "Oh, and, Abbie, would you mind bringing some strawberry jam with you? You'll find it in the fridge."

Chapter Ten

Strawberry jam?

Cain is inventive, I'll allow him that. After a leisurely half an hour spent under the streaming jets, caressing each other, smoothing soap into some very sensitive places, shampooing, rinsing and generally working each other into a frenzy of lust, we're at last back in the bedroom. In the shower Cain brought me repeatedly to the brink of orgasm, then back again, and now I'm quivering wildly each time he lays so much as a fingertip on me. Draped loosely in a large bath sheet, I kneel in the center of his huge bed, waiting for whatever he decides is to come next. I sincerely hope it's to be me, but with Cain there's no telling.

I'm right. His own towel looped tightly around his hips, Cain instructs me to lose mine and to lie down on my back. Naturally, I obey. Picking up the strawberry jam from the bedside table where I left it, he unscrews the top of the jar.

"Put your hands behind your head and keep really still. I'm going to coat your nipples in jam, then lick it off. That sound like fun to you?"

He stands beside the bed, his eyes are running up and down my nude body admiringly, but he's clearly waiting for an answer. I nod slowly. It does sound like fun. It also sounds like it's going to tickle and I seriously doubt I'll be keeping still for very long. I say as much to Cain.

"My jam, my bed, my rules. I want you to keep still, and if you don't think you can, I'm happy to help. Would you object if I were to tie you up?"

I look at him, stunned. I hadn't anticipated this. But as I reflect on the idea, a wisp of delighted anticipation curls inside me. It grows, and I know I want to try it. This might be very nice indeed.

I try not to sound too eager though. "I, well, maybe. If you'd like to. Here?"

"Yes, here. I want to tie your wrists to the bed head."

"But why? I mean, what then?"

"I think you know what then. I'll tie your ankles too, your legs spread nice and wide. Then, you're mine. I'll touch you, play with you, spread jam anywhere on your body I like and lick it off. Then I'll do it all again. And make you come as I feel like it. And I'll fuck you. How does all that sound?"

It sounds quite delightful, but he really has no need to tie me to the bed. If that's the deal, I'm going nowhere. I say as much.

Cain smiles. "Ah, but helplessness is such a powerful aphrodisiac. Just think of it. Naked. Spread out on the bed. Mine. Can you hand over control to me, sweetheart? Will you let me have your body to do as I like with it?"

I consider, but only for a moment. "Yes, I think so. I trust you. Would you untie me if I ask you to?"

He doesn't answer that question at first. Instead, he places the jar of jam back on the bedside table then he stretches out alongside me. He's still wearing his towel, while I'm completely nude, but somehow the dynamic doesn't feel too imbalanced. He kisses me, lightly at first, then deepening as he slips his tongue into my mouth. I've completely forgotten my question by the time he finally lifts his mouth from mine, but he hasn't.

"Yes, I would untie you. But we do need to talk about safe words."

"About what?" This sounds heavy, dangerous even.

He nuzzles my nose with his, to lighten the mood perhaps, but I know that this is a serious conversation. His tone betrayed that much. I was able to detect that subtle but certain shift I'm coming to recognize, that thread of steel in his voice that tells me to listen, to concentrate, to make sure I understand him. He props himself up on one elbow, caressing my face with his other hand. He doesn't intend to intimidate me just now, but he does mean for me to pay attention. I give it. Undivided.

"If you and I are going to play these games together, and, sweetheart, it's clear to me that we are, then I need to make sure you know how to protect yourself. You remember the other day when I spanked you, I told you what to say to make me stop. I even asked you to count, and when you stopped counting, I knew you'd had enough. As a submissive, you need to be able to call a halt if something happens that you can't tolerate, or if you've simply had enough. You need to be able to tell your Dom how you're feeling."

I was right, this *is* heavy. And he does keep on using that same word. "Submissive? Is that really what I am? I thought we were just—having fun. Maybe some of the things I asked you to do to me were a bit unusual, but…" My voice trails away. I'm not sure what I ought to be asking, or what I actually want to know. If he gives it—this thing between us, this kinky fun—a name, it makes it all so much more real. I appreciate that, for me at least, this has already gone beyond light-hearted, no strings bed-romping. A fuck-fest as he likes to call it. I'm not trying to kid myself that none of it really matters. Cain certainly seems to have other ideas now, and I really should be pleased about that. I am.

His expression is kind, patient, he's ready to explain, to help me understand, but I know our relationship is shifting. Solidifying. That gives me a warm feeling. This is more than just my pussy responding, though heaven knows that's happening too.

"If you let me spank you, tie you up and maybe do other things to you as well, then, sweetheart, that's you submitting. So you are a submissive. And I know full well that I'm a Dom. And we *do* need safe words."

I concede that, but I'm still inclined to think he might be over-complicating this. "I could just say no. Or stop. Will that do?"

"Yes, up to a point. We made do with that the other day. But that was just a mild spanking. And this morning it was all about pleasure. It was intense, I know that, and I did offer to stop. I went very slowly with you, and did a lot of checking. And when I spanked you before, I did add in the counting thing, which worked well. Whether you realized it or not at the time, that got you out of trouble. The problem is, you might say words like no and stop anyway, when you really mean the exact opposite. Indeed, I'm pretty sure you will be in the next few minutes. And especially if you're feeling something really intense. It's possible to be misunderstood. I prefer you to have a safe word that you'd never normally say. Then, if I hear it, I know you mean it."

He rolls onto his back, pulling me up onto his chest. He holds my gaze as he continues this amazing discussion. "Actually, I want you to have two safe words. One will be your signal for me to stop, no questions, just stop immediately. Sort of like a red traffic light. The second safe word will be your amber light, a signal for me to slow down, that you need me to check, to be careful. It will tell me you're struggling, upset, not sure, that you're close to your limit. Maybe that you need to talk, or ask me something. Does this make sense?"

Yes. No.

"What? What sorts of things might you do to me? What could you do that would be so awful that I'd need to..." My voice trails away as I try to imagine the sorts of activities he might be planning. I have a sudden mental image of Cain looming over me with a whip in his hand. I'm not at all convinced I entirely like that notion, though it does hold a certain...allure. And if he *is* contemplating something like that, what on earth does he see in me—recognize in me—that I never knew was there?

I can only stare, bewildered, as he continues to hold my gaze.

Then he continues, "I can see you're scared now, but you've no need to be, Abbie, I'll never, ever do anything to you without your consent. I haven't so far, have I?"

I shake my head, still unable to find any words.

"And I won't. This isn't about me attacking you, hurting and scaring you. This isn't about helpless victims and violence. This is kinky fun, with a bit of an edge. So, if you let me tie you to the bed, as I want you to, you have my promise I'll untie you if you use a safe word. No question. Is that good enough?"

Is it? Yes, possibly. Probably. I lie still, our eyes locked together, and I see honesty in his. And gentleness, despite the unwelcome image of the whip. I see caring, maybe even tenderness. He'll take care of me, give me what I want and keep me safe too. So I really think his promise *is* good enough. Better than good, even. I find myself nodding, slowly, but with a growing degree of certainty. I trust Cain Parrish, in this matter, definitely.

He smiles at me again. "Right. So, unless you have something else in mind, what about we use the traffic lights then. Red means stop, amber means slow down. Will that do?"

Again I nod. Then, "What will you use? To tie me up, I mean? I don't want to be handcuffed."

His smile broadens, and now it's tinged with a truly wicked glint. My pussy clenches in response.

"No handcuffs then. How about silk rope?"

Silk rope? Now that does sound rather acceptable. So I tell him that will do very nicely indeed. He smiles and suggests I make myself comfortable on the bed.

The rope is black and very soft. Supple. Cain produces it, two long pieces from the innocuous-looking blanket chest under the window. Except I'm now perfectly clear that it's not a blanket chest—well, not entirely. He keeps a few other interesting bits and pieces in there too. I'm relieved that there are no whips or chains or anything terribly frightening. Just toys. Toys he promises to share with me, if I like.

I might like. I might indeed.

"I want you on your back, I think, this time. I did promise you a spanking, though, and you should have had it yesterday, but you were indisposed. So maybe we'll start with that."

As I stand beside the blanket chest, still pondering the mysteries within, Cain tosses the lengths of rope casually onto the bed and sits on the edge. His curt hand gesture is clear—get over here, now, and lay yourself across my knees. Moisture is gathering between my legs just at the thought, and my bottom clenches in anticipation. To lie across his lap, both of us naked, seems so much more intimate, more connected somehow, than the table did. Still, I move slowly. I take my time positioning myself, and he seems to be in no hurry either.

I place my hands on his thigh to steady myself as I lean forward. He doesn't offer assistance, and I'm glad of that. Neither of us has said as much, but it's an intrinsic part of this, a core part of our deal if you like, that I place myself here willingly. That this is by my own choice. At last I'm comfortable—my head close to his ankles, my hands resting on the carpeted floor. My hair is trailing on the carpet and my bottom is presented perkily for his attention. Only now does he touch me.

His caress is light as he trails his palm across my buttocks, tracing the lower curve with his fingertips. He slides his hand along the deep groove between my arse cheeks, continuing down to ease through my now very wet folds.

"Ah, yes, little Abbie. Anticipation is everything..." he murmurs as he slowly circles my now dripping pussy. "Open your legs, love."

I spread my thighs, and my reward for compliance is swift and certain. He takes my clit between his fingers and squeezes it. I gasp, caught between pain and pleasure. He releases me, only to rub the sensitized nub firmly with the pad of his thumb. Now the pleasure is pure, intense and unambiguous. My orgasm is there, rushing through me before I take my next breath. I'm shaking and shuddering under his skilled caresses while he continues to roll my clit between his fingers, my nerve endings all standing to attention. He takes his time, drawing every last ripple and surge of delight from me. He's hardly started, and already I'm dissolving. I feel as though I could just melt into a puddle at his feet, a warm pool of delight soaking into his knee-deep shag pile.

At last I'm back, my body my own again, in a manner of speaking. In truth, I'm his to do with as he will—we've pretty much agreed that. I'm utterly relaxed, absolutely content. I lie still now, my bottom quivering while I wait for him to deliver the first swat.

I hiss sharply when the first spank lands across my right buttock. It's hard, sharp. More intense than my first experience of this, downstairs in the kitchen. But I need that, want more. I wait for the next one, but instead I hear his low, sexy voice.

"Count, please, Abbie."

"One." My voice is clear, strong. Why I should feel at my most powerful when I'm really at my most vulnerable is another mystery to address later, along with the contents of the blanket chest perhaps. But for now I'm just going to absorb what this moment has to offer.

"Hard enough?"

"Harder, please." *Now, where did that come from?*

I give a small yelp as the next slap catches my left buttock. My arse clenches wildly now, and the heat starts to radiate.

"Two. Harder still, if you could." *Amazing!*

"Oh, I certainly could, Abbie."

And he's not wrong. I yelp again when he swats my right buttock once more, right in the same spot as he did previously.

"Three. Thank you. Four. Five."

I continue to count while he continues to land the blows, each one unerringly hitting the same spot on each buttock, alternating between them. He's accurate and consistent, each spank is just the right intensity to hurt me, to push my limits, but not quite enough to make it really unpleasant. It's almost unpleasant, almost too much, but not quite. Just enough. My bottom is hot, burning up, the tender skin absorbing the slaps as he delivers one after the other.

"Ten. Eleven. Ahh. Twelve." I can't bite back my scream, but this time it doesn't stop his next slap.

"Amber." I'm not sure what I'm asking, what I want exactly. I don't want him to stop, not yet, but it's just too, too...

His palm lands on my bottom again, but now it's gentle. He slowly caresses my quivering, skin. I sigh, loving the tenderness in his touch. He draws his fingers lightly across the most sore places, and I rub my cheek against his leg in grateful response.

"My hand print is here, in vivid red on your bum. It looks gorgeous." I wince as he traces the outline of his hand, etched on my skin. "A minute's break, then six more, but not as hard. Okay with you?"

I shift on his lap. "Only six?"

"Six. If you get that far. Remember your safe word."

I won't be needing that. This is nothing. Not really. I just need to relax, accept, enjoy.

I do all these things, but I still safe word after the fourth slap. Cain massages my sore bottom again, once more slipping his fingers between my thighs to test my pussy's reaction to all this. I'm absolutely soaking. There are wet sounds as he slides two fingers deep inside me, finger-fucking me hard and fast as I open my legs wide again. His other hand reaches for my clit. A few seconds, and my orgasm is once more rippling through me as I spin delightfully out of control. My pussy clenches around his fingers, greedily seeking more friction, grabbing at him. He chuckles and deliberately slows his thrusts. It's too late, my body is beyond recall and I thrust my hips wildly to maintain the pressure, tightening around his fingers and wringing the last dregs of release from my body myself.

At last, I lie still. I'm satisfied, utterly content.

But Cain is not. "Stand up." His voice has taken on that hard edge again, sublime but so powerful, demanding obedience.

I stand.

"Lie down, on your back."

I glance at him balefully. My bottom is smarting, I'd really prefer to lie face down. One look is enough to convince me not to argue. I dutifully scramble onto the bed and carefully ease myself onto my back. It's not too uncomfortable, on reflection. As long as I don't move.

Cain stands, watches me trying to find a way to lie still without irritating my sore bum any further. His lip quirks, but he says nothing. He doesn't have to. I make a mental note to safe word earlier next time.

He picks up one of his lengths of rope and makes a smallish loop at one end. He holds that out to me, and I slip my left hand through it. Without speaking to me now, he quickly ties both my wrists to the bed posts. I know he'll have done a thorough job, and he's obviously not new to this, but still I try a couple of experimental tugs to see if there's any give. There isn't.

Cain takes a little more time carefully checking his knots, asking me if my wrists hurt at all. I shake my head. I'm tied up well and truly, but the ropes are soft and supple against my skin, and not so tight that they affect my circulation. Satisfied it seems, he picks up the second length of rope and quickly repeats the process but this time tying my ankles to the bottom bedposts. I'm not tall enough to actually reach, so this time there's more rope involved to cover the extra distance. And by the time he's finished, his knots checked and my wellbeing assured, I'm quite immobile, naked on his bed, my legs spread wide, and completely at his mercy.

Wonderful!

"You've had two orgasms already. I think you might be able to show a little restraint now, no pun intended." He seats himself on the bed beside me, idly circling my left nipple with his fingers.

It tickles, sort of, and I wriggle slightly. He stops his tormenting, smiles at me then deliberately starts again.

"Look at me, Abbie. If I didn't want you to watch, you'd be blindfolded."

My eyelids snap open, a shiver of unease rippling through me. I really am helpless and quite literally in his hands. He reaches for the jar of jam, still sitting on the bedside table. He dips his finger in then offers it to me to lick. I do, curling my tongue around his middle finger, tasting the jam but also my own juices from being finger-fucked just a few minutes ago.

"Nice?" He asks the question casually. I manage an equally noncommittal tilt of my head. His lip quirks.

"Not sure? Try this then?" He dips his finger again, and this time smears the jam across my lips.

I snake my tongue out to lick it away. His eyebrow is raised, silently asking my opinion now. I lick my lips again, managing to exhibit a little more enthusiasm.

His reply is just a slow, sexy smile. He dips two fingers into the jar, scooping out a more generous helping of the sticky red jam. Even though I know it's going onto my nipple, I still jerk as he trails his fingertips around my areola then smears the stickiness all over the swelling peak of my left breast.

"Cold?" His question is delivered so dispassionately he might have been discussing tomorrow's weather.

I shake my head. "Not cold. I told you, I'm ticklish."

"Ah yes, so you did." And he proceeds to do exactly the same thing to my right nipple before stopping to admire his creation.

I strain my neck to glance down at my vivid red nipples, now smeared with stickiness and standing to attention under the jam. I expect Cain to dip his head and start to lick it off, but he's not ready for that yet. Instead he slides his fingers through the goo on my left nipple, pinching my swollen bud between his thumb and finger ends. I jerk again as he squeezes hard enough to hurt. His response is to take my right nipple in his other hand and apply the same pressure there too. I moan softly, arching under his touch despite the discomfort. He increases the pressure, only slightly, but enough to make me yelp as real pain bites. He releases me and lowers his mouth to my breasts to start the long and painstaking process of licking my nipples clean. He laps the jam away, then he takes one hard pink pebble into his mouth and sucks on it. The pleasure is intense, and I cry out.

"Please, I can't..."

He stops sucking, but doesn't release my nipple from his mouth. His 'I told you so' glance up at me is enough to silence me for a while as he starts once more. Moments later I'm writhing under him, as far as my restraints will allow me to, as he shifts his attention to the other side and starts all over again. I'm so incredibly aroused my pussy is clutching on the void within. I want to close my legs, squeeze my clit, anything to gain some relief. But I'm held securely in place, helpless, my legs spread wide.

At last he lifts his head, and reaches for the jam jar again. I groan, expecting the process to start all over again. As indeed it does. He carefully spreads jam across my breasts, not just the nipples, and I find myself hoping the jar was closer to full than empty. Now that I'm becoming accustomed to the sensation, and to the restraints, it really is very, very nice. Not enough yet to bring me to orgasm, but definitely getting there.

This time Cain doesn't stop with my breasts. Satisfied I'm suitably coated, he gets up and to my astonishment heads for the bedroom door. Surely he isn't going to leave me here... Wordlessly he leaves the room, but I trust him and I wait. In moments he's back, a warm, wet flannel and a towel in his hands. He wipes his fingers then grabs a pillow from behind my head and shoves it under my bum to raise my bottom from the bed. Idly, I note that the soreness from my spanking is almost gone. He then lifts my hips again, this time to slip the towel underneath.

"This bit can get messy." He winks at me as he picks up the jar again.

I hold my breath as he takes two heaped fingerfuls of jam, then using the fingers of his spare hand to open my inner lips, he smooths it thickly over my clit and labia. He's now shifted his position so he's lying across the bed, between my wide open thighs, propped on one elbow as he proceeds to dip his fingers again and paint more of my pussy with the sticky jam. He's very thorough, smearing the cool, fruity concoction everywhere. I just know, no matter how diligent his attempts to lick it off, I'll be back in the shower before this evening's over.

I lay there, perfectly still, acutely conscious of every sweep of his fingers across my clit, my labia, my pussy. He even dips his fingers into between my lips to deposit a blob there, before continuing around to coat my tight little arsehole with the stuff. Now I do gasp. This is new. This is something previously unexplored. I'm not sure what I make of this.

Cain ignores my shocked hiss as I wriggle, trying to shift my vulnerable and previously untroubled anus from his attention. If anything, his efforts there are intensified.

"Please, I don't think..." I'm not sure what it is I want to say, but some form of protest seems to be called for.

He glances up at me, his fingertip now firmly inserted into my arse. "Safe word, Abbie. Or you keep still and let me do this." His gaze holds mine, but his fingers remain still as he lets me process what's happening to me.

I turn it all over in my head. I'm acutely aware of the intrusion, his finger is in my arse, for God's sake. But, I don't use my safe word. I don't even use my amber light. Instead, I deliberately close my eyes, and force my body to relax, to go limp. I give myself over to him.

"Good girl." His words are softly murmured, then he returns to his task.

Once I've accepted the indignity, I have to confess that it feels rather nice as he eases his finger deeper into my bum. He's not rough, not forcing me at all, just slowly gaining entry, my muscles relaxing and opening to allow it. As his second knuckle disappears inside me, I can't contain another small gasp. He isn't hurting me, but it does feel strange. And slightly scary. And more than slightly wicked. Cain quickly settles that little interruption though by scraping his thumb lightly over my clit. My hips lift, my whole body arches—his to do with as he likes. The final inch of his finger sinks into me, and I lie still, utterly relaxed, utterly trusting as he continues to stroke my clit.

My orgasm a few seconds later is beautiful, an intense sensual experience. It's almost spiritual, my connection to Cain so absolute in these ecstatic moments. I shiver, my body shuddering and convulsing in its release. I'm quite helpless to do anything but accept what he's doing to me. For me. It's as though all my nerve endings are directly connected to my clit, and everything he does to me is intensified by the intimacy of his final penetration. I thrash my head from side to side, the only part of me that can move, as wave after wave of pleasure washes across me, through me. All I know is, he's touching me, I'm allowing him to do whatever he chooses to me, and it's wonderful beyond compare.

Cain slides his finger from my arse, but makes no move to untie me. Instead, he lowers his face to my pussy and starts to lick. Slowly, delicately, as though he's savoring every sweet mouthful he laps at every inch of my exposed cunt. He draws the tip of his tongue along my slit to tease out the jam coating my entrance, and I make a little throaty sound in appreciation. It feels so good, so decadent, so sweetly kinky. He takes his time, careful not to leave any part of me untasted. I'm flexing my fingers, twisting my hands in my restraints, tugging at the ropes binding me. Cain sees, knows, but still doesn't release me. I could ask him to, but this is his show, and I'm content to play it his way.

The now familiar churn of orgasm is welling again, my pussy clenching and squeezing. The need to be filled is almost overwhelming. I want him inside me, now.

"Fuck me. Please, fuck me…" I'm moaning now, the plea desperate as my body starts to spasm again.

"Soon, baby. One more orgasm first. Come for me now." His tone is low, but insistent. He slides two fingers deep into my cunt, twisting and separating them inside to scrape against the walls of my channel.

He finds and strokes my G-spot, rubbing harder as I stretch and strain against the ropes.

"I need…" My voice trails away—I don't know how to articulate what I need.

Cain seems to sense it anyway. "I know, sweetheart. You'll have what you need. First, I want you to come. Now. Come for me, hard, fast."

His fingers are urging me on, and his words only serve to intensify the sensations. In moments I'm imploding again, my senses scattering as my release rips through me. This time my climax is powerful, intense, almost brutal in its severity. The tidal wave of pleasure sweeps any rational thought aside as I'm carried along, spinning helplessly — weightless in the grip of this intensity of feeling. At last it passes, and I drift slowly back to reality. I may have forgotten to breathe, I'm gasping now, the air shuddering into my lungs as I drag oxygen in. Cain withdraws his fingers again and rolls off the bed. He quickly unties my ankles, but leaves my wrists bound. The sharp snap of the condom foil precedes his entry by mere seconds. He plunges his cock fully inside me, thrusting hard as he quickly sets up a rhythm.

"Oh, God. Cain. I — that's..." I can't find anything sensible to say, so I give up the effort. I open my eyes to find Cain's gray gaze fixed on me.

"You are so beautiful, babe. So bloody gorgeous..." His voice is ragged, lowered now to little more than a growl.

Still supporting his weight on his arms, he leans down to place his lips over my mouth. His breath mingles with mine and I can taste the sweet, sensuous mix of strawberries and my own musk on his lips. I open my mouth and suck his tongue in, loving the double penetration. He lowers himself down onto his elbows, cradling my face in his hands as he continues to fuck me hard. His kiss deepens, and I lift my legs to anchor them around his waist. The angle increases his penetration, and the slight shift in direction pushes his cock hard against my G-spot with every stroke. In moments I'm coming again, my pussy tightening around him, milking every last tingle of pleasure from his cock.

"Christ, baby, yes. Squeeze me. God, you're so fucking tight. So hot..."

His cock is like a piston, pounding into me, bumping hard against my cervix with every stroke. He rocks his hips sharply under my heels as I cling around him. I shake and shudder, and give myself over to yet another powerful orgasm. This time though, I'm not alone. Cain stiffens, his cock jerking hard inside me as he rams it home in one final thrust, then holds still as the semen pours from his body.

At last we're both sated, lying still and spent. Cain withdraws, disposing of the condom quickly before he reaches up to free my wrists. I roll onto my side and snuggle up to him. He loops his arm around me, pulling me in close as he drops a light kiss on the top of my head.

"Well, that should keep us going for an hour or so. Just about enough time to grab a bite to eat."

I rub my cheek against his chest. "Mmm, and I need another shower. I'm all sticky." I snuggle in closer though, in no hurry to go anywhere for a while. Cain seems inclined to agree, tightening his arm around me. And in moments, we're both asleep.

Chapter Eleven

"Tell me about this thing you're doing in Rothbury."

"Sorry...?" Cain glances up from his position crouching in front of the dishwasher. I pass him another two plates to stack in there.

"This building site you went to today. In Rothbury? What are you building?" I may not have much interest in the paperwork side, but I am genuinely intrigued by the construction process itself. I know that much of the work is physical and hard, but it also has a delicate technicality about it, requires careful planning, meticulous organization to make sure everything goes together just as it should. Or so I imagine.

Cain stands up, dries his hands then passes me the tea towel.

"It's what *we're* building, actually. Parrish Construction is you *and* me, plus about a dozen or so other employees and sub-contractors. But the development in Rothbury isn't just us. It's a refurb of an old woollen mill, going to be luxury apartments overlooking the river. Nice spot. The principal contractor, A.R.T., is a multi-national, but we — Parrish

Construction—specialize in period stuff. They've brought us in to do the internal dressed stone work and lay some new Yorkshire stone flooring. We'll be on site for another three or four weeks."

It sounds fascinating, and I'm full of questions. "How did we get in on a massive job like that then? Do we advertise?" I'm thinking of the flyers I stuffed into envelopes today.

"Yes, sometimes. And we have a reputation in the trade for this sort of work. We've done a lot for A.R.T. in the last couple of years and they usually call us in on jobs like this one."

"Do we do anything else? Other sorts of building?"

"Sweetheart, times are hard. We do anything that comes our way. We're doing okay, but I never turn down work. This specialist stuff pays well though."

"So, what other things have you—sorry, we—built?"

"Come on, I'll show you." He holds out his hand.

I take it and follow him from the kitchen. He leads the way to the small home office at the back of the house, the room where I first found him as I explored the house the afternoon I arrived here and was intimidated by Oscar. Speaking of whom, the silent gray shadow has trotted down the hallway after us and is now slinking across the office to take up residence in his usual chair. Cain ignores him as he pulls open the top drawer of a filing cabinet.

"Here, that's our brochure. It's on our website too. It has details of some of our previous projects." He hands me a glossy booklet. "Have a look through that if you like."

I take it cautiously and open it at random. Then I heave a sigh of relief as I realize it's mostly pictures. Glossy images of building projects in various states of completion. I smile my thanks, and drop into the only chair in the room to thumb through it more slowly. There are words on the pages too, but in his marketing, Cain Parrish clearly relies more on showing rather than telling. I'm glad of that, and I find the brochure quite fascinating. I'm suddenly full of questions.

"Where is that? What was this project? How long ago? Which bit did we do? Why do you…? What's this for?"

Cain leans against the door frame, answering me patiently, explaining in more detail as I quiz him. One picture particularly intrigues me. It's a converted church, a huge building which has been cleverly sliced into beautiful apartments, whilst somehow managing to maintain the full height of the massive space in the middle. The entrance is photographed and spread across the center pages of the brochure. There's a huge restored stained glass window with light streaming through, washing the whole building in a multi-colored glow. It's clever, artistic and I have a powerful urge to paint it.

"Where is this place?" I point to the stained glass window.

"Leeds. Rather off our usual patch, but it was a special job. Couldn't resist it. That was a derelict church, a listed building. It'd been empty for over twenty years—unless you count the pigeons, that is. Christ, what a mess that was when we started."

"It's lovely now. Which part of it did we do?"

"That part mostly. The entrance foyer. The exposed stonework needed to be cleaned and dressed, and a lot of it was chipped and damaged. We restored the ecclesiastical features, the stone carvings and so on. It was difficult to do because of the height. We had to use a cherry picker and internal scaffolding to reach the ceiling. We brought in a specialist glass artisan for the window, obviously. That was a one-off."

"Is it open to the public? I'd like to see it. Paint it possibly…?"

He gazes at me, considering. "That's the entrance, so yes, you could probably get in to see that much. In fact, the Civic Trust down in Leeds probably do tours there. They were never away from the place while the work was going on, constantly checking we weren't about to rip out some irreplaceable bit of Pugin architecture. You'd need permission from one of the current residents to go into any of the apartments though."

"It's this bit I'd like to see, with the stained glass window. Could we go there sometime?"

"I don't see why not, if you like. And, Abbie, if you want to paint it, we could probably use your picture in some of our future publicity. We've tended to rely on photography up until now, but other forms of art would be interesting as well."

I gaze at him, an idea forming of how I might be able to add some value here after all, how I can make my contribution. My literacy and numeracy skills haven't equipped me for a role managing the office, and I'd hate that in any case. But the prospect of visiting these various refurbished buildings, painting them, drawing out their historical essence skillfully restored and reinvented for a twenty-first century lifestyle. Now that—that is me. I'm at home suddenly, sure of myself, a fish that had been floundering on the river bank, unexpectedly toppling back into the cool, fresh water. I've found my niche.

Cain sees it too. He's smiling at me, and on impulse I throw my arms around him. He returns my hug, and lifts me off my feet to swing me in a circle. The tiny office was never designed for such nonsense and we manage to send a stack of trade magazines flying. Neither of us minds much though, and even Oscar seems unmoved by the commotion.

"Sounds like a plan, sweetheart. I'll check with the Civic Voice when we could get in there. First chance we get, right?"

I kiss him, liking it very much indeed.

* * * *

"Where are you going today?"

We're eating a rushed breakfast again, having invested the half hour or so we might have used making bacon sandwiches in a frantic fuck-fest. Neither of us is complaining, but I'm starting to contemplate my coming day with a distinct lack of enthusiasm. I've noticed that whilst yesterday Cain dressed in old work clothes, today he's a lot smarter. He's wearing gray Chinos, a black T-shirt and a dark gray leather jacket. His battered work boots have been abandoned in favor of shiny black leather shoes, and he's been in the office stuffing papers into a document carrier. I somehow don't think he's looking forward to another day crawling around in muddy holes with the clerk of works.

"Rothbury, same as yesterday." He slugs down the dregs of his coffee and picks up the keys to the van. "Are you ready?"

I nod and pick up my jacket. "How come you're not wearing building site clothes then?"

"Ah, right. Today I'm in the site office all day. We have some meetings with the architects, and we're interviewing for an electrical contractor. I agreed to sit in on the panel."

"Could I come? With you I mean? I wouldn't get in the way." Anything to avoid another day staring at that computer screen and trying to pretend to Phyllis that any of it makes sense. And actually, the prospect of sitting in on discussions with an architect is quite interesting. I don't suppose I'd be much help choosing an electrician, but I could perhaps look around the site.

Cain pauses on his way to the door, glancing back at me over his shoulder. At first I think he's going to tell me he's too busy, that I would be in the way.

"Okay, I don't see why not. We'll need to make a detour though, call in at the yard first."

"Yes, of course. I'll need to tell Phyllis where I am."

"That, yes, but we'll also need to pick up some gear for you. Building sites are dangerous places. You'll need a hard hat, a high-vis jacket and some steel toe caps."

I stare at him in astonishment. It had never occurred to me I'd need all that. He catches my amazed expression

"No safety gear, no entry to the site. Health and safety rules. The site foreman *will* check. I know, I appointed him. Do you have any jeans you could wear?"

I glance down at my knee length floral skirt. Very decent, but probably not suitable for a construction site.

"Give me a minute." I shoot past him and bolt back up the stairs. Five minutes later I'm hopping into the passenger seat, appropriately dressed in my blue denims and trainers.

Our stop off at the yard is brief. Just enough time to explain our plans to Phyllis, who is otherwise preoccupied in any case as the computer on my desk seems to be playing up this morning. I shuffle past guiltily as I remember my hasty exit yesterday and my doomed search for the start button. The sooner I can get myself established as the resident artist and not the admin assistant, the sooner I'll stop being such a liability.

Cain retrieves his hard hat and high-vis jacket from where he left them yesterday on top of Phyllis' filing cabinet. He opens the bottom drawer and rummages around in there, before pulling out another similar jacket and a hat.

"Just try that. It might need adjusting, but it's the smallest I can find." He perches the hat on my head, and adjusts the plastic strap at the back to fit me. He taps the top of the hat lightly with his knuckles. "So far so good. Now we just need some steel toe caps for you. We'll have to buy those though as we don't keep a stock. Come on."

He hurries me out of the office again and bundles me back in the van, complete with my hard hat and jacket. Our next stop is a specialist trade footwear shop on the edge of the town center. He shepherds me inside, and I'm stunned at the range of styles and colors I can choose from. I'd expected to have to wear something ugly and bulky, and very masculine. Not so at all. The ladies shelves have a wide selection, and I end up with a pair of light gray and purple work boots that look not unlike my own trainers. And they're just about as comfortable too. Cain insists on paying, and pockets the receipt to pass on to Phyllis later.

"Let the tax man pay for your shoes, love," he explains as he gestures for me to head back to the van. "I always do."

The site in Rothbury is about an hour drive, and by the time we've finished getting me kitted out we manage to hit the rush hour traffic. I use the time spent crawling along the dual carriageway to quiz Cain about the project we'll be on today.

"It's an old textile warehouse, three storeys, on the banks of the river. We're adding verandas, designed for fishing. And moorings for boats. There'll be a communal rooftop garden too. It'll appeal to the angling fraternity, retired mostly I'd imagine. The planners have insisted on traditional materials and design throughout, original where possible, which is why we're there. There'll be twelve apartments on each floor, so it's not a massive development. Some complicated fireproofing needed though. These old warehouses tend to be steeped in the oils from the wool that was stored there, and that's highly flammable. You'll have seen on the news how these places can go up like a torch if they ever catch fire. Well, that's no use if people are going to be living there, so we need to treat the stone and the timbers to make them safe."

That makes sense to me, and I continue to bombard him with questions about just how they might be able to fireproof the building. If my interest amuses or surprises him, Cain doesn't show it. He answers my queries patiently, and in no time it seems to me we're pulling into the parking pace alongside the warehouse. The building itself is surrounded by scaffolding, and is a hive of activity as construction workers scurry up and down ladders and along the external platforms.

Cain heads for the site entrance, a double decker portakabin erected alongside the main warehouse, and I trot after him. There's a poster-sized notice at the side of the entrance, covered in tightly packed small print and diagrams. Cain points to it.

"As you're not a regular on construction sites you're supposed to read that. You need to be familiar with health and safety regulations." He pauses by the door, allowing me time to read the notice. Or so he thinks.

I make a pretense of staring at it, paying particular attention to the symbols as those might make some sense, and wondering how long this should take. My heart is sinking. Even when I think I might have found something I can do, something that really interests me, my bloody reading trips me up, and I find myself lying again. Covering my tracks. Again. Cain helps me out after a few minutes.

"Have you nearly done?"

I nod hastily. "Yes, yes I'm fine."

"Okay then." He opens the door of the portakabin and gestures me inside. I step through, into a sort of makeshift canteen. There are long tables, lined with plastic chairs, a few of them occupied. At the far end is a water boiler, and on the table next to it a huge tin of coffee, a pile of teabags, a half-used up bag of sugar and a stack of polystyrene cups. Workmen are gathered around the tables, in two groups mainly. They all have cups of something steaming in front of them, and there's a scattering of newspapers being passed around. Cain nods to one or two of the men, and I wonder if they're part of our team here. I don't have time to ask though before he's heading for another door, this time leading into the busy site office.

"Morning, Rachel. Is Steve here yet?" Cain's question is addressed to the woman behind the closest desk.

Of the other four or five desks arranged around the room only two are occupied, both by middle aged men who ignore us as we enter. Rachel is aged around thirty, I'd say, and is dressed rather like I am, jeans, a sweatshirt and a high-vis jacket. There the similarity ends though, as she looks up at Cain, and answers him without her fingers ever faltering in their lightning dash across her keyboard.

"Yes. In the meeting room. They're just starting. Do you want a coffee bringing in?" Her final remark is aimed at both of us, her smile friendly and welcoming.

"Yes, if you would please." Cain is stepping around her desk, now headed for the meeting room I imagine.

I trail behind him.

"Yours is black, I know that. What about you…?"

Cain stops, turns back to face Rachel. "Sorry. I should have introduced you. This is Abigail Fischer, co-owner of Parrish Construction. She's accompanying me today."

This news doesn't seem to be at all out of place. "Pleased to meet you, Miss Fischer. I'm Rachel, Site Administrator and general dogsbody." She gets up from her desk, and offers me her hand.

I take it, and shake briefly. This is a far cry from cleaning schools. No one ever shakes your hand there.

I smile back. "Abigail, please. And I'd like mine white if that's okay. With three sugars."

"Coming right up. I'll be in in a minute."

I follow Cain across the main office and through the only other door. Four men are already in there seated casually around a table on yet more plastic chairs. Cain gestures me to take the one remaining spare chair then turns to go back into the main office. The men all smile politely at me, and one of them, a burly middle aged chap, stands and leans across the table to offer me his hand.

"Morning. I'm Steve Williams, Project Manager."

I shake his hand, and remember Cain's introduction when I met Rachel. Taking inspiration from that, I announce myself as the co-owner of Parrish Construction, just as Cain returns with two more chairs, possibly borrowed from the canteen. He places one next to me and the other opposite us. As he takes his seat, Rachel arrives, carrying a tray full of cups. One of the men stands and takes it from her, and she turns on her heel to dash out again, only to return moments later. This time she's carrying a pile of files, drawings and other important looking documents which she dumps in the middle of the table. She extricates a large notepad from among the pile and takes the one remaining vacant seat.

"Right. Now we're all here, do we need introductions?" Steve starts the proceedings.

Soon I learn that as well as Steve, Rachel and Cain, I'm in the company of David Mitchell and Sam Berrisford, both architects, and Jack Naylor, A.R.T.'s regional head of finance. No one questions my presence, so I settle in to listen.

The discussion is mainly about complying with planning regulations, and Cain's endeavours yesterday were apparently all to do with ensuring that the foundations for the building are strong enough to support the additional weight once new floors and extra internal walls go in. This is not normally Parrish Construction's responsibility, but A.R.T. hired Cain as a consultant to accompany the clerk of works on his inspection and report back today. Cain does most of the talking for the first half hour or so, and everyone listens. He's clearly someone who knows his stuff.

He's confident, self-assured, and I desperately wish I could be more like that. Perhaps, one day…

Even though there's a fair amount of incomprehensible jargon being bandied about, I find I can follow most of what's being explained. The conversation moves on, and we discuss the finances of the scheme. Mr Naylor appears content that everything is on budget, and I understand that concept well enough too. The only tricky issue remaining is one of timing as it seems the electricians and the decorators both want to be on site at the same time. The clash has arisen because the decorating sub-contractor is now insisting on coming a week earlier than previously agreed. For her part, Rachel insists that can't happen as the electricians will be burying cabling in the walls, and the plasterers would then have to do their thing before the painters could start. She proposes phasing the works so that the electricians start at one end, closely followed by the plasterers then by the decorators. She makes a note to insure the cabling supplies are delivered in time for the electrical crew to get set up and under way.

As I listen to the conversation, I realize that this is primarily what Rachel's job consists of—making sure everything and everyone is in the right place at the right time. She tells the men how it's going to be, and they do as she says. That's what happens, I suppose, when you're good at your job and everyone knows better than to argue.

The morning flies past and before I know it, it's half-past ten and a pile of bacon sandwiches arrive, delivered, I gather, from the mobile vending trailer which has set up next door to the site to sell greasy burgers and such like to the hungry construction workers. The men insist that Rachel and I help ourselves first, but the conversation hardly flags as we munch and plan. Well, they do. I munch and listen.

Soon, it's lunch time, and by then we've covered revisions to the internal layout of the individual apartments to create a slightly larger kitchen. The planners like big kitchens apparently. I know how they feel. A.R.T. also need to upgrade the heating system, but Mr Naylor is happy with that as the extra cost will be covered from savings they can make on internal decorations and generally speeding up the work. As well as appeasing the decorators, Rachel's queuing system is actually quicker, and therefore costs less to do. They all like the sound of that.

By the time Cain and I wander out to the burger van to see what else might be on offer by way of suitable lunch-time refreshment, my head is buzzing with questions. I'm finding all this absolutely enthralling, and I want to learn all I can about how a scheme like this goes together. Cain answers as best he can, but eventually has to concede defeat to Rachel who's joined us after we returned to the canteen. We chew on our hot beef sandwiches while she picks at her plastic tub of mixed salad. Rachel seems happy enough to satisfy my rampant curiosity, and even offers to take me with her when she does her round of the site later. She has to do a progress review each week, and today's the day. I accept gratefully, especially as I know Cain will be caught up in the interviews and I'd otherwise be at a loose end.

* * * *

While Cain is closeted with the rest of the panel meeting with potential electrical contractors, I get to spend a very enjoyable couple of hours scrambling up ladders and over scaffolding with Rachel. She moves from one floor to the next, chatting to foremen and supervisors, checking that there are enough materials on hand or on order to enable work to progress without any hold-ups. She makes notes of any issues she needs to deal with later. As we make our way back to the site office, I ask her how she got into this job.

"I just sort of drifted here, I suppose. My dad is a plumber, and I sometimes went to jobs with him. I've been hanging around building sites since I was a kid, and I like the atmosphere. My first job was in a bank, but I hated that. So when A.R.T. advertised for clerical staff, I applied. I've worked for them about ten years now, and my job has grown to this. I like the variety, moving around as developments are completed."

"Don't you have to have some sort of special qualification? A degree in building or something?"

She shrugs. "There are qualifications. Most of our engineers are graduates. Not me though. I've done courses along the way, in project management, health and safety, equal opportunities, that sort of thing. But mostly I've just picked things up as I've gone along." She pauses to count the rows in a stack of breeze blocks before turning back to me. "So, what about you? What do you do at Parrish Construction? Apart from fucking Cain, obviously."

I stare at her. Did I hear that right? Apparently I did, because she's standing there, grinning at me. There's nothing malicious in her expression, but she does seem interested, And amused by my reaction.

"Come on, don't be coy. He's an attractive man, who wouldn't?"

Who indeed? Rachel?

"If I was into men, I'd probably shag him myself. As it is, you're more my type. But I'm fixed up already so don't look so horrified. I won't be jumping your bones any time soon. Unless you'd like me to, of course…?"

I shake my head, not sure how to respond to that offer. "Er, no, no thank you. I mean, I'm sure that would be nice, but…"

"God, Abbie, you're so easy to wind up. I can tell why Cain adores you. Come on, let's find out if they're done yet. And you still haven't told me what your job there is."

I trail behind her as we make our way along the last section of scaffolding and down the final ladder to the ground, wondering what to say. I settle on something which is not too far from the truth — or at least the truth as I'd like it to be.

"I've not been there long. This is my first week, actually. I think I'll be helping out with publicity though, advertising."

"Right. You do look like one of those creative types, come to think of it."

I'm not sure if that's a compliment or not but decide to take it as one. "Thanks. I suppose I am, a bit. I'm a painter."

"I see. But not an emulsion merchant, I assume."

"No. I do mainly watercolours, sometimes oils. And I draw. In fact, I was wondering if anyone would object to me making a few sketches while I'm here?"

She waves her arm expansively around her. "Feel free. I'm going in for a brew now though, so I'll see you back inside." She tucks her clipboard decisively under her arm and leaves me to it.

I spend the next hour or so busily sketching various scenes and angles. No one takes any notice of me, or if they do they're either too busy themselves, or too polite, to comment. I capture the sense of ordered chaos as assorted troops of workers scurry around, each engrossed in their own part of this big jigsaw, each seemingly confident that if they do their own little bit, all the rest will fall into place around them. I'm sure they're right, but that happy outcome is largely down to Rachel, I suspect.

Eventually Cain finds me perched on a stack of paving slabs, engrossed in sketching a JCB as it trundles up and down its roughly pressed track, delivering stone to a team who I suppose must be Parrish Construction. I recall Cain telling me we're doing the dressed stone work, and yesterday morning he mentioned wanting to supervise a delivery. This must be it. I don't see him approaching until he hitches his hip onto the slab alongside me.

"Rachel said you were drawing. Can I look?"

He's peering over my shoulder, so I angle the sketchpad so he can see better as I continue to put the final strokes of my pencil in place.

"Hey, now that's good. Really good. In fact..." He looks carefully at my drawing, his head cocked to one side. "I know you draw what you see, but I wonder, could you put a sign in the foreground, just here" — he points with his finger to show where he means — "and write 'Parrish Construction' on it? Then we could use that in our advertising. Or better still, write it on the side of the JCB. That'd be smaller, more subtle..."

He breaks off as I snatch my sketchpad back and slam it shut. I can no more write 'Parrish Construction' on a sign than I can fly up to the top of the scaffolding on the building in front of us.

"Hey, what's wrong? It was just an idea..."

And it was a good idea. How many more good ideas will I not be able to take up because of this, this problem of mine?

I mumble my excuse. "You're right, I only sketch what I see. If you like though, I'll draw the sign that's outside the yard onto the picture. When we get back. Will that do?" I can copy the lettering from the sign easily enough, if it's in front of me.

He shrugs. "Sure. However you want to do it's fine with me." He stands, his smile now ever so slightly puzzled, as though he knows something's not quite right here, but he can't figure it out. Yet.

I hold my breath, tensing for whatever his next question might be, but it doesn't come. I'm off the hook again. For the moment at least. Instead, he stands and tilts his head in the direction of our van. "I'm ready to be getting off now, if you are?"

I nod, gathering my stuff together and putting it in my bag with my pad. "I'll just say goodbye to Rachel though."

"Ah, yes, your new best friend. Did she proposition you?"

My blush gives it away, and he chuckles. "Christ, she's rampant. I should have given you the head's up. Sorry."

"It's fine, really. She's very nice."

"Nice?" His eyebrows lower and he eyes me suspiciously

I punch his arm. "Yes. Nice. But not my type."

His eyebrows relax again. "Ah. I'm so relieved. Right, you go do your farewells then. I'll see you in the van."

Chapter Twelve

The first half hour or so of the journey back is spent in silence. I'm contemplating how to smooth over the awkwardness created by my irrational response to his suggestion, and Cain is no doubt reflecting on what a moody cow I am. I'm the one to crack first. I never could bear an unpleasant atmosphere.

"Thanks for bringing me along today. I enjoyed it."

He shoots me a quick glance before returning his attention to the traffic. "I'm glad. So, would you come with me again?"

"Yes! I'd love it. Where are we going tomorrow? Same place?"

He smiles, no doubt amused by my enthusiasm. "Sadly not. Tomorrow I'm doing real work—installing your new boiler. Phyllis emailed to say it's been delivered so we can get it fitted and working."

"Ah. Right." I'm not sure what I think of that prospect. *My* new boiler. *My* new flat. No reason to stay at Cain's any longer then, once the heating's fixed.

A few minutes pass, more silence, only slightly less awkward now.

Cain is first to speak. "I've enjoyed having you around. At my house, I mean. And not just because of the mind-blowing sex."

Now it's my turn to slant him a glance. "I've enjoyed being there. You've made me feel very welcome. And not just because of the sex…"

He smiles. "No. But it definitely helps."

"We could still, you know… Even if I'm living in the flat I mean."

"Are you saying you'd still let me spank you? And fuck you? Even if you're living in the flat?"

I'm not convinced he needs to be quite so blunt about it, but that is basically my point and I see no benefit in confusing the issue. "Yes. I would. If that's what you want too, obviously."

"Obviously. Not as convenient though. Maybe you should stay with me a bit longer, see how it goes for a while…?"

His eyes never leave the traffic as I stare at his profile and ponder what it is he's actually saying to me. Convenient? I might have hoped for a little more enthusiasm, especially as he seems to be inviting me to stay with him indefinitely. Is he asking me to move in? I only met him a month ago, we've been sleeping together for just a matter of days. Surely it's too soon…?

As if my doubts and confusion were spoken out loud, he interrupts my thoughts. "Don't overthink it, Abbie. The flat'll still be there whatever. And once I've put the new boiler in, it'll be warm. I like you, you like me. Or you seem to. I'm just saying we could leave matters as they are, see what develops."

He makes it sound so reasonable, not a big deal at all. Why not?

Because he'll hurt me, that's why not. And not just physically. If—when—he finds out what I've been hiding, he'll dump me. He's sure to—I'd be a liability as a business partner, and not terribly interesting as a companion. And the sex might be good, better than good, but that'll soon fade. What man wants a stupid girlfriend, lover, submissive or whatever I might be? He'd be embarrassed by me, ashamed of me. Nearly as ashamed as I am of myself.

But even knowing all that, the prospect of moving into the flat, however warm it might be, alone, is completely unappealing. I want to stay with Cain, it's that simple. For however long it lasts. I might well be on a collision course as my reality threatens to derail this erotic fantasy I'm living in, but that will come soon enough without me hurrying matters along.

"Okay, fine. I'll stay. For a while, see what develops, like you say."

He turns to me, flashes me a quick but still absolutely dazzling smile. He really can ramp up the sex appeal when he wants to. "I was hoping you'd say that. So, are you up for a little spank-fest later?"

Spank-fest! My bottom quivers in response and my pussy moistens delightfully. No harm in playing it cool though. For a while. "That sounds quite…nice."

He's not buying that, sadly. "Nice? Miss Fischer, you're squirming in your seat. And I do believe you might be blushing. Who'd have ever imagined that? There's a lay-by just up ahead—maybe I should pull over and have you show me your clit. I wouldn't mind betting it's already swollen. Is your sweet little tush wet, Miss Fischer? Should I check?"

He flicks the indicator on the steering wheel to signal left, makes as though he is about to pull in.

"No! That won't be necessary."

"Miss Fischer?"

"Yes, I'm wet. Okay?"

"And your clit?"

"Yes. Probably."

"Probably what?"

"Swollen. Pink." We pass the lay-by, and I start to relax, but he soon puts a stop to that.

"What about your nipples?"

I glare at him, but can do nothing to stop the physical response his words are evoking. I'm acutely conscious of my nipples, now rubbing against the soft silkiness of my bra as they also swell and harden, and of the gathering wetness between my legs. Not to worry, I somehow doubt I'll be keeping my existing knickers on for very much longer.

"Miss Fischer, I'm waiting. Are your nipples hard yet? If you're in any doubt I'd be happy to check them for you."

"Thank you, but that won't be needed either. Yes, my nipples are hard. And sore now, thank you very much."

"Don't mention it, my pleasure. So, shall we have a little music then? There's Coldplay in the glove box. Or you could try and find something on the radio."

"I don't care about bloody music..." I mutter grumpily, squeezing my thighs together in the hope of creating even a tiny bit of friction around my clit. It doesn't make much difference, and Cain isn't letting up.

"I'd like some music. The CD, please. And Miss Fischer, you'll find all that wriggling around much more effective if you just unzip your jeans and shove your hand down the front. Would you like me to pull over and demonstrate? It's no trouble."

"No! Thank you." I continue to squirm.

"Miss Fischer. Zip. Hand. Now."

What? "Are you serious?"

"I am. And I'm running out of patience. Did I not make myself entirely clear? I reckon we've about ten minutes before we get back to the yard. That should be enough time for you to make yourself come at least once, maybe more. So get on with it, if you would."

I don't move, just continue to stare at him.

"You're wasting time, Miss Fischer. Maybe you need that demonstration after all." He signals left again and the van starts to slow down.

I reach for the button on my jeans and unsnap it. "I'm doing it, I'm doing it."

"At last. Hurry up then."

I pull down my zip, and before I can think over what I'm doing, I slide my hand inside.

"I want to see. Lift up your bum and push your jeans right down. To your ankles. You'll need to be able to get your knees apart."

I gasp. "What if someone sees?"

"The windows are tinted, and no one will see what you're up to anyway. So do as I say, please."

And I do it. I really do it. In broad daylight, as we drive smoothly through the rush hour traffic on the A1, headed toward of Berwick-upon-Tweed, I actually shove my jeans and pants down around my ankles and spread my knees wide. Even before he asks me to, I lift up the hem of my T-shirt to give him an unimpeded view. Then I slip my hand back between my legs and get started.

I slide my fingers through my slick folds, testing the wetness there. Quite impressive. I trace the outline of my pussy, leaning back in the seat and lifting my hips slightly. I can feel his eyes on me as he divides his attention between me and the road. We pull up at a roundabout, and I sink lower in my seat, hoping that a curious passer-by won't glance into the van, but I'm becoming a little less concerned at that anyway as my arousal starts to spike. The van is stationary and I know he's watching me as I slip two fingers inside my pussy. I'm hot and tight. And very, very wet. I squeeze the muscles of my pussy around my fingers. This is what he feels when he finger-fucks me. My response is erotic, I love the feel of my pussy clenching around my hand, and I imagine it's his cock in there.

I lay my head back against the headrest and groan.

"Feeling good, Miss Fischer?"

The motion of the van tells me we're moving again as I gasp my response. "Yes. You?"

"Oh, I'm feeling very good indeed, love. You'll find your G-spot at the front, about a third of the way in."

I follow his route map, and thrust my hips forward as I hit that sensitive place. And keep on hitting it. I rub harder, angling my hand to be able to slip a third finger in, and place the pad of my thumb over my clit.

"I see you've found your technique, Abbie. Now let's see what you can produce."

He has the grace to keep quiet, well, almost, for the next couple of minutes as I concentrate on producing not one but two beautiful climaxes. The first is there in moments, whipping sinuously through my tingling body as I thrust my fingers deep inside my pussy, rubbing hard against my G-spot with each stroke. I flick and caress my clit with my thumb, and the combined sensations are overwhelming. I shudder and groan my way through the orgasm, concentrating on not letting up the pressure even as my senses scatter. As I start to calm again, I withdraw my fingers from my pussy to turn my full attention to my throbbing, demanding clit. I slide my middle and index finger along each side, smoothing out the hood now shielding only a small portion as the little nub swells even more under my touch. Using my right hand to position and expose the sensitive bud, I lay the middle finger of my left hand on the tip and press lightly.

I start a circling motion. It feels good. I flick. That feels good too. I rub the pad of my finger up and down, and from side to side. I feel my arousal start to build again, hovering there, just below the brink. Nearly, nearly, not quite.

"When we get home, you're going to do that again, but this time you'll have my cock inside you." His tone is low, even, indescribably sexy.

It's enough, and I shatter again.

I'm still buzzing as we pull up outside the gates to the Parrish Construction yard. It's all locked up as Phyllis will have left at lunchtime to get back to her Stan. Cain gets out to open the gates, as I reach down to pull up my pants.

"Take those right off. Have you ever tried nude drawing?" The van door swings on its hinge as he hops down, leaving his words hanging in the air.

"What?" *Did I hear that right?*

But he's already walking around the bonnet to unlock the gate so I have to wait until he returns to the cab before I can check. Meanwhile though, I know I'd better do as he says. I unbuckle my seatbelt and reach down to untie the laces of my still shiny new safety shoes and toe them off my feet. My socks follow, then I kick my crumpled jeans and underwear from around my ankles. I turn to face him as he climbs back into the van.

"Did you say nude? I don't draw nudes. Well, I never have…"

"I wasn't asking you to draw a nude. I mean *you'll* be nude as you do the drawing." He edges the van forward through the gate to park in front of the office door. He turns to me. "You promised you'd draw that sign for me. Onto the picture you did back at the site. I want you to do that please, if you would. And I want you to be naked when you do it."

"But, why…?" I'm not entirely opposed to the idea, but it has rather arrived out of left field.

He shrugs. "I'd enjoy it. And I feel you owe me some sort of penance for your behavior back there at the site."

Ah, right. That. I start to apologize, but his raised hand stops me.

"You can say you're sorry later. After you've followed me inside, taken off the rest of your kit, drawn me that sign, and then bent over your desk for a spanking. Then you can apologize if you still want to." His gaze is serious, level. He means it, and this feels like a subtle shift in our relationship.

He's not threatening me with anything I won't love doing, but somehow there is a hint of discipline in this too. A whisper of retribution for my rudeness, my unreasonable reaction to his request. I drop my eyes, studying my hands now folded together and resting on my still-bare thighs.

I'm confused, uncertain about this new and as yet unexplored element to our play. But at the same time I know instinctively that I'm going to do it, going to allow it. How could I not when the thought of submitting in this way is even more exciting than the first time he spanked my bottom?

I chew my lip thoughtfully as he waits for my response. He doesn't rush me, and I'm glad of that. I need these moments to process, to adjust and accept. And eventually, when I'm ready, I meet his gaze again.

"Will you be naked too?"

"No."

"I see. How many spanks?"

"Ten. But hard."

"Ten. Yes. But I prefer to lie across your lap."

"The desk, Miss Fischer." His gaze is unwavering, and his attitude uncompromising.

He's in charge, his call. My pussy clenches in enthusiastic response.

"Very well." I turn to reach for the door handle, then suddenly think of a problem. A big problem. "I'll need to be able to see the sign. If I'm inside…"

"I'm sure you'll manage very well from memory, Miss Fischer. But just in case, there's another one inside. A plaque on the wall."

At his prompt I remember seeing the plaque yesterday, sporting the same red and gold lettering as on the side of the van. And I know I can do this. I nod then open the van door.

I follow Cain into the building, then stand beside him as he disables the alarm. My clothes and shoes are bundled in my arms, and I deposit those on Phyllis' desk for now. My own desk will be required for other matters. The alarm sorted out, the outer door now closed, Cain leans on the door frame to watch me. The plaque is beside him, fastened to the wall.

"Whenever you're ready, Miss Fischer." He steps forward to hand me my bag which he very kindly carried in for me from the van as my hands were full. I extricate the pad and turn to the correct page, glancing at the drawing of the JCB and at the space in the picture where Cain wants his sign to go. I lay the sketchpad on the desk.

"Just here?" I point to the spot in the foreground.

He simply nods, leaning back to watch me, his arms folded.

I don't require any further instructions — the process now is clear and simple enough. I stand and remove my jacket. I hang that over the back of my chair, and pull off my T-shirt. My bra follows quickly. Naked, I obligingly stand still for a few moments. I know he'll want to look at me. He runs his eyes up and down my body before making a circling motion with his finger. Obedient, I turn around.

"Bend over, Abbie. Show me your pussy."

The fierce clenching in my lower body forces me to hesitate for a couple of seconds before I lean forward to do as he's said. I struggle to remain still as he continues to study me from his vantage point by the door.

"Hold onto the chair if you need to steady yourself. Open your legs wide for me."

I do it, grateful for the stability offered by the sturdy chair as I spread my legs for his examination.

"You're still very wet. And very pink. Your clit's swollen — I can see it from here. It's all but waving at me. I think you're enjoying this, Miss Fischer. What a hot little slut you are when the mood takes you. I do hope you won't stain your chair. Maybe I should have you do the drawing standing up?"

My stomach twists again at his words, and there's a fresh dribbling of moisture from my wide open cunt. He's right. I am a slut. And that being the case, I can't help thinking how very acceptable it would be if he could see his way clear to ramming that thick, hard cock of his into my pussy right now. More wetness, more dribbles. *Christ!*

"I'd prefer to sit, if I may. Perhaps there's a towel or something...?"

"Perhaps. I'll check. Don't move."

I remain in position as he strolls past me to the tiny kitchenette area. He emerges almost immediately with a tea towel. I'm sure there must be hygiene implications, but I keep those concerns to myself as he lays the towel across the seat of my chair.

"You can sit down now, and get started please."

I dutifully take my seat, appreciating the roughness of the fabric under my throbbing pussy. I pick up my sketch pad, at the same time wriggling against the towel, my legs spread wide as I try to press my aching clit into it.

"Sit up and keep still. The quicker you finish the drawing, and we get your spanking done with, the quicker I'll fuck you. And that *is* what you want, isn't it?"

I do my best to sit normally as I glance at him, now lounging in Phyllis' chair, his feet propped on her desk. "Yes. Thank you."

His answering smile is almost imperceptible, and the next few minutes are spent in highly charged silence. Or near enough. The only sound is the faint scratching of my pencil across the paper as I quickly sketch a signboard, which I can do freehand, then carefully copy in the details from the plaque. Despite my current circumstances, I do manage to concentrate fully on my task. I can read the lettering, pretty much, but I know I need to take care over the details.

"Should I do the small writing as well? The numbers?"

"Of course. Those are our contact details. We'll need those in our advertising. We want people to be able to find us."

I nod briefly and return to the task, now peering closely at the plaque to be sure I don't make any mistakes. I could do this much more quickly if he weren't here, watching every move. The tension is almost palpable as I work even more slowly to avoid any mistakes. Well, to me it is. He seems perfectly relaxed.

At last I lay my pencil down on the desk and pass my sketchpad to Cain for his inspection. He looks at my efforts then glances across at me.

"Perfect, Abbie. We can use this as the cover for our next brochure." He eyes me curiously, then stands and comes to crouch in front of me. He's looking up into my face, clearly concerned.

"You're scared. I can see it in your eyes. Are you afraid I'll hurt you?"

I shake my head, but can't prevent the prickling of tears at the backs of my eyes. I *am* afraid, but not of the spanking as he seems to think. As he watches me, my face crumples and suddenly I'm sobbing.

"Holy fuck, Abbie." He stands and scoops me from the chair, turning to sit down himself with me now cradled in his arms.

He holds me, murmuring words of comfort and reassurance as I weep into his shirt. He traces large circles on my bare back with his palm, and I loop my arms around his neck and cling on. At last my sobs subside, and I'm reduced to a rather unattractive gulping sound. Cain reaches across to Phyllis' desk for her box of tissues, which he thrusts into my hands. I make good use of them, tidying my ravaged face up as best I can before I dare look him in the eye again.

"You a bit calmer now?" His tone is gentle, caring. I nod gratefully.

"Abbie, anytime you want to stop, you can use your safe word. You do know that, don't you?"

I nod. "Yes. I know. It wasn't that…"

"What then?"

What indeed? How can I even start to explain why I was so terrified as he studied my drawing, dreading that he might find something wrong. A letter copied the wrong way round, something missing. Anything at all to betray the fact that I can't actually read it. And when he declared my reproduction perfect, I was so overwhelmed with relief that the floodgates just opened.

"It's nothing. Just me. I get, sort of…emotional. I'm sorry, it won't happen again."

He hugs me closer. "It might, love, and if it does, that's fine. I like emotion, it shows we're connecting. I like you to be afraid too, up to a point. But you looked to me as though you were really scared back then, and you weren't supposed to feel like that. Can't you tell me why it was? So I can make sure it doesn't happen again."

I shake my head. "Please, it was just me being silly. Can we leave it? Please, Cain?"

He kisses my hair. "We will talk this through, and I will get to the bottom of it. But not now. Not if you don't want to. And speaking of bottoms…" He pauses to caress mine. "Would you prefer to just get dressed and I'll take you home?"

"No! I mean, what about…?" I glance at my desk.

He smiles. "Ah, my little Abbie. What a pain freak you're turning out to be. How lovely. But on this occasion, and because I scared you before, you can lie across my knee if you want that."

I shake my head emphatically. "The desk. That's what you said." And, as an afterthought, "Why are you being so nice to me? This is a punishment isn't it? I thought Doms were supposed to be stern. And hard."

He doesn't answer at first, but his expression is serious, considering. I'm conscious that our relationship is shifting, deepening. Perhaps he knows it too.

Eventually, he replies, "Doms are supposed to be whatever their subs need at the time. When you need stern and hard, you'll get it. And when you need cuddling while you sob, you'll get that too. And you're quite correct, this is a punishment. So right now it seems you need to be spanked, and if you wouldn't mind assuming the position, I'll deliver that too."

So, he *is* my Dom. And I suppose that makes me his sub. I'm glad to have that clear, and on impulse I frame his face in my hands and kiss his mouth quickly, before scrambling to my feet. He smiles at me, his expression one of warmth now, and approval. He doesn't ask me what the kiss was for. There's no need. He knows.

And if I thought my emotional state was vulnerable before, I'm quite clearly a goner now.

* * * *

"Eight." My bottom is hurting now, really hurting, but my voice remains steady.

"Aah! Nine." This time I can't bite back the scream, but I manage not to shift from my position spread out across the desk.

"Are you okay? Last one?" He waits a moment for my response.

Despite the pain now radiating across the skin on my backside, I'm certain of my answer. "Yes, please. Do it." My buttocks are clenched so tight, every muscle in my bottom and thighs tensed, waiting for the final slap. My weight is braced on the desk, the cool beech veneer surface smooth against my breasts and stomach.

Cain does not disappoint.

"Ten. Oh, Jesus, that hurts."

Cain insisted that I count the spanks, and despite my moment of fragility earlier, he definitely does not hold back now. He promised me hard, and I got hard. My bottom feels to be on fire.

"Stay there. I want to be able to admire your beautiful red arse as I fuck you. God, you're glowing, girl."

"You have a heavy hand. Sir."

"Maybe it's you. You bring out the worst in me. Or the best, depending on how you look at it. Open your legs."

The best, I'd say. I groan as I move, every muscle protesting. But I do as I was told. I hear the sound of Cain unzipping his jeans, then the thud of his wallet landing on the desk alongside me. The snap of foil, and moments later his cock sinks into me, right to the hilt.

I groan again, but this time in gratitude. And just for good measure, "Thank you, Sir."

"You're welcome."

There's no more talking now as he sets up a rhythm, hard, brisk, each stroke perfectly angled to hit that special, sensitive spot. I'm clutching the edge of the desk, my arms stretched out in front of me. Cain's hands are on my hips, holding me steady for his penetration. He leans forward, lifting my right leg to place my knee on the edge of the table, opening me farther. He reaches around and under me to take my clit between his thumb and finger. Instead of his usual stroking or flicking though, this time he squeezes it. Hard. And tugs it. Also hard. It's painful. I yelp. He tugs again, harder.

I come instantly, the exquisite blend of pleasure and pain irresistible. How does he know? How the fuck does he know when I'm really hurting and when it's just that he's shoved me right to the very edge of pleasure? I have no time to contemplate that mystery though as my pussy convulses around him. My hips are gyrating, my cunt tightening and pulsating around his width, none of this under my conscious control. He thrusts harder, bumping my cervix with the head of his cock. His climax is soon there. He curses, leaning forward to bury his face in my hair as he plunges one last time into me and holds still, his body throbbing with its release just as mine is. Through my own climax, still ricocheting around my senses, I'm aware of the rush of warmth as the hot wash of semen fills the condom, and at last we're both still.

Cain withdraws, quickly disposes of the condom in the loo then comes back to find me still draped across the desk.

"My hand prints are fading now, love. If you don't shift from that absolutely delightful position, I'm going to start touching them up again."

My buttocks quiver. It's a nice thought, but I know when I'm beat. I wriggle my hands under me and start to push myself up. Cain's arms are quickly around me, which is fortunate as I stagger when my legs protest at being asked to resume their normal function. He steadies me then considerately helps me to pull my outer clothes back on. I see no reason to bother with underwear.

"I was going to suggest we stop to eat at the pub on the way back, but neither of us is exactly fit to be out among decent folk just now. Straight home?" Cain grins at me as he picks up the van keys.

"Yes please." I'm hungry, but I'll settle for whatever's in Cain's freezer. What I really fancy more than anything right now is a long soak in the bath. I ask him if that's a possibility.

"Of course. Before or after food?"

"After I suppose. It's my turn to cook."

"Sweetheart, you've missed your turn every day since you arrived. I'm not about to get picky now. You soak while I cook." He hands me the keys so I can go and get in the van while he re-sets the alarm.

My bottom is still making its views felt as I settle into the passenger seat, but I decide it's a pleasant, warm sort of soreness.

I could get used to this.

Chapter Thirteen

We arrive at the yard-cum-office before Phyllis the following morning, despite having indulged in our usual wake-up ritual. Hot, down and dirty sex is one sweet way to start the day. Definitely sets me up till lunchtime. Probably better than hot, sweet coffee. I think. Up to now I've not had to choose between them.

"You just get on with whatever you feel like, I'll get started on that boiler." Cain leaves me perched on my chair—scene of so much more pleasant activity yesterday—as he hauls his massive toolbox up the narrow internal staircase to the upstairs flat.

The computer is sitting quietly, minding its own business. I see no reason to disturb it so I head into the kitchen to put the kettle on. The sound of the door tells me Phyllis has arrived so I reach for a third mug from the cupboard.

"Morning," she calls out.

I answer her, and there's a distant 'morning' from upstairs too. I finish making the drinks and I place her cup of weak, milky tea on her desk. I take Cain's coffee up to him. All that's visible is his rather tight and seriously attractive bum hanging out of the airing cupboard. I place the coffee on the floor behind him and pat his arse smartly as I turn to leave.

"You'll get yours, Abbie…" The voice is muffled, but he's doing his best to sound stern.

"I do hope so. Sir."

Back downstairs Phyllis has obligingly turned on my computer as well as her own so at least I can put off having to ask her how it's done for a little longer. My desktop is now glowing happily on the screen, waiting for me. I sit at the desk and stare at it. A few minutes later, Phyllis notices my lack of any productive activity.

"Did you forget your glasses again, love?"

"What?" I turn to her, puzzled.

"Your glasses. On Monday you said you couldn't read the screen without them. I was just wondering…"

I seize the excuse, hoping she hasn't spotted my slip. It's true what they say, that liars need exceptionally good memories. Mine could stand some improvement. "Oh, yes, right. Yes, I left them at home again. Is there any more envelope stuffing I can do?"

"No. All done. I blame you."

"What?" I've no idea what she can mean.

"Me? Why? What have I done?" Cain's voice from just behind me gives me a surprise. I never heard him coming down the stairs.

"You keep rushing this poor girl out in the morning without her specs. She'll strain her eyes. You need to take her home to collect them." Phyllis is also doing her best to be stern this morning, it seems. And I'm sure it would have had a sporting chance of working if Cain had a clue what she was talking about.

"What glasses? Abbie doesn't wear any."

I look from one to the other, desperately casting around for some sort of excuse or explanation. They both look to me to clarify matters.

"I do. Sometimes. For close work. And computers."

His eyebrows lift in mild surprise. "Oh, right. Well I need to nip home for my electric screwdriver. I'll pick them up for you. Where are they?" Cain grabs the keys to the van and waits expectantly for further instructions.

"I-I-I'm not sure. I don't use them that much."

"No. Can't say I've ever seen you in them. And I haven't seen them anywhere around the house. Could they be in the spare room?"

I'm conscious that Phyllis' ears have pricked up. She's clearly not above a little friendly curiosity regarding our sleeping arrangements.

"No. Yes. No."

Cain hesitates by the door, clearly perplexed now. "Abbie?"

"I don't think I brought them with me. From Bradford."

"But, don't you need them?" Phyllis is looking concerned. And confused. "I never go anywhere without mine."

"Well, I do. I forgot, that's all." I make to get up, intending to head for the loo. Cain soon puts a stop to that.

"Abbie, sit down."

I drop back into my chair immediately. What is it about that voice, that certain inflexion that demands immediate obedience? He comes back across the room to hitch his hip on the corner of my desk, and takes his time studying me as I perch uncomfortably in my chair.

"What is all this? You don't need glasses, love." His tone has softened, maybe, a tad, and he reaches to pick up my sketchpad from yesterday, still lying open on Phyllis' desk where he left it last night. "This is close work, some really intricate stuff in here. You had no trouble drawing these."

"Ooh, is that your stuff? I wondered who drew these. They're lovely. I like the building site..." Phyllis reaches for the sketchpad and Cain hands it to her.

"Yes, Abbie's very talented it seems." He cups my chin in his hand. "But unfortunately not above telling a few fibs to get out of something she doesn't want to do."

He doesn't know the half of it.

He turns his attention back fully onto me. "Abbie, I appreciate this is not your cup of tea, I really do get that. You said all along you don't want to work in an office and I don't expect you to do it indefinitely. I can see we'll have to advertise for another admin assistant for Phyllis, and then you'll be able to concentrate on the artwork for our promotional stuff. It's a much better use of your talents in any case, I *can* see that. But until we get someone else in, I expect you to help out here as we agreed, to do what needs doing and not make excuses. We all need to do things we're not exactly happy about sometimes. You can't always pick and choose. I won't ask you to spend all day, every day in the office, but I do expect you to pull your weight. And not to dream up lies to get out of working. Are we clear?"

I gaze at him, and see my excuses and alternatives falling away. Put like that, I can see how my pathetic fabrication would look to him. I feel ashamed that he'd believe I was lazy or being selective in what I'm prepared to do, but the truth is even more damning. I really have no option but to do my best to make myself useful. He sees my acceptance in my eyes, and smiles at me.

"Thanks, sweetheart. I'm sorry to have to get heavy with you but I need you to understand how important this is. It won't be for long, I promise. Phyllis can place an ad today..." He glances at her, enquiring.

"Oh yes," she chimes in brightly. "It'll be in the Observer next week. We could have someone starting in two or three weeks' time. There's always bright young folk looking for work round here."

How encouraging. Until then, though, I'm stuck.

* * * *

Cain is soon back with his missing screwdriver, and returns to his task upstairs in the flat. I pass the next hour or so pointing and clicking and desperately hoping I don't stumble across anything on the computer that I could inflict irreparable damage to. If Phyllis notices my lack of productive effort, she's too kind to comment, and I'm happy for the reprieve when she observes that it's about time for a nice cup of tea.

"I'll get it." I'm up and headed into the tiny kitchen before she can volunteer, and I quickly rustle up three drinks. I've memorized everyone's preferences so it doesn't take me long. I carry Cain's black coffee upstairs to him, not sure of my reception after this morning's bit of nonsense. I needn't have worried. His smile is as dazzling as ever as he turns to me, wiping his hands on a rather disreputable piece of rag. I can't decide what I prefer to see him in—dirty and worn work clothes like now, or the smart casuals that he wore yesterday to visit the site in Rothbury. Or nothing at all, the state he's in when we wake up and he treats me to his own brand of morning service. The latter probably, on reflection.

"Thanks, Abbie." He takes the mug from me and tosses the rag back into his huge toolbox. Most of his tools are back in there too, and a glance at the new boiler now on the wall over the sink, its green lights blinking happily, suggests he's just about done here.

Sure enough, "That's me finished. Give it twenty-four hours for the system to get up to strength again, and it'll be warm as toast. Not that you'll be needing it…?"

I smile back. "No, seems not. Should we rent the flat out?"

"Could do. Or Phyllis' new assistant might want to live here. We'll see." Then, in a sudden shift of direction, "Are you busy this afternoon?"

I glance at him, surprised. I may be a lot of things, but busy is not one of them. I shake my head.

"Right. Well, I'm going over to Morpeth to see a new client who wants a quote for a job. Small, but fairly specialist. A cottage refurb and extension. Do you fancy coming with me?"

Do I? What's that about bears shitting in woods? Still, no harm in playing it just a little bit cool.

"Sure. I don't think there's anything that won't wait until tomorrow. Shall I just check with Phyllis?"

He grins, knowing full well I'm bluffing. "You do that, Miss Fischer. Be ready to get off in half an hour. I'll just finish up here and I'll see you downstairs."

* * * *

The drive to Morpeth is as interesting as yesterday's expedition to Rothbury was. Although most of the journey is on the busy A1, the Northumberland scenery is stunning. I've never been a landscape artist especially, but I could easily develop a taste.

"Have you always lived here?" I think he probably hasn't, Cain doesn't have the distinctive Berwick accent I've been hearing all around me, an almost Scottish brogue. His speech sounds not too different from mine.

"No. I grew up in Leeds. Only came up here when I started working for my uncle. It's been about ten years now though."

"Do you like it? Berwick, I mean. The north east."

He shrugs. "Not at first, too isolated and too fucking cold and windy for my taste. No decent entertainment nearer than Newcastle or Edinburgh. Remember, I was a randy lad of nineteen then…"

"Right. And now you're a randy lad of what—thirty?"

"Twenty-nine."

But I note he doesn't deny being randy. How fortunate.

"Since I started taking over more and more of the business, I've not had time to worry about my limited access to the fleshpots of Newcastle. I get enough entertainment scrambling up and down scaffolding, and until you came and started disrupting my domestic arrangements, I usually spent my evenings doing the paperwork. Occasional clubbing, just to avoid becoming a total recluse, you understand. You've corrupted me, Miss Fischer."

Good thing too. And I can imagine the sort of clubs he frequents. I don't point any of that out though. Instead, I enquire about the project we're going to look at.

"It's a period cottage, two bedrooms, eighteenth century. The new owners want to extend it to three bedrooms, but want the job to be done tastefully. Sympathetically. I gather the building isn't listed, so that simplifies things. We'll meet the owner and architect, get a feel for what they want to do, take some measurements and then let them have a price for the job."

"What do you want me to do?"

"Watch, listen, learn. Take some notes perhaps."

I stiffen, but manage not to let my voice give away my sudden nervousness. "I didn't bring a notepad or pen."

"No problem. I always have that stuff. We'll do fine."

Well, that remains to be seen. The rest of the journey passes in near silence. I don't doubt Cain's thoughts are focused on the intricacies of sympathetically extending a two hundred year old rural cottage. Mine are on how to hide my inadequacies yet again.

We find the cottage easily enough and Cain does a quick assessment from outside. The client meets us there and immediately launches into an outline of her thoughts on how the place might be improved.

"Two storeys, stone, with slate roof. The ground floor room will be a kitchen-diner, the upstairs an additional bedroom. We want the interior to be in keeping with the period—stone floors, mullioned windows. The less you can see the join, the better I'll like it."

We're standing in a little huddle in front of the cottage, gazing at the soon-to-be-transformed frontage. The owner, Mrs Henderson, is the head teacher of a primary school in Newcastle. The cottage is to be her rural country retreat, her place of solitude and seclusion where she can unwind and recover from the stresses of trying to impart wisdom and learning to the young minds of Blythe. Cain shoved a notepad into my hands as soon as we arrived, clearly expecting me to make notes of Mrs Henderson's detailed requirements. Instead, I've been sketching.

Our client-to-be has very clear ideas regarding how she wants her new home to look, and as she describes her vision, I've been quickly committing it to paper. I've sketched the new window configuration, the roofline, the gable end where the extension will re-shape the proportions of the house. I've even embellished the whole thing by sketching a new forecourt and patio for her, optional of course. The architect is a nondescript little individual, whose name I can't recall. He follows us around, agreeing with everything Mrs Henderson says. It's quite clear who is the creative mind here.

"What about heating? Will you be wanting to extend the existing system? I'm not sure the boiler will take the extra load." Cain is peering into the airing cupboard under the stairs, assessing the rather ancient looking boiler in there.

"Ah, no" — Mrs Henderson waives her hand airily — "that clapped out old thing, it owes us nowt."

Her strong Yorkshire accent reminds me of home, and I quickly add a Yorkshire terrier to my impression of her future garden.

"Rip that out and put in something new. Something efficient, economical." She's quite definite, and I suspect she'll get no argument out of Cain.

Sure enough, Cain nods his agreement, clearly relieved not to have to attempt to wrestle the last dregs of life from the noble old boiler. "And the kitchen? Will you want us to fit it, or do you have other plans?"

"No, lad. I want it all sorted at once. Traditional units. And an Aga, naturally."

"Naturally. We'll cost all the internal fitments separately. Could you make a note of that, please, Abbie?" Cain glances at me expectantly.

I nod, and quickly sketch my impression of an Aga.

"Right. Now some measurements." Cain pulls a gadget not unlike a mobile phone from his pocket. "We can handle this bit. I'll come and find you when we're done."

Mrs Henderson seems perfectly content to leave the measuring to us and bustles off inside. I'm expecting to be given one end of a tape to hold, so I'm somewhat perplexed when Cain just starts striding about pointing his gadget in various directions.

"Do you have your pencil handy?"

"What, yes, of course…" I'm not sure how I'm going to handle this, but ever the optimist I dutifully poise my pencil anyway.

"External dimensions first then. Length, five-point-five meters. Width six-point-two. Total height to apex, nine-point-nine."

I heave a sigh of relief. I can do numbers. Pretty much. I write down the figures as he calls them out to me, concentrating hard.

"Windows. One-point-two by two meters, three on this elevation. Hardwood, sash type."

This is harder, but I jot down the numbers, and draw a sash window. Then we're on to the door, which is apparently to be a stable type. I draw that, and write down its measurements as dictated by Cain. He's hardly glancing in my direction now as he quickly, efficiently, gathers the information he'll need to be able to calculate the cost of the work. I follow him around, managing to keep up as he calls out more and more numbers which I just add to my growing list.

At last we're done. Cain turns to me. "Did you get all that?"

I nod hopefully, my notepad clutched to my stomach.

"Let me see?" He holds out his hand, and I have no option but to pass him my notebook.

He studies my unorthodox approach to recording the dimensions of our project, and looks up quizzically.

"Christ, Abbie, your writing's bloody awful. I hope you can read this because I sure as hell can't. Doubt if Phyllis'll be able to either. You'll have to go through the costings with her tomorrow. Nice pictures though." With an amused smile he hands me my notepad back, and turns to go find Mrs Henderson.

* * * *

We're just clambering back into the van as Cain's phone rings. He swipes the screen to take the call.

"Hi, Beth. How's things?" He pauses, then, "Right. I'm in Morpeth so I can call at the builders' merchants and pick some up. I'll be there in an hour or so." He ends the call and turns to me. "Beth's my plumbing subbie. Remember, I mentioned her before? She needs some sealant. Do you mind?"

I shake my head. "No, no problem. Do we get to do the shopping then?"

He laughs. "Well, I prefer to think of it as logistics, but yes, it boils down to shopping today. Making sure all my — our — sub-contractors are on site and working to capacity. So, to that end, Beth needs sealant."

The rest of the afternoon is spent, very pleasantly in my view, purchasing several large tubes of some waterproof sealant from a builders' supplier then taking it to a job on the outskirts of Newcastle where the formidable Beth is elbows deep in installing a new bathroom in a smart semi-detached house. She comes out to collect the supplies from us.

"Beth, meet Abbie. Abbie's now a co-owner at Parrish's. She's learning how we do things and meeting our most valued associates. One of which is you."

Beth grins at us as she pulls her long blonde hair back into a severe pony-tail, securing it with a rather grimy scrunchy. Despite the vivid green overalls, I have never seen a less likely looking plumber. Beth would do justice to any magazine cover, she's absolutely lovely. Blonde, seriously sexy curves, vivid blue eyes, peachy complexion. She holds out her hand, and I shake it. I'm not sure if I ought to admire her or hate her. I settle for returning her infectious smile.

"Pleased to meet you, Abbie. Please remind him how valued an associate I am when it comes time to settle my invoice." She turns to Cain. "Almost done here. Now I've got the sealant, I'll stay and finish off. My mum will have to collect Jacob from school."

"Thanks, Beth, I appreciate it. How are you fixed for a central heating installation next week? I'll need an extra pair of hands."

"That should be fine. I'm taking Monday and Tuesday off because Jacob's off school. Teacher training or some such. Anyhow, I'm all yours from Wednesday."

He dumps the tubes of sealant into her arms. "I'll text you the address. And I'm hoping we'll have another decent extension to do soon. Just been to meet the client and take a few measurements. We'll submit a price and see how that goes. I'll let you know."

She smiles brightly, ready to start work again now she's supplied with sealant. "It all counts. See you soon." She nods at me, mock salutes Cain and saunters back into the house.

I stare after her. "I wouldn't have had her down as a plumber. A glamorous receptionist maybe, or a model."

Cain heads back toward the van. "Well, appearances can be deceptive. And a self-employed plumber will always make more money than a receptionist. Plus, the hours are better for a lone parent than modeling would be. And, she's her own boss."

I haul myself back into the passenger seat, contemplating yet more missed chances and wasted opportunities. Plumbing might not seem the most obvious career choice, but I envy Beth her independence. My regrets are coming thick and fast now. Sometime soon I really must do something about this little issue of mine. Maybe I'll give Sally a ring later, find out if her offer of help is still open.

Chapter Fourteen

When I wake the following morning, I'm alone. Cain's side of the bed is long cold. I recall he told me he was setting off early for a meeting in Edinburgh, and that I'd need to make my own way to the yard.

I glance across at the clock. *Christ!* Eight-fifteen. I need to get moving. I throw the duvet back and aim my feet at the carpet, wincing as my weight rests on my well spanked bum. Cain is definitely a most diligent Dom. I suspect I'll be reminded of his attentions all day. I'm feeling distinctly contented with life as I shower quickly then pull on some clothes. I had intended to wear jeans, but they rub my tender buttocks so I opt instead for a loose skirt.

Downstairs I grab a bowl of cereal, fill Oscar's bowl with his catty breakfast, make sure he has plenty of water then head for the door. It's a pleasant half hour walk to the yard, and I arrive just before nine-thirty. Phyllis is already well ensconced at her desk, looking as though she's been here for hours. Maybe she has. She's efficiently typing in that way she has, where she doesn't even need to look at the keyboard. She never breaks her speed as I come in and she calls out her cheery greeting. I hang up my coat and head for the kitchen to get us both a drink, noting as I pass my desk that Phyllis has kindly fired up my computer as well.

Ten minutes later, unable to put it off any longer, I lower myself carefully into my chair. My bum doesn't hurt too much. I settle myself into a reasonably comfortable position and stare disconsolately at my desktop.

"Cain emailed. He says you have the measurements from yesterday and he wants the costings for that job worked out as soon as possible." Phyllis' voice is matter of fact, business like.

And I'm rescued again. I dig in my bag under the desk for my battered notepad.

"Yes. I have them here. I don't know how to work out the costings though…"

"Not to worry, love. That's the easy bit. You just yell 'em out and I'll put 'em into the spreadsheet. The machine does the calculations for us."

Ah, how convenient.

I flick through the pages of my notebook until I come to my scribblings from yesterday. I stare hard at the first page, the jumble of numbers, and try to remember exactly what Cain said. Luckily, I have a good memory. I've had to cultivate one.

"External measurements first. It's five-five, six-two."

"Five-five, six-two what?" Phyllis' nimble fingers are poised over the keyboard

"Length was five-five, width was six-two." I'm sure it was that way round, so I look up at her confidently. "Are you ready for the windows yet?"

Apparently not. Phyllis has more questions. And now it's getting really technical. "Are we talking imperial or metric measurements here?"

"What?"

"Feet and inches? Or meters?"

Feet and inches. Must be. So that's what I tell her.

"Are you sure, love? Cain usually deals in metric. I just ask because five-five, and six-two sound more like imperial. Feet and inches."

I know exactly what he said, I wrote the numbers down as he yelled them out to me. So there's no doubt in my mind as I assure Phyllis that we are indeed discussing feet and inches.

"It seems like a tiny extension then, that's all I can say. Hardly worth bothering with. Right then, go on love, fire away."

"It was a small cottage," I offer, by way of explanation. "Windows now?"

Phyllis nods briefly, fingers at the ready again. "Windows."

* * * *

I spend the rest of the morning sketching an impression of how I expect the extended and refurbished cottage will look, based on Mrs Henderson's description. Maybe we could send her my drawing along with the quote for the work, sort of an added bonus. A free gift.

Phyllis has printed off the figures, based on my measurements, and leaves the sheet on her desk, stapled to what I now understand is our standard schedule of work. She's altered the details to suit the specifics, no two jobs are exactly the same, but the general framework doesn't seem to vary much. I guess

I'm managing to pick up some of the basics, and I've not even been here a week yet.

Phyllis leaves at twelve as usual, but not before asking if I'd mind spending some time this afternoon checking for any unpaid invoices that we ought to be sending out reminders for. At my perplexed expression she explains that I need to look through the file of invoices—helpfully she dumps a large, red folder on my desk—then I need to compare each invoice against the spreadsheet in our accounts where payments coming in are listed. She shows me how to navigate to the accounts section on my computer, and brings up the correct spreadsheet on my screen. Any invoices without a matching payment in, and where the date of the invoice is more than a month ago, are late and need chasing. We'll send them our standard reminder letter. If the bill is more than three months overdue we get heavier, she explains. That's when we start mentioning the prospect of legal action.

This is not going to be easy, I know that. But I can probably manage to compare names, especially as I'll have all afternoon to do it, and no one watching me. At least she doesn't seem to expect me to send out the reminder letters. I nod, smile encouragingly and tell her to have a nice afternoon.

"You too, dear. See you in the morning." She buttons up her coat and is out of the door, leaving me, my file of invoices and my spreadsheet. *Happy days.*

The next two hours crawl past. I need to study the paperwork so carefully to be sure I'm looking for the correct name in the column on the left of the spreadsheet, and when I don't find it I'm not entirely convinced it's actually because the invoice is overdue. It could just as easily be that I've made a mistake. We could end up sending out nasty letters to really good customers, customers who've settled their bills on time and would have perhaps put more work our way if I hadn't pissed them off.

The more time I spend struggling with the task, the more nervous I become. This can't go on. I need to come clean before I do some real damage to this business that Cain has worked so hard to build. I look across at the small pile of supposedly overdue bills, wondering if I should perhaps check again that they're not lurking somewhere on that spreadsheet. I turn back to study the screen again, reach for the mouse.

And it disappears. The screen is blank. Well almost. There's a pattern of empty oblong shapes, nothing more. There should be numbers and words in those boxes, not this screen full of absolutely nothing. A moment ago it was all there, now it's gone. I click the mouse. Nothing. I click both buttons, starting to panic. A list of words appears, none of them make any sense. They're not my spreadsheet of paid invoices. Christ! I'm clicking desperately now, the little arrow darting across the screen as I frantically, futilely, search for the missing information.

I manage to find my way back to the desktop, the rows of familiar looking icons. From there, telling myself to calm down, to breathe, I carefully retrace the steps Phyllis took to find my way back into the company accounts. I heave a sigh of relief, it all looks to be there. Wherever it went to, it's back now. All of it, as far as I can see. I carefully scroll down the sheet, the words and numbers whizzing past my eyes. It looks the same. I think.

But I've had enough. Enough shocks and pressure and enough of bloody computers. I glance at the clock on the wall. It's only just after three o'clock, and I didn't even start work until half-past nine so I really can't slope off home this early. I look around the cluttered office. Everything here requires reading, writing, numbers. There's absolutely nothing I can safely do—anything I touch has the potential for disaster. My ignorance could, will, do real damage. I nearly wiped out half the accounts just now. I might be on the point of upsetting lots of really good clients. It can't go on. It really can't.

On impulse, I dig in my bag for my phone and find Sally on my speed dial. School should be finished by now and hopefully she'll have turned her phone back on. Sure enough, she answers after the second ring.

"Hey, Abs. How are you?" She sounds so happy, so cheerful, and so familiar. A wave of homesick longing hits me from nowhere. I hadn't even realized I was missing Sally, missing my old home. But I definitely miss my old job. At least I knew where I was back then, mopping classroom floors and wiping down the school toilets. I had no invoices to worry about then, no computer hiding files from me and giving me heart attacks, no one banging on about imperial or metric whatever those might be. But in that moment I know, however safe and familiar it might have seemed, I don't want to go back. All this might be beyond me now, but it doesn't have to be. I've seen things here in Berwick, working with Cain, that really interest me, really spark my imagination. I can use my talents here, but I need to do some basic work first. Otherwise I'm just an unguided missile, a disaster waiting to happen.

"I'm great. You?"

"Not bad. Missing you though. How are you making out with your builder buddy?"

Builder buddy? And the rest. Sally's my closest friend, but some stuff is just too private. I'm not about to tell her anything about my out of hours relationship with my new business partner. Instead, I go for it, the real reason for this call, and I need to get it over with before I lose my courage.

"Is your offer still open?"

"My offer?"

"To teach me to read."

There's a brief, stunned silence, then, "Hell, yes! Anytime. Are you coming back then?"

I consider that. I suppose I'll have to, at least for a while. "Yes, I guess I am. How long will it take?"

Sally seems uncertain. "That's impossible to say for sure. But, Abs, you're not starting from scratch are you. You can read a bit. It's more that you need practice, familiarity and to build your confidence with written words. It really could come together pretty quickly you know, if you set your mind to it."

"My mind *is* set, Sal. I want to do this. How soon can we…?"

"School breaks up for half-term in a week. I've nothing planned. What about if we do one week, all day every day, intensive reading recovery, and see how far we get? How would that suit?"

"Sal, you're a star. Shall I come to yours?"

"Yes, that's best. I'll make sure I have lots of suitable resources here ready to go. I don't suppose you fancy practicing on kids' books do you? Although Bob the Builder might be suitable…"

"Something more adult, if you don't mind." Although the opportunity to practice some new skills on my very own, personal Bob the Builder has been perfectly acceptable over the last few days. Not that this need concern Sally.

"Do you mean 'Fifty Shades' adult, or something more wholesome?"

"Fifty Shades? What's that?"

"My friend, you really do need to read more. Do you want to practice on mucky books, erotic fiction or something else? Do you fancy adventure, romance, science fiction, crime thrillers? What sort of stories do you want to read first?"

Although the mucky books sound like the sport of stuff I really could do with reading, we settle for a selection. I promise to show up at Sally's house on the first Saturday of the school holidays, ready to throw myself into this project.

At last, the end is in sight, light at the end of my tunnel. And with any luck, it won't be a train coming.

* * * *

"Hello, anyone here?"

I jerk up from the cupboard under the sink in our tiny office kitchenette, banging my head. Now that I've made my plans, spoken to Sally, agreed where and when my great re-awakening is to begin, I feel justified in abandoning my allotted tasks. I'll do all the things Cain and Phyllis want, and more, in time. And I'll do it well, or if not well at least competently. But not now. Not today. Today, I'll stick to what I know, which is cleaning out the kitchen cupboards.

I scramble to my feet, rubbing my head as I stand up. I peel off my rubber gloves and head back into the office.

"Ah, there you are. The door was open..."

It's Mrs Henderson, the lady with the cottage in Morpeth. I hadn't expected her, we don't usually get our clients actually coming to our offices. But I do my best to extend suitable hospitality to what I hope is to become a valued customer.

"Good afternoon, Mrs Henderson. Please, won't you sit down? I was just about to make a coffee, could I offer you something?"

She politely declines the offer of refreshments, but does take a seat, at Phyllis' desk. "I was passing, on my way to a conference in Edinburgh. Well, sort of passing..." She pauses.

I smile my encouragement. I'm glad she decided to call. The A1 is the route to Edinburgh, and it runs about a mile west of where we now are. Not too much of a detour, not really.

She continues, "I need to be getting off soon, but I thought I'd call in and see if you've had a chance to work out the figures for my extension. I need to talk to my bank you see, and I was hoping to be able to do that before the weekend."

I nod, nervously scanning Phyllis' desk for the print out of the costed proposal. It's my own sketch that identifies the correct bundle of papers from among the piles of everything looking exactly the same.

"Of course, we did it earlier. It's here." I pick up the proposal and hand it to her, my own sketch on the top. "I think Cain was intending to post it, but since you're here."

"That's what I was thinking, save me some time and you a stamp. Oh, what a pretty drawing..." She breaks off to study the sketch. "Who did this?"

"I did. It's what I imagine your house could look like, after the work has been done, obviously. I embellished it a bit, added the patio, and the pot plants. And the dog..."

"It looks lovely. And this is exactly the end result I'm hoping for. You've clearly understood the brief perfectly. And this picture is just what I need to convince me I'm right to do the alterations. Can I keep it?"

"Of course, it's meant for you. I'm glad you like it."

She's leafing through the sheets pinned to the back of the sketch, nodding slowly. "I do. And I like these figures too. Yours is by far the cheapest quote. And your drawing tells me you really do understand what I want to achieve. The job's yours, Miss…"

"Fischer, Abigail Fischer. I'm one of the partners here." I stick out my hand and she grasps it, shakes warmly.

"I'll email of course, formally accepting the quote and confirming Parrish Construction as my selected contractor and agreeing the start date. It's been nice doing business with you, Miss Fischer."

I smile at her, pleased to have done my bit. "And with you…"

She waves cheerily at me as she heads for the door, the papers tucked safely under her arm, looking for all the world like a seriously satisfied customer.

Chapter Fifteen

I'm lost in thought as I stroll along the main road heading out of Berwick toward our house. The rocky shoreline is to my right, the gray waters of the North Sea rippling darkly. This is dramatic coastline, and I know those waters are exceptionally cold, even in the summer. It's mid-October now, and even the most determined paddlers would think twice. I keep stopping to admire the swooping, screeching seagulls, though I know the locals detest them. Phyllis calls them a menace, says they make a mess and are too noisy. Maybe if I live here long enough I'll come to share that view, but for now I love them.

"Need a lift, miss? Would you like to come and show me your etchings?"

I turn sharply to see Cain hanging out of the van window, curb crawling beside me.

"You'll get us both locked up." But even so, I'm pleased to see him. I open the passenger door and hop into the van beside him.

"Good trip?"

"Yes, not bad. What about your day?" He grins at me as he puts the van into gear and pulls away.

I think for a moment. It's been a weird sort of day, on reflection. A day of ups and downs. And of momentous, hopefully life-changing decisions. Which reminds me, I need to explain to Cain that I'll be going back to Bradford for a week. But not yet.

"It's been good. Really good. We got that job in Morpeth, Mrs Henderson's cottage."

He glances at me, puzzled. "How come? I didn't sign off the quote yet."

"Oh, well, Phyllis did the costings from the measurements we took yesterday, and printed it all off. Mrs Henderson called in about an hour ago, on her way to Edinburgh, so I gave her the figures. I didn't realize it needed signing off. But anyway, she said it was the cheapest quote she'd had and the job's ours. And I did a sketch, a sort of artist's impression of how her house will look when we've finished. She loved that, said it showed we'd been listening and understood what she wanted."

"Oh, she did, did she? Nice touch then, maybe you can do more of those — it could be our USP."

"USP?"

"Unique Selling Point. Something that sets us apart from other building firms. Those sorts of things are important, this is a competitive trade we're in, Abbie. But in future, I want to see all quotes before they go to the client. Sometimes I can find ways to reduce costs, increase our edge a bit. Sounds like that wasn't needed this time though. So, where do you want to eat tonight?"

"At home?"

"Could do. But since we're both fairly presentable, how about we adjourn to the Fisherman for a pub meal? It'd save on washing up."

I smile happily as he signals left to pull into the car park behind the pub. It's going to be another exceptionally pleasant evening.

* * * *

Cain shoves his empty plate aside as he leans over to pull his phone from his pocket. He's just done justice to a huge steak and ale pie, with roast potatoes and vegetables. My chilli con carne jacket potato was more modest in comparison, but delicious even so.

"Would you mind going to the bar, order us some coffee. Unless you want something stronger? I'll just skim through my emails."

"No problem. And just coffee's fine for me. You want black, as usual?"

"Naturally. Get them to add it to our bill."

I'm uncomfortable at the mention of the bill. So far, Cain has paid for everything, and it just won't do. For heaven's sake, I'm going to be earning twice as much as he does from the business. We need to talk about money. I return to our table, coffees safely ordered to find Cain staring at his phone, his brow furrowed. He looks up sharply as I retake my seat.

"Fiona Henderson has confirmed that contract." The news is not unexpected, nor is it unwelcome as far as I know, but he doesn't look as pleased by it as I might have expected.

"Yes, she said she would. Is there a problem?"

"Yes, could be. The price she seems to think we quoted—where did she get that from?"

Seems to think?

The Three Rs

"It was there, in the papers. Phyllis worked it out from the measurements."

He shakes his head, and I can tell by his darkening expression that something is seriously amiss. "No way those measurements arrived at this price. We couldn't build her a garden shed for this."

"If there's been a mistake, maybe we could give her a ring, tell her what the cost really is..." My voice trails off at his disgusted glower.

"I'll say there's been a fucking mistake. And there's no way we can go back to a customer, after a contract has been offered and accepted, and say 'oh, by the way, it won't cost what we said, it'll actually cost nearly ten times as much'."

"Ten times as much? How could we be that far out? Surely..."

He's not listening to me. He punches numbers into his phone, glaring at me as he waits for someone to answer.

"Phyllis? Hello. Cain here. Sorry to bother you at home..." He waits, evidently being told it's quite all right. Then he launches in. "Those figures for the Henderson job, where did you get them from?" He waits a few moments. "Yes, but what Abbie wrote down was correct, I checked it while we were still on site. How come the build cost has come out at about ten percent of what I would have expected? Less than six grand for a two story stone built extension, for fuck's sake." He pauses again, then, "What?" He looks sharply at me, still listening intently.

My stomach feels heavy, that chilli con carne now sitting awkwardly.

"Imperial? Who the fuck uses imperial measurements these days?"

I have a really, really bad feeling now. I've messed up. Messed up royally. And worse still, I've dragged Phyllis into my screw-up as well. Cain gestures at me, pointing to my bag.

"Do you have the notebook with you?"

I fumble in my bag and pass it to him. He flicks through to the page where my scrawled numbers and drawings record the all-important data from yesterday. He glances through again, still speaking into the phone.

"Yes, here it is. Five-point-five, by six-point-two..." Another silence at his end, then, "She said what? But, didn't you think to check? You must have known the figures didn't make sense."

He continues to listen to whatever Phyllis is saying, his eyes closed as he leans his head back against the seat.

"She came into the office this afternoon, apparently, and Abbie gave her the printout. She left a happy woman, and now we know why." His tone is calmer, more resigned. Another brief silence, then, "Okay. You weren't to know the client would show up. And Abbie wasn't to know the figures weren't the final ones. Shit!"

Our coffees arrive, but Cain ignores his, still intent on making sense of this unfolding disaster. At last he tells Phyllis he'll see her in the morning, and ends the call.

"Phyllis says she asked you if the measurements were metric or imperial, and that you were very definite that they were imperial. Feet and inches, Abbie. Why the hell did you say that?"

I stare at him, totally confused. I have no idea, none at all, what he means by 'metric' and 'imperial'. I have heard of feet and inches, so naturally that's what I thought the measurements meant. I don't say any of that, though—I don't know where to start trying to explain. Instead, I settle for a whispered, "Sorry."

"Sorry! Is that the best you can do? Christ, Abbie, five-point-two means five-point-two *meters*. Five meters and twenty centimetres. Not five feet and two inches. Five-point-two meters is about seventeen feet. We've under costed for the materials we'll need, and the labor time. We've only priced for a five-foot-five, by six-foot-two extension, nine-foot-nine inches high. What the client wants is nearly ten times that size. Five-point-two meters wide, by nine-point-nine meters high converts to seventeen feet wide by thirty-two feet high, more or less. That's a hell of a difference. We'll lose thousands on this job. What were you thinking, Abbie?"

What indeed? I have no answer. I'm not even completely sure I understand how the problem arose. He's babbling about random numbers that seem to make some sense to him, but he lost me at the first mention of meters and centimetres. I can only repeat my apology.

His expression now is one of disbelief. "Sorry! For fuck's sake, Abbie, how could you be so..."

I don't let him finish. I can't let him say it. I might say it to myself, but from him it would be just too painful, quite, quite unbearable.

"Don't you dare call me stupid! It was a mistake, I've apologized. Don't you ever make a mistake?" I'm already grabbing my notepad and ramming it back into my bag, my half-finished coffee abandoned.

Cain seems to agree the meal's over. He stands, shoves his phone back into his pocket and pulls out the van keys. He stalks over to the bar to settle our bill while I make my way outside. He joins me a few minutes later, his face still a mask of furious incredulity. He unlocks the van, opening my door for me.

"This conversation is *not* over, Abbie. You've a lot of explaining still to do."

Like hell. No way am I explaining anything to him, at least not while he's in this mood. I sit mutinously in my seat, and a couple of minutes later I fling the door open as he pulls up in front of the house. I leap down and head for the front door, Cain hard on my heels.

"I wasn't about to call you stupid back there. I know you're not stupid. That's what makes this all the more ridiculous."

I round on him again, my temper spiking and every defensive instinct leaping straight to red alert. "Don't call me ridiculous either. Who do you think you are? I didn't do it on purpose, I've said that. It was a genuine mistake."

"A fucking expensive mistake. That quote should have been nearer to fifty grand than five."

"Well you'll just have to talk to Mrs Henderson then. She must have realized. She'll know it was a mistake."

"Why the fuck should she? You didn't. Or so you say."

"What's that supposed to mean? Are you saying I'm lying?"

"Well it makes no sense to me…"

I see red. I've heard enough. Defensiveness, humiliation and bone-deep fear of being found out is a powerful cocktail, I find. I lose my temper completely. I just want out of there, and to be rid of him. "Go fuck yourself. Because you're sure as hell not fucking me again."

I dart past him, making for the stairs.

"Abbie, don't you dare walk out on me when I'm talking to you."

Arrogant bastard. I yell my answer from the top of the stairs, "You can talk to yourself from now on. I'm leaving." I slam the bedroom door behind me.

Moments later he bursts into the room, to find me turning all my clothes out of the drawers. I reach under the bed for my holdall.

"What the fuck are you doing?"

"Like I said, I'm leaving."

The door slams again. "Oh, right. And where do you think you're going?"

"I'm moving into my flat. Will you give me a lift or do I have to walk there?"

"What? Abbie, for fuck's sake. I don't want you to leave."

"No? Well you give a pretty good impression of it. But it's not up to you. I've had enough of your accusations. I screwed up, I know that. And I said I'm sorry, but that's not good enough for you, is it? You think I'm stupid, or ridiculous. Or both. You're even suggesting now that I did it on purpose. Well, like I said, fuck you."

All the time that I've been yelling at him I've been throwing my stuff into my bag and now I pull the zip around roughly. It doesn't fasten, but I'm well past caring. My signature hot—and as often as not self-destructive—temper, is in full flow now, and he's getting both barrels of it.

Not that this seems to bother him unduly. He leans casually against the door, watching my antics. I grab my bag and round on him furiously.

"Please get out of my way."

He doesn't shift. "I don't want you to leave, Abbie. Not like this. I didn't mean to insult you. I just want to understand how this happened."

"No? Well I'm past caring what you did and didn't mean and what you want. Excuse me please."

I make to push past him, and at last he stands politely aside. I take my chance and shove past him into the hallway, only to have him turn and stroll along after me.

"Right, I'll drive you then if you're so bloody determined to go. But I'm telling you now, Abbie, this is temporary. I want you back here where you belong. When you cool down you'll see that."

My temper flares again. I dump my bag on the floor and turn to square up to him. Nose to nose now, I hurl my anger in his face. "Oh will I? How come you're such an expert then? Maybe when I cool down I'll see you for the over-bearing arrogant bully that you are. Have you considered that?"

The cool bastard seems quite unimpressed by my aggressive stance, but my choice of words does appear to get to him. He frowns and has the grace to look genuinely concerned. "Bully? When did I ever bully you?"

I'm not backing down. "Think back. What about the first time I ever clapped eyes on you, when you waylaid me in the street as I was leaving work? You insulted me then as well, come to think of it. And threatened me. I should have known better than to get involved with you."

I reach down to grab the handles of my holdall and start to lug my bag along the upstairs hallway, only to have him take it from me and lead the way downstairs. He reaches the front door and turns to me again.

"Abbie, please stay. Let's talk."

I have a momentary pang of conscience. He *is* being reasonable. More or less. But rational, reasonable debate does not come easily to me at the best of times, and certainly not when I'm caught like this, on the back foot, feeling defensive, vulnerable and threatened—my dark secret on the point of being exposed. And just as I'd finally reached out and grabbed the solution. The solution that had seemed out of reach, had appeared to be quite unattainable. Until now. How frustrating to come so close, and to be found out, to fall at the final hurdle. I glare at him, just wanting to be out of there. "I'm done talking to you."

He shrugs, clearly baffled but resigned now to the inevitable. He reaches for the door handle, opens the front door and gestures me through. "Okay, get in the van."

Ten minutes later I'm alone, in the middle of my new living room, my bag bursting its contents all over my carpet. The sound of Cain's van pulling away reaches my ears, then fades as he drives back along the road. As the silence surrounds me I sink to my knees, sobbing.

Chapter Sixteen

Somehow I manage to lie awake most of the night then oversleep the next morning. By the time I open my eyes, it's bright daylight. I reach out of bed and grope around on the floor for my phone. I manage to locate it and turn it on to display the time. Nine-fifteen. I roll onto my back, staring at the ceiling and contemplating the wreckage which is my new life. Cain hates me, doesn't trust me – thinks I'm an idiot. Or worse. And I loathe him. I do. Really.

Except I don't. I easily could, not least as he's turning out to be right about things looking different in the cool light of morning. But I don't hate him – I couldn't. Can't even really dislike him. He had every right to be disgusted with me last night. My blunder has cost us thousands, and even I know that a small firm like ours can't stand those sorts of losses. I might well have cost someone their job.

Oh, Christ, not Phyllis! Let it not be dear, loyal, long-serving Phyllis who gets sacked. Because I know he can't fire me – I own more of the company than he does. I suppose that means I do the sacking.

I groan and roll onto my side, shoving my face back under the duvet as I contemplate the possibility that Phyllis might be held responsible for my screw-up. My instinctive reaction now is to dive right back under the duvet and stay here, but I know I owe Phyllis an apology. I daresay I owe the same to Cain, plus the little matter of forty odd thousand pounds if I've understood correctly the full implications of whatever I did wrong yesterday. I poke my head out again, timid but with a growing determination to make at least some of this right. I listen carefully for any sounds from downstairs. In particular, for voices. I want to know if Cain is here. I can't recall what he said he was doing today, where he was going. Maybe he never did say…

I ease my legs out of bed and get to my feet, tiptoeing over to the window. My bedroom doesn't look out directly onto the yard, but if I open the window and strain my neck a bit I should be able to see the back end of his van if it's parked outside. With some contortion I come to the conclusion that he doesn't seem to be here. I've also concluded by now that I really have no alternative but to make an appearance downstairs. Even without the pressing matter of making my peace with Phyllis, I have no coffee up here. No supplies of any sort at all. I need to go out and buy some groceries to make my new home liveable.

I head for the loo, relieved to find half a roll of toilet paper dangling helpfully from the dispenser, and a modest sliver of soap. I manage to make myself as presentable as I can without a toothbrush or toothpaste — mine are still in Cain's bathroom. I dig in my bag for a hairbrush. At least I had the presence of mind to bring that. Or maybe I just never bothered to unpack it from when I came up here from Bradford. Was that only last week? Whatever, I'm thankful for small mercies, and twenty minutes after I woke up, I'm making my way down the narrow staircase into the rear of the office, ready to grovel to Phyllis at least. Grovelling to Cain will be a lot harder, but I'm beginning to accept the reality that this may also be necessary.

"Morning, love. Kettle's on." Phyllis is cheerful and as welcoming as ever, giving me the distinct impression she's not just been fired and neither has she had a dressing down from Cain.

No doubt he's saving that for me then. I stand in the doorway, hesitant, still unsure of my reception. Phyllis gets up from her desk and bustles past me with a smile, heading for the kitchenette. "I bet you've had no breakfast, have you? I nipped out and got some crumpets. And some cornflakes. Wasn't sure what you'd like…"

I gape at her, astonished. Not only does she seem unmoved by my transgressions, she's actually being nice to me. Caring about me. Looking after me. I follow her into the tiny kitchen space to see her pouring water into two cups. She hands me one, and I reach automatically for the milk bottle and sugar bowl on top of the tiny fridge. I see that they have been joined by a small pack of cornflakes and half a dozen crumpets. Phyllis picks up her own mug and squeezes past me in the doorway as she heads back to her desk.

"You just help yourself, love. There's plenty of milk, and butter in the fridge if you want the crumpets. No hurry."

My stomach growls, and I settle on the cornflakes. I poke around in the cupboard and find a small bowl. I dump a generous helping of cornflakes in then take the bowl, the milk bottle and a teaspoon back to my desk. I sit down, noting that the computer is not turned on today — thank God for that — and splash milk all over the cereal. Phyllis just glances across at me as I start to munch, then diverts her attention back to her screen. We spend the next five minutes or so in silence, well near enough silence. I defy anyone to devour a bowl of crunchy cornflakes without making a sound. Eventually I stand and take my bowl back to the kitchen. I return with my now cooling coffee and take my seat again. I gulp down several fortifying sips before I look again in Phyllis' direction.

Now, I have her full attention too. I can't put it off any longer. I smile tremulously, and go for it.

"I'm so sorry. Really I am. I never meant for you to get in trouble. It's all my fault, obviously. I'll tell Cain that, so he can't blame you…"

Phyllis shrugs. "No need, love, Cain doesn't blame me. Come to think of it, I didn't get the impression he blames you either. It was just one of those things. I'd no idea Mrs Henderson might come in before I had a chance to talk to Cain about which version was right. Who could have expected that?"

Just one of those things? My mistake might wipe out months of profits. Years even, for all I know. Then I pick up on her remark.

"Which version was right? Was there more than one version?"

"Oh yes, I did two. One using your imperial measurements, and another using the metric ones. I was fairly sure it must be metric, but you seemed so convinced… Anyway, I ran both sets of figures through the system and came up with two prices. If you just look over there, you'll find the second tender. It was underneath the one you handed to Mrs

Henderson. Just bad luck really that I left the wrong one at the top of the pile."

As she's talking she gestures to a pile of papers on the corner of her desk, closer to me than to her. I eye the documents malevolently, cursing the dumb bad luck that seems after all to be at the bottom of all this. Well, bad luck and the fact that I didn't understand the measurements I was writing down.

"Would you mind passing the other tender to me, love? I just need to check I included for planning fees. Cain thinks it might be worth talking to Mrs Henderson, see if we can agree on a compromise. He's thinking of offering a deal on the labor if she'll meet the full cost of the materials..." She breaks off to look across at me, her hand outstretched expectantly.

"Er, which one is it?" I pick up the top set of papers from the pile and make to hand it over.

"No, it's farther down. I'm not sure just where..."

She's watching me carefully now as I stand and start to slowly pick up each set of papers in turn, peering hopefully at the jumble of letters and numbers closely squashed onto the front of each one. I've examined maybe six or seven potential candidates before I lift my gaze to meet hers again.

"Are you sure it's here? I can't seem to..."

"Does Cain know?" Her expression is inscrutable, but I can see it in her eyes. That dawning recognition, that light bulb moment where it all clicks into place.

Even so, old habits die hard. It's so ingrained in me that I make one last ditch effort. "Does he know what?"

"Does Cain know you can't read?"

"I... I... Who says...? Why would you think that?" Old habits again.

"Well, okay then, read to me what's on the front of that one in your hand." She leans back in her chair, watching me closely now. Waiting.

I look at the bundle of papers I'm clutching, the words now dancing merrily all over the white background. I might have some sort of chance if they'd only keep still. Long moments pass before Phyllis stands, comes around her desk and gently peels my fingers away from the sheaf of papers. She puts it back on top of the pile, shuffles through the ones I'd already checked before pulling out the second from the top of the pile.

"It's this one." She tosses the Henderson tender onto her own desk then picks up my now empty mug. "We need another drink, dear. I'll get it."

Phyllis gets up and heads into the kitchen, leaving me to contemplate the awful implications of this latest catastrophe.

My secret's out.

Shit. Holy fucking shit.

"So, how did this happen then?"

Phyllis is seated alongside me now, her refreshed cup in her hand as mine sits on my desk.

"What do you mean? How did what happen?"

"I mean, how did a bright, inquisitive, talented young woman like you manage to get this far without ever learning to read and write. Except you can write, can't you? Cain said you wrote down the measurements so he must have seen you do it. And I could read them, just about. What's going on, Abbie?"

What indeed? But there's no point continuing with my façade. The game's up now.

"I can write. Numbers definitely and some words. Words I know and see a lot. Like my name, address. Well, my old address. Cat, dog. Yes, no. But new words take a lot of sorting out. I can manage a bit, if I have loads of time. And if no one's watching me…" My voice trails off, I'm so acutely embarrassed at having to confess this, at having to explain myself to a virtual stranger even though Phyllis has not breathed so much as a murmur of judgment over me.

"I knew there was something, just couldn't put my finger on it. The way you seemed to struggle with the computer when most people your age can work them in their sleep. And that stuff about needing your glasses. That was just to avoid having to read, wasn't it?"

I nod, my eyes now fixed on my cup of coffee. "I'm sorry. I didn't like lying to you. To Cain."

"I take it he doesn't know then?"

I shake my head, tears now threatening. She'll tell him. Or she'll insist I do. Either way, he'll be disgusted. Or worse still, he might be kind, pretend to understand. I couldn't bear that, couldn't stand his condescension. Especially now, when I'm on the point of sorting myself out at last.

"I was hoping I'd never need to tell him."

"Love, he'll figure it out soon enough. Men can be dim-witted, we all know that. But they usually get there eventually. He knows there's something amiss, he's completely baffled about how you made that mistake…"

"Has he said something?"

"No, not to me. He wouldn't though, would he? It's between you two. But sooner or later, he'll work it out."

I'm oddly comforted at Phyllis' assurance that Cain wouldn't talk about me behind my back, but at the same time keen to convince her I can manage to keep this under wraps. If only she'll help me. I need her to co-operate. I need her to keep my secret a little longer.

"He might not. I've arranged to have lessons. Private lessons. Some intensive tuition. Next week in fact."

Her eyebrows go up, she's very interested, seem impressed even. "Oh, well that sounds like an excellent plan. Is it through the high school?"

"High school?" I'm long done with school. Nothing would induce me to go back. Except to clean, naturally.

She goes on to explain, "There's no college in Berwick. Nearest is Newcastle, or Edinburgh. That's too far for lots of the young people to go every day so the high school does some of that further education stuff."

I snort derisively. "I'd hardly call learning to read 'further education'."

"Well, you know what I mean. So, not the high school then?"

I shake my head. "No. I'm going to spend all next week with my friend, back in Bradford. She's a primary school teacher, but with an extra qualification in teaching remedial reading. She's been on at me for years, and I've decided to take her up on her offer. She's getting me some books. Adult books. I don't want to learn to read on Noddy and The Tweenies."

"I should think not. You should try that Fifty Shades thing — that's adult. I'll lend you mine."

Sally said something similar. I decide this Fifty Shades thing could well be exactly my sort of book, though if I'm understanding everyone correctly, I'm not so sure I'd have thought it was Phyllis' cup of tea. But who am I to judge? I thank her, pointedly ignoring the tell-tale flush rising up my neck as I recall my own recent excursions into the joys of spanking and bondage. Sadly, there'll be no more of that. I well and truly burned my boats with Cain last night. Which reminds me...

"Please, don't tell Cain. About me, I mean. And the reading stuff."

"Won't he wonder where you've got to? Next week? How will you explain taking off like that? How long will you be gone for, anyway?"

"Sally's only off work for a week. But we can get a lot done in a week, she says. Then after that it'll be a matter of practice. And now that you know, maybe you could help me to understand the computer a bit better...?"

"Of course I'll help you, love. You only ever needed to ask. And I'll help with the reading as well. You can practice here, in the office. And Cain'll help too."

My body bristles to attention. "Oh no, he can't know. Not ever. That's why I'm learning now, after all this time. I don't want him to know. Please, promise me you won't say anything. Please, Phyllis."

She shakes her head sadly. "Of course I'm not going to say anything. I'm not one to interfere. It's your secret, not mine. But, love, he *would* understand. He *would* help."

"He wouldn't. He would never understand."

"You know what I mean. He'd be okay with this." Phyllis' tone has firmed up at the mention of Cain. She may not be given to idle gossip and interference, but she has a point to make now and she continues undaunted. "I've worked here for over twenty years, I knew Cain when he arrived, a skinny lad with big ideas. He's bright, he's determined. He works hard. He turned this business around when his uncle had let it get run down. Everyone who works for him likes him. Respects him. Because he's kind, and he's fair.

He expects a lot, but he gives a lot back. If he knew you were working to fix this, he'd be behind you. Whether or not he understood." Her voice softens, "I *do* get the impression he cares about you."

"He thinks I'm out to steal his business. And now he probably thinks I'm out to wreck it too."

"None of us understood why old Mr Parrish didn't leave everything to Cain outright. It's what we all expected. But he must have had his reasons. And whatever he might have said, Cain does care about you. I'm sure he does."

"Not now. Not since last night. We argued…"

"Well I worked that out for myself when I had a text from Cain to say you were at the flat. That's how I knew to get you some breakfast on my way here. Will you be staying up there for a few days then? If so, you'll need to go shopping…"

I nod. "Yes, I expect so. At least until I come back from Bradford. If I go back to Cain's, he's sure to find out. And I don't want him to. At least, not until after…"

Phyllis' dubious shrug suggests she doesn't think much of my logic. Nor perhaps of my chances of convincing Cain I should be living in the flat and not at his house. But she opts to keep those views to herself.

"There's a supermarket up on the North Road. Do you know it?"

I nod. We've passed it on our way home each evening. Except that Cain's is not my home anymore.

"Right. You can go and get yourself some bits and pieces then. Cain said if you need an advance on your director's salary I was to sort that out for you. Do you?"

I stare at her, totally perplexed. It never occurred to me I might be able to get money from the business, to tide me over. Cain may well be angry with me, and he has every reason to be, but he's still thinking about my welfare. The more I reflect on what happened, the more I recognize that. And the more I cringe when I think of the way I spoke to him last night. Correction, screamed at him. Yet still, he hasn't left me in the lurch. He knew I had no money and made arrangements to deal with that. I really couldn't feel more ashamed of myself or any smaller than I do right now. And I know I'm going to have to face him soon.

"Where is he? Is he coming in today?"

"Rothbury this morning, then pricing a job in Hexham I think. Hasn't he texted you?"

He might have. For obvious reasons I tend not to check texts too often. I dig in my bag for my phone, and sure enough, there are three texts waiting for me. I peer at the first.

RU OK? Txt me.

The words are meaningless. Helplessly I hand my phone to Phyllis.

"Are you okay? Text me. Bloody text speak. As if the English language wasn't mangled enough." She passes it back and I scroll to the next one. This is easier, now that Phyllis has translated.

Abbie? RU OK?

I scroll to the third one.

Back about 6. I'll come to ur flat

Again I hand my phone to Phyllis.

"He's coming round to the flat when he gets back. About six o'clock." She glances up at me and smiles. "Best buy some chocolate biscuits when you go to the supermarket. He likes those."

Chapter Seventeen

Cain arrives soon after six. I hear his van outside then the sound of the door downstairs being unlocked, the alarm system disarmed. By the time he arrives at the foot of the internal staircase, I'm at the top, waiting for him.

"Can I come up?" His tone is calm, as ever, low and even.

My stomach lurches as I realize how much I've missed him, just in those few hours since I stormed from his house. I nod and step back inside my flat, closely followed by Cain. As soon as the door closes behind him, I'm desperate to start my apology. I need to get it out, before my courage deserts me. I've been giving some considerable thought to how I might make amends, earn his forgiveness for both my huge and costly mistake, and for the appalling way I carried on last night. I have an idea, but he may not go for it.

I launch straight in, before he gets so much as a sniff of a chocolate hobnob, "I'm sorry. I don't know what got into me..." *Not entirely true, but still...*

Cain stops my babbling with one upraised finger. "What are you apologizing for, Abbie? Exactly?"

I stare at him blankly. Isn't it obvious? "For losing us all that money. You can take it back from my share, obviously. I don't want anyone else to be going short because of me."

"I think you know already that the terms of James' will won't allow that, even if I was prepared to let you. What happened was a mistake. It was unfortunate, but it wasn't your fault. Not really."

Now I'm completely bemused. Of course it was my fault. My stupid fault for not knowing the simple difference between meters and feet and inches. Apparently Cain does not see it that way though, as he goes on to explain, "Our normal system for these things is that Phyllis prepares tenders based on my instructions, my figures, and I do a final check before it goes out. It's a good system. It works. Yesterday, the problem was no one told you about it, so you didn't know not to hand that proposal over to the client before I'd seen it. And there was no way we could have predicted that she'd just come waltzing in like that. In the normal course of things, Phyllis would have put both sets of figures in front of me, I'd have spotted straight away which was the correct one and Mrs Henderson would have got the right quote. Now you know what our process is, we've plugged that leak. It's done with."

I find his calm acceptance little short of amazing. We've lost thousands. I blurt out my protest, perhaps the latent business-woman in me finally surfacing, "But it isn't. It can't be. What about all that money?"

"I'm going to have a word with Fiona Henderson, we might yet be able to negotiate a deal. I'd have spoken to her already, but apparently she's away until Monday."

I nod. "Yes, that's why she was here. In Berwick. She was on her way to a conference in Edinburgh. She was passing."

He gives a short snort of mock laughter. "I see, that explains it. I had been curious as to why she was here in Berwick. But as I said, that wasn't your fault. It was just an unfortunate combination of circumstances." He smiles wryly, and I suppose there is an element of sod's law about it. Whatever can go wrong, will go wrong. "So," he continues, "now we've got that out of the way, is there anything else you need to apologize for?"

There is. I know there is. I behaved like a total brat last night. I completely lost my temper, driven no doubt by fear of being found out for the illiterate dunce I am, but even so. I was an absolute cow. Admitted, Cain was less than polite when he first discovered the cock-up, but in the circumstances, his reaction wasn't disproportionate. And I now realize it was not directed at me. I can't say the same for my tirade at him, the names I called him.

"I'm sorry I was so rude. I shouldn't have lost my temper."

He shrugs. "We all lose our rag sometimes. I knew you had a fiery temperament, right from the beginning. I don't mind you yelling at me. Well, up to a point. And you were nowhere near that point yesterday. We were both upset, a bit stunned perhaps. Things got said, like they do. No harm done. So, what else?"

Now I'm at a loss. I've said I'm sorry, both for the awesome screw up and for yelling like a Banshee. He's dismissed both as though they don't matter. What else could there be?

"Abbie? What did I specifically ask you not to do? But you did it anyway."

I'm staring at him, genuinely bewildered. And slightly nervous. His tone has taken on an edge I'm starting to find familiar. A steeliness has crept into his voice that tells me my bottom might be tingling soon, and not necessarily in a good way. At least, not initially. But I can't work out why.

Cain decides to help me out, "I asked you not to leave. I asked you to stay and talk, to finish the conversation. But you walked out on me."

"I— Yes, but..."

"Didn't you?" His tone is implacable, he expects an answer.

He gets defensive babble, "I needed some space, time on my own to calm down."

His eyes harden, narrowing just slightly. "No you didn't. You left because you didn't want to talk to me anymore. Or maybe you didn't want to listen to me. I hadn't finished. I asked you to stay. But you refused. I would never have walked out on you in the middle of an argument, Abbie. Not when there were things you still wanted to say to me."

There is no hint of reproach in his tone, but there is disappointment. Displeasure. Both sting me, though I'm not sure why. I'm only now starting to recognize how important Cain Parrish's good opinion is. In part, that's what got me into this situation, my desperate attempts to avoid him finding out the real reason for the incorrect measurements, and consequently losing his respect. I seem to have lost that regardless, and much else besides.

And no, I believe he wouldn't walk out on an argument. But then, he's not a hot tempered ex-redhead with low self-esteem. I've been storming out on people all my life, whenever the going gets rough. I'm beginning to think though that those days might be numbered. Cain clearly won't accept it.

Sure enough, "I intend to punish you for leaving me last night, as you deserve. Will you accept that from me?"

"Accept? What do you mean? What are you going to do?" I'm whispering, playing for time. I'm pretty sure I know exactly what he means, exactly what he intends to do. And to be fair, my thinking had been developing along the same lines. But inviting Cain to spank me is a long way removed from him claiming that right. This is a shift—a big shift in our relationship.

He continues to press his point. "I intend to spank you. Hard. You've earned a seriously sore bum for the way you behaved. So, will you lie down over my knee, lift your skirt, pull down your pants and accept your punishment? Then it's over. Then, I fuck you and take you home. Or maybe take you home first, then fuck you. I'll decide when we get to that point. What do you say to all that, Abbie?"

I had intended to plead with Cain to allow me to stay at the flat, just until I go to Bradford for my intensive reading lessons, but in this moment I can see that will never be acceptable. The spanking might, just might, be negotiable, but not the separation. He wants me back. He's demanding it. And in truth, I want to go back. Maybe I should hesitate, take longer to consider my options, the implications. I do neither.

"Yes. All right. Now?"

"Of course now." He walks toward me, and I back away instinctively. He pauses, his head tilted in warning. "Are you scared of me? Of this?"

I shake my head. I'm nervous, not sure exactly what to expect from this new side of my usually light-hearted, sensual Dom. I'm only now properly encountering Cain's stern side, that part of his Dom nature that demands obedience from me. And respect. And delivers retribution. I'm not scared, not really, but I have every reason to be wary.

"No? Then don't back away from me. I'll never do anything to you that you weren't expecting, that you haven't consented to. So, the bedroom, I think."

He strides past me, across my small living room and into the bedroom. I trail in his wake, noting that he seems to be very familiar with the layout of my flat. Not that it would be easy to get lost in here, but still. In the bedroom he pauses, glances around him.

"I used to live here. Until James died, and I inherited his old house and decided to move in there. I miss the place sometimes."

Well that explains it. Obvious really. Meanwhile I'm still hovering by the bedroom door, unsure what to say or do now. "I—yes. It's a nice flat."

He turns, regards me solemnly for a few moments. "It is. But don't get too attached to it." With that he seats himself on the edge of the bed and turns that cool, steely gaze full on me.

"Take off your underwear, Abbie, and assume the position." He pats his knee, as if his meaning was not entirely clear enough already.

I hesitate, not really intending to resist but still needing a few moments to gear up for what's about to happen. An erotic spanking is one thing, but to allow him to spank me as a punishment, well, that requires a completely new bit of head space. This is me accepting his authority, his right to discipline me. What if it's too much? What if he really hurts me?

Cain seems to understand what's happening in my head and doesn't rush me. He allows me to adjust, to realign my thinking as our relationship shifts and re-forms. This is no longer casual, just a bit of fun while it lasts. This is something more, but I'm not yet sure what the 'more' is, what he's offering, or what I might want to accept. What I might offer in exchange.

"I won't just spank you and then dump you. I'm doing this because I care about you, and about us. I'll be here afterwards, to fuck you and to look after you. You *will* be all right with me, Abbie. You'll be safe." Intuitive as ever, Cain provides the reassurance I need.

"Can I use my safe words, if it's too much?"

"If what I'm doing is truly intolerable, then yes, of course. You always have your safe words. But remember, Abbie, this is a punishment. I'm not setting out to arouse you. It's not intended to feel good. It *will* hurt. But you're a grown woman. I expect you to face up to what you've done and the consequences, and to accept your punishment gracefully. Can you do that?"

I take a deep breath. And another, before I nod. Our talking is done. With no further ado, I reach down, lift my skirt to peel away my pants and tights. Cain watches me in silence as I place my discarded underwear on a chair beneath the window, then he beckons me to him. I walk across the room, and whilst my heart is thumping hard, I'm strangely calm. At ease. Cain's slight smile of approval as I lean over his lap and place my stomach across his knees is all the further encouragement I need.

He waits until I'm settled, lying still, then, "Lift your skirt up, Abbie. Right up above your waist."

I do it, conscious of the cool air on my bottom as my buttocks are exposed. My thighs are pressed close together, my muscles tense. I wince as Cain's palm connects with my right buttock, even though his touch is light, a sensual caress.

"How many swats, do you think? What have you deserved, Abbie? What will it take to teach you the lesson you need to learn?"

I have no idea, no frame of reference for this. I've managed twenty spanks in the past, and been all right with that. But this is different. This is meant to instil in me some sort of lesson, a warning for the future.

"Twenty-five? Would that be enough, do you think?" I can but hope.

He's stroking my bottom, his palm smoothing across the sensitive skin, his fingertips sinking into the fleshy part. It feels so good. I wonder if he'll still be inclined to pleasure me after this. And will I still want him to?

"You're new to all this, so yes, twenty-five will be enough, I think. On this occasion. I can make your sweet little arse smart well enough with that. Once I start, I expect you to keep still. Scream if you want, but don't wriggle or try to cover your bum with your hands. Remember what I said to you just now. You're an adult, a submissive who's earned a punishment, so act like one. Are you ready?"

"Yes. I'm ready." I'm not sure I'll ever be completely ready, but this is a near as I'm going to get. Then I yelp in pain and my body jerks upwards as the first swat lands.

Cain says nothing, but his palm on my back between my shoulder blades makes it clear I'm to get back in position and stay down. He waits until I go still again, then, "I'll let that one go, but do not move again, Abbie. If you do, I'll repeat that slap. The sooner you get yourself under control, the sooner we're done here and can get on to the fucking, which I'm sure we're both looking forward to. Well, I am."

I grit my teeth. "Sorry. I *will* keep still. I promise."

"Good girl."

I scream again as the second slap lands, but by the third I'm managing to ride the pain better. My body tenses up with each blow, but by sheer effort of will I'm remaining in place. He delivers the next three strokes swiftly, each one landing just below its predecessor, and alternating between the cheeks of my bum. I'm counting the spanks silently in my head, wondering if I'll be able to accept all twenty-five without even a time out. I hope so, I don't want to drag this out.

"How many is that, Abbie?" His voice is low and sexy. He caresses my seriously sore bottom with his palm as he waits for me to reply.

"Ten, I think."

"Mmm, I agree. Ten. Nearly half way there. How are you doing?"

"I'm fine. A bit sore, but I'm okay."

"Good. Because these next few will be harder. Punishment, remember?"

And he's right, they are. I'm screaming in earnest as the next five spanks land, hard and heavy on my tender skin. My bottom feels to be on fire, the pain radiating everywhere. But still I manage to hold my position, not wriggling, and by the time he's approaching twenty, I've stopped screaming again, settling for gentle but persistent weeping instead. Christ, this is hard.

"Open your legs, Abbie."

Oh God, he intends to slap my pussy. I gasp, and whimper quietly, but I do as he's asked, obediently exposing my most delicate and sensitive area for his punishment. He doesn't spin this out. His palm connects with my cunt but less forcefully than I had feared. The lips of my pussy are already swollen and slick, and his slap causes me to clench uncontrollably.

"Mmm, interesting. What a hot and sexy little sub you are, Abbie. Even when you're receiving the spanking of your life you can still manage to get wet. Shall I just check how you're doing?"

He thrusts three fingers inside my pussy, hard and fast. And deep. Now I moan in earnest, and the wriggle I can't manage to suppress earns me another rebuke.

"I told you to keep still. For that you've earned an extra slap."

I squeeze my pussy around his fingers, determined not to make matters any worse, as he finger-fucks me relentlessly. "This is a punishment, you get your rewards later. Don't you dare come until I tell you you can."

"Please, it's hard. I can't help how I feel…"

"Yes you can. Concentrate. Control yourself. And wait." He thrusts his fingers deep inside me again, angling to hit my G-spot, the bastard.

I grind my teeth together, desperate to suppress my response. I'm managing, after a fashion, until he suddenly switches tack and withdraws his fingers, only to take my clit between his finger and thumb and squeeze it hard. My orgasm is instantaneous, rocking my body and sending deep shudders through every inch of me, rippling from my core and out through my fingers and toes. It's unstoppable, as he surely knew it would be.

As the tremors die away and my body returns to something resembling normal—well, the sort of normality that entails being draped over a Dom's lap, accepting a severe punishment spanking, whilst climaxing wildly—Cain's low, sardonic voice interrupts my attempts at composure. "You need to practice your self-control, Abbie. That little performance has earned you ten more slaps. By my reckoning, that's now fifteen still to go. Shall we continue?"

I'm lying limp across his lap now, and past caring what happens. I just want this to be done with. I don't answer, just wait for the next blow to land. It doesn't.

"Abbie, I won't continue until you tell me to. Are you ready?"

"Yes." My response is whispered, but he hears me.

The next five spanks are delivered swiftly. I may be mistaken, but it feels as though he might be letting up slightly. Or maybe I'm just getting accustomed to this, my tolerance level rising, the endorphins making a belated appearance to help me through the ordeal. The next five are manageable enough too. By the time we've reached thirty, tears are streaming down my face, I'm gulping for air, but I'm holding it together.

He pauses. "Abbie? Are you still okay? You've gone quiet."

It does occur to me to offer some sassy remark, but I decide on discretion. "I'm fine. Please, just finish it. I want this to be over."

"Happy to oblige. Open your legs again please."

With a groan I do as he's asked, only now becoming conscious that my thighs had been clenched tight together. I'm ready to plead. "Please, Cain, don't touch me again. I can't manage to stop whatever happens, and I'm really hurting now."

"I think you know by now that I'll touch you when and how I like. But I'll take that as an amber light."

He lands a swat on my pussy, a direct hit on the swollen, sensitive lips. I gasp, it's painful, but incredibly erotic too.

"Again?"

He waits, and I drag in a deep breath as the sweet sensation pulses through me.

"Yes. Please."

He spanks my dripping tush again, and at my whispered response, he does it once more. I'm groaning softly, my body a tangled confusion of pain and pleasure. I'm no longer sure where one ends and the other begins.

"You want the last two here as well?"

Ah, no longer punishment perhaps. "Yes. Please. Harder."

"My sweet and sexy little slut. I intend to fuck you until you can't stand, you do realize that, I hope."

"Is that a promise? Sir?"

"Indeed so, little sub."

And I scream as he swats my cunt twice more, hard and sharp. The powerful ripples of pleasure/pain surge through my body again, and I scream my approval. Moments later he's scooped me from across his lap and I'm on my back, spread out on the bed, my legs open wide as he kneels between my thighs. I watch through half-closed eyes as he drags a condom from his back pocket before unzipping his jeans. He covers himself quickly then reaches for my right knee. He lifts it, opening me wide, my skirt still hitched around my waist. He takes my other knee, opening me fully before he thrusts his cock deep into my pussy.

He never said anything about suppressing my orgasm this time, and it's just as well because my climax is there immediately. My pussy clenches around him, beyond my conscious control. My ankles are in the small of his back and I hook them together as I reach for him, latching my hands onto his shoulders. I cling on and he drives his cock into me, each plunge deep and hard—the head of his erection connecting with my cervix. I cry out, caught up in the sheer erotic beauty of this moment, completely overpowered, overwhelmed. Falling headlong in love.

As my climax recedes, I go limp underneath him. Cain clearly notices and slows his rhythm.

"Am I hurting you, love?"

"No. It feels wonderful. It's just so, so…"

"Intense?"

"Yes. And overwhelming. It feels so tight…"

"Christ, yes. So fucking tight I think my balls might explode."

"That would be a pity."

His low chuckle rumbles in my ear. I can hardly believe he's just spanked me to the very limits of what I can endure, he's now fucking me so deep and hard I think I might just faint, and I can still manage to poke fun at him. And he'll actually let me.

"Less sass, more paying attention to what my cock's doing to your tight little pussy. Squeeze me, Abbie, let me feel how tight you are…"

I do, my reward a low groan as he resumes his rhythm, each stroke deep and long. As ever, he finds the perfect angle to create the friction I need right on my G-spot, and my second orgasm is soon bubbling to the surface.

"Come for me, sweetheart. Let me know how much you want this."

My scream of ecstasy is muffled against his shoulder as I arch up into his body, and he rakes his fingers through my hair to tilt my head back. My face positioned for his kiss, he lays his mouth over mine and plunges his tongue deep, mimicking the action of his cock. I open, welcoming him, loving him.

Even as my climax recedes, he's sliding his hand between our bodies to find my clit, and this time when he squeezes it, my response is welcomed, encouraged with low murmurs. It wouldn't make any difference any way, I'm past any attempt at control. My body is his to use, responding mindlessly to his touch. I come a third time, my pussy spasming around his cock as he too rushes toward his release. He stiffens, then surges forward, his cock filling me entirely before he holds still, buried deep within me. He twitches, jerks hard as he starts to climax. There's a rush of familiar warmth as his semen fills the condom. I squeeze again, more in accepting affection than involuntary response, a way of silently communicating how much I treasure this connection between us.

His kiss dropped softly on my ear is his reply. His murmured, "I missed you. Let's go home" completes the story.

* * * *

"Would you mind if I went away next week? On a sort of holiday?"

Cain rolls from his position behind me, my bum tucked up tight against his stomach, his softening cock nestled between my legs. It's a position I like, seems such a shame to move. But still, I have to ask.

It's now been two days since Cain came to my flat, spanked me and reclaimed me, brought me back to this house which has rapidly come to feel like ours rather than his. Two days in which we've spent a glorious weekend together. There's been sex. A lot of sex. Glorious, mind-blowing fucking, but countless tender moments too. Moments when Cain massaged my feet, or helped me to wash and comb my hair, even though I insisted I'd been doing it for myself since I was seven. Moments when we lay, naked and exhausted on the rug in the living room, watched by Oscar who, if he finds the antics of his new owners less than decorous has not protested unduly.

Moments when Cain lay still while I straddled him, only lowering myself slowly onto his throbbing erection when he threatened me with a spanking to top the one he provided on Friday evening. There have been many such intimate moments, and easily as many moments when we fucked frantically and mindlessly, unable to get enough of each other. Moments when we've vented our emotions and our delight. I can't get enough of him and it does seem as though the feeling is mutual. And deeply satisfying.

On Sunday afternoon we even took time out to go exploring the rocky Northumberland shoreline again, this time driving a few miles south to the village of Beal, and from there walking across the causeway at low tide to reach the island of Lindisfarne. Cain sat on a low section of tumble-down wall, watching as I sketched the beautiful ruins of the priory. One of the things I most love about drawing is the artistic license I can claim, to embellish as I see fit. So inspired by the evocative narrative of the local guide whose job it is to greet visitors and deliver a potted version of the history of the island, I add my own touches. I sketch in a few haunting images of peaceful monks from days gone by, fleeing from marauding Vikings, with horned helmets and snarling, bearded faces, all adding to the rich historic tapestry I'm creating. Well that's my story. Or maybe I just didn't want to pass up an excuse to draw Vikings.

I glanced across at Cain, observing that he'd have passed well enough for a Viking in an earlier age. His arrival at my flat on Friday, his implacable insistence on totally dominating me, all add to that image. And totally make my toes curl and my pussy twist into a tight little knot of desire. I grew wet just remembering how he'd completely overwhelmed me and, after my initial nervousness, I'd been delighted to let him. In true Viking tradition, I do feel distinctly pillaged. Maybe he's right, maybe I *am* a natural submissive. It certainly seems like it.

We drove back to Berwick, neither of us saying much. For me, my head was full of what the coming week might bring. Will Phyllis respect my privacy, keep my secret? I know she feels compromised at being less than honest with Cain, she believes I should tell him the whole truth. Maybe one day. Soon. When it's fixed. It'll be easier in retrospect, I'll feel less exposed.

I have no idea what Cain's thoughts were on that journey, though his insistence on spending most of the evening in our customary naked state, eating our supper in bed, is a clue regarding his state of mind. Our love-making — or fucking as Cain usually terms it — has been sweetly vanilla since then, at least by our standards. By unspoken agreement, my body is too sore for anything kinkier. I'm pleasantly tender, harboring absolutely no regrets or misgivings about what happened. The redness has now faded from my bottom, though it glowed prettily for at least thirty-six hours, so maybe soon… We're huddled together in a contented after-glow. Shame I need to wreck it. But I have to say something.

If Cain insists I should stay here, I'm not entirely sure what I'll do. Maybe then I'll come clean. For sure, I can't be derailed now. For the first time ever, as far as I can recall, I have both motivation and opportunity, in the same place at the same time. That's enough, that's all I need. The rest is just a matter of getting on and doing it. So he has to agree, he has to let me go. It's that simple.

He props himself up on one elbow, and I can feel his eyes on me though I resist the urge to turn to him.

"A holiday? Where are we going then? Somewhere warm?"

We! That does get my attention. I roll onto my back, looking up at his curious expression. He doesn't seem unduly ruffled by the prospect of this sudden change in plans. He may soon.

"I was thinking I'd go on my own." *Ah, right, not so relaxed now.*

"Is something wrong, Abbie?"

I shake my head emphatically "No, absolutely not. It's perfect. We're perfect. I-I've never been more happy than I am at this moment."

He narrows his eyes. "Okay. That's good. So...?"

"I need to visit my friend. Sally? I think I mentioned her. We used to work together, at that school in Bradford. It, it's just something we arranged a while ago. It's half term next week you see. We like to spend time a bit of together, hit the shops, that sort of thing. I won't arrange any other trips if you don't want me to..." *Please, God, it's a white lie, don't let him find out.*

Miraculously, he smiles. "Abbie, if you want to nip off and visit a friend for a few days, that's fine. You don't need my permission. Arrange as many trips as you like. I'll come on them sometimes, although at least one of us could do with being here. I have work stacked up as it is so couldn't easily manage time off at short notice, but I don't mind at all if this is what you want to do. And the joy of being the boss, one of the few perks in my view, is you can take time off work when it suits you. More or less. So, where are you and Sally going then?"

"Oh, nowhere really. We just want to spend some girlie time together, maybe some shopping, a few art galleries..."

"Sounds like more your sort of thing than mine. Enjoy. When are you planning to go?"

He's agreed! He's actually bloody agreed. No arguing, no pleading. Shit!

"Friday, if that's all right. I can catch the train sometime in the afternoon. Go via Leeds."

"If you wait until the evening I don't mind driving you."

"No!" My response comes out more sharply than I intended, but I need to get him off that notion fast. No way can I let him get wind of the real purpose of this visit. I don't want him meeting Sally, and if he drives me all the way back to Bradford on Friday evening there'll be no good reason for not asking him to stay over at least for the night, maybe the whole weekend. And every day counts. Every hour almost. I need all the time I can get for this project.

"No? Are you sure?" If he's noticed my vehemence — and I have to suspect he has, he's not calling me on it. Not yet anyway.

"I'm sure. There's a train every hour, it's only a couple of hours to York, then another hour across the Bradford. It's quicker than driving..."

He rolls onto his back, seemingly ready to accept that I've made independent plans. "I'll miss you. When will you be back?"

"On the Sunday? The second Sunday. I'll be gone nine nights. Is that okay?" If he insists, I might have to think about returning earlier than I intended, which would sort of undermine the whole purpose of the trip.

"I see. I'll *really* miss you then. I suppose I'll just have to find something else to keep me busy. And get back into the habit of feeding old Oscar."

Amazingly, he hasn't objected. His response is admirably philosophical, really. And not at all what I was anticipating, given his apparent possessiveness a couple of days ago. I draw a deep sigh of relief. He's accepted it, no questions asked really. I roll over, now propping myself on my elbows on his chest, gazing down into his amused gray eyes. Impulsively I lean in to drop a kiss on his mouth.

"Thank you."

"You can do better than that. Thank me properly." His lips quirk in mock challenge.

I manage to wipe the smile off his face with my follow up kiss, full and deep and open-mouthed, exploring his mouth, using my tongue to find and tangle with his as we roll across the bed. Moments later he's reaching for another condom, snapping the foil and unrolling it over his re-kindled erection. He breaks the kiss, maneuvering me underneath as he pins me to the bed.

"If it makes you this enthusiastic, maybe I should pay for your train ticket as well. Would that get me a chance to fuck your arse too?"

I wriggle under him, arching suggestively. "Help yourself. I'm all yours."

"So you are, my sweet and sexy little sub. So you are."

I moan my appreciation as he sinks his cock into my welcoming, slick channel, at the same time hooking his arms under my knees to lift and open me for his deeper penetration. It's fast, it's hard and it's probably not especially pretty. But it is truly wonderful and I cling on as he fucks me expertly, screaming my orgasm moments later. He's not the only one who will be counting down those nine nights.

Chapter Eighteen

The next morning, Monday, Cain drops me off at the yard but doesn't come in. He has meetings in Newcastle. He's seeing his accountant and he wants to track down Fiona Henderson if he can. He did invite me along, and I was tempted. But I'm keen to see Phyllis and reassure her that Cain and I are fine again. And that my plans for addressing my little problem are well in place, so she won't be in this awkward position for much longer.

Phyllis is already at her desk, embroiled in what I gather is the usual Monday morning backlog of emails, requests for quotes, messages from clients with leaky roofs or patios that won't stay flat. I make myself useful in the kitchen. Ten minutes later, plied with a fortifying mug of genuine builders' tea, she turns to regard me solemnly.

"So, how was it?"

"It?" Surely she can't know how we solved our little dilemma…?

"It. You and Cain. Are you back at the house then? I suppose you must be—you came in the front door and not down those stairs." She nods in the direction of the staircase up to the flat.

I take a sip of my sweet coffee, not quite able to meet her eyes. I have no regrets, no doubts at all about how things are between myself and Cain Parrish — the spankings, the hot and more than slightly kinky sex — but I can't see me discussing any of that with Phyllis. I settle for a bit of code. "Yes. He can be very persuasive."

"Mmm, I expect he can. Let's hope the Parrish charm works on Mrs Henderson too."

In a manner of speaking. I settle for a non-committal sort of grunt, and take refuge behind my coffee cup again.

"Is everything all right about next week then? Are you still going to study with your friend?" Phyllis is clearly keen to pursue our discussion of Friday.

Study? I never thought of myself as a student, but I suppose I am, now. And it feels quite nice. Wholesome. Sort of productive. I nod, feeling rather proud of myself as I look up at Phyllis.

"I mentioned it to Cain, about me being away all week. He was fine about it. I had to convince him not to drive me down there though."

"He still doesn't know what you're going for then?"

"No. Not yet. I thought I might tell him. After."

"I see. I still think it'd all be a lot easier if he knew the score. He'd be able to help you."

I don't doubt he would. And by now I know him well enough to believe he's not the sort who'd say anything unkind or derisive, at least not deliberately. But I've no way of knowing what his private thoughts might be, apart from astonishment. That's a given. Would he think less of me? Surely he would. Anyone would.

It'll be difficult enough telling him afterwards that I've somehow managed to get to the advanced age of twenty-two and can't read as well as the average seven-year-old. But once it's fixed I can start to move on from this, and distance will make the self-loathing easier to face. This is what I *used* to be, how it *was*. It's not the 'me' I am now. This 'me' is clever, determined, successful. Moving forward. This 'me' is someone I'm proud of. Or I will be. Roll on Friday.

"Abbie? Are you okay?" Phyllis is looking at me, concerned.

I glance at her, shaking my head to clear it. "Sorry, I was miles away. I'm fine. Just a bit tired. It was a heavy weekend. Nice, but busy." Encouraged by her answering smile, I go on to tell her about our excursion to Lindisfarne, pulling out my sketchpad to show her the pictures I drew.

She particularly likes my Vikings, and comments on the more than passing similarity between my pillager-in-chief and a certain Cain Parrish. I have to accept she has a point.

I spend the rest of that morning bent over my sketchbook putting the finishing touches to a number of drawings I've started since leaving my old home. The Angel of the North, the building site, Lindisfarne. I'm going to add water colors, but that doesn't seem quite the right activity for a day in the office. Phyllis doesn't agree.

"To be fair, love, you're not going to be much use doing invoices or checking the trade press for jobs we could tender for. Why not get on with what you're good at? There'll be plenty for you to do later."

"I'd have to go home for my paints."

"Well go then. The walk'll do you good."

I don't need asking twice. I'm headed for the door, my jacket over my arm before she can change her mind and find some envelopes for me to stuff. I pause in the doorway, remembering my last attempt at mastering invoices.

"By the way, I did have a go at finding the unpaid invoices last week. Like you asked. I'm not sure I did it right though. I left the ones I thought needed chasing in a separate pile." I point to the papers on my desk. "I was wondering if maybe you could check them...?"

She glances up at me wryly as she continues her rapid fire typing. "Probably best, love. I'll have a look tomorrow."

* * * *

She doesn't do it tomorrow though. The next morning Cain and I arrive at the office together, to find the door still locked and no Phyllis. Once inside, there's a message on the telephone answering machine telling us that her Stan is under the weather and she needs to stay with him today, that she'll make up the hours later.

"Does she have to do that? Make up the time, I mean?" It seems to me that Phyllis already does more than her share.

Cain seems to think so too. "Well, I'm not counting. She'll probably have some work she can do at home anyway, knowing her. Could you phone her back and tell her it's okay and not to worry? We'll manage." He glances up at me from the pile of envelopes he's busily splitting open in Phyllis' absence. "Well, you will. Do you mind staying here on your own, love? We could do with having someone to deal with phone calls if nothing else. And this lot." He tosses the rest of the unopened mail onto Phyllis' desk. "I need to get off to Morpeth, sweet talk Mrs H and her bloody architect. She seems ready to be reasonable, but that little shit's kicking up a fuss. You'd think the massive cost saving that dropped in her lap was his doing, the way he's carrying on..."

I cringe. No matter how kind, how generous both Cain and Phyllis are, whichever way you slice it, it was my doing. I hope Cain does manage to salvage something, and the least I can do is agree to hold the fort. I'm not relishing the prospect of spending the day here on my own though. Still, I have my paints now. And needs must.

"I'll be fine. You get off. Drive safe." I smile brightly, and Cain drops a quick kiss on my mouth as he heads for the great outdoors. "Put anything important or interesting on Phyllis' desk, and shred the junk." He gestures at the rest of today's post, just before the door swings shut behind him.

Ten minutes later, my customary first coffee of the day steaming merrily on my desk, I haul the post toward me. Might as well make a start. I've no intention of shredding anything, too much potential there for absolute disaster. I may be thick, but I'm not totally stupid.

Most of the post looks like junk to me. Advertising stuff, bright and glossy with pictures of such interesting items as power tools, uPVC window frames, paving slabs. I pile those up for Phyllis. At least now that she knows about my issues I won't need to try to justify why I haven't been more discriminating. The rest I can't make head nor tail of, frankly. Official looking stuff, closely typed sheets, could be anything. I leave those neatly stacked for

Phyllis too, and get on with coloring up my pictures. Needless to say, I leave the computer well alone.

The phone rings a few times. Someone enquiring about whether we do gardening — I tell them we don't. Another caller tries to sell us a subscription to something called *Plumb Line,* which sounds like a magazine. I agree they can send us their brochure. Cain phones to ask how my day's going, I tell him I'm fine. I'm even finer when he tells me that Mrs Henderson has overruled her bolshy architect and has agreed to a quote of forty thousand pounds all in for the extension. Cain thinks we can do it for that — no profit, but no massive loss either. It's a result.

* * * *

Phyllis' Stan is still not himself according to her message on the answering machine the next morning so she's taking another day off. She promises faithfully to be in tomorrow. Even if Stan's still poorly, her neighbor has agreed to sit with him if need be. I'm not enthusiastic about another solitary day in the office, but I don't make a fuss as Cain heads off for Rothbury and that wonderful building site. After that he's meeting Beth the glamorous plumber to get started on a central heating installation in Morpeth. I ask him to give my regards to Rachel and to Beth, as I start on this morning's post.

Today's crop is much the same as Monday's, just there's less of it. The piles of promotional glossies and other boring stuff on Phyllis' desk are growing, but still I resist the lure of the shredder. And the computer. Myself, my water colors and my sketchpad spend a quiet day together, interrupted only occasionally by the phone. I make appointments for

Cain to price up a job in Hexham and another in Alnwick. Next I agree to send our brochure to a developer based in Edinburgh who needs a specialist traditional stone mason to do some sub-contracted work. He's found us on the Internet so Cain's marketing must be working. This sounds like the sort of thing Cain likes best. Beth phones to confirm she's available for the central heating job and on her way to the address Cain texted her over the weekend. Again, I consider plumbing as a career choice. It would be nice to actually work with Cain properly—doing something useful and skilled. My resolve firms even more. I *will* make next week count.

On Thursday morning Cain drops me off just before eight. He has to get to Morpeth for another hot date with Beth and the intricacies of eco-friendly heating systems. I find the door unlocked, and Phyllis looks to have been at her desk for at least an hour already. Her computer is fired up, and so is mine.

"Morning, love. I'll be with you in a moment. Just wading through all these emails."

I feel a shooting pang of guilt that it's all been just left for her, while I've spent two days painting. Not for much longer. I make her a cup of tea, it's the least I can do.

"That pile looks to me like just advertising stuff, junk mail." I point to the stack of glossies. "Let me know which you want shredding, I'll do it later. Not so sure about those though." I tilt my head in the direction of the 'official' pile.

"Most of that's probably junk as well. I'll check after I've got my inbox cleared."

She's clearly busy, I leave her to it as I attack today's post and add to the growing mountains of correspondence yet to be dealt with.

The Three Rs

It's half an hour later—just as I'm contemplating a second cup of coffee—that Phyllis' muttered expletive reverberates around the tiny office. "Shit! Shit, shit *shit*! When did this come?"

I turn, alarmed. She never normally speaks like this.

"What? When did what come?"

"This." She's brandishing something from the boring pile. I abandon my immediate plans for renewing our beverages and take the sheet she's waving at me. I glance at it, and I'm no wiser really. Apart from the initials in the heading—H.S.E—I can't manage to decipher anything else especially meaningful.

"I don't... What is it?"

But Phyllis isn't paying any attention to me. She's already on the phone, dialing Cain's mobile number.

"Cain? Yes, yes it's me. Yes, I'm back. He's fine. Much better. Look, you need to get to Newcastle, the Health and Safety Exec offices. Yes, now." She pauses, no doubt listening to whatever Cain's saying on the other end, but she interrupts him.

"They want to interview you, about that incident last month in Rothbury, when Rob broke his arm. Apparently there's been a complaint about safety procedures..." She pauses again, briefly, before breaking into his flow, "It's not short notice. Not really. The letter's dated the beginning of last week, but it only arrived in this week's post. Must have got held up on its way here. It arrived Tuesday, I think. Your appointment was yesterday."

She pauses, then, "Yes, of course. I'll scan it and email you a pdf. And I'll phone them and make our excuses for yesterday, tell them it was because I was off sick. I'll let them know you'll be there today."

She hangs up, then turns to me, "Well, that settles it. You'll have to tell him now."

"Why? What? Tell him what? What's happened?" I'm baffled, totally at a loss. Something momentous seems to be going wrong—both Phyllis and Cain are rushing around, dropping everything to attend to whatever's on that sheet of paper. And I haven't a clue what's happening. If anything, this is even more terrifying than when the solicitor's letter arrived all those weeks ago, back in Bradford, disrupting my, up till then, reasonably untroubled existence. At least then I could prop the offending article unopened beside my breakfast cereals, make it wait until I was ready. This situation is hurtling forward, out of control. And I've no idea what's coming next.

Phyllis draws a deep breath and sinks onto her chair. "Last month one of our scaffolders, Rob, fell from a platform and broke his wrist. Nothing too serious—could have been a lot worse. But any accident on a site gets reported and is investigated by the HSE—Health and Safety Executive. They came, did their checks, spoke to the other workers, interviewed Cain, looked at the paperwork, and it seemed everything was in order. But now it appears Rob's made a complaint, probably to do with insurance, but even so, the HSE are back on it. They're entitled to call in managers, developers, site supervisors, anyone with responsibility for health and safety stuff. Here, that's Cain. They wanted to see him at their offices in Newcastle on Wednesday, and it's a fineable offense just not turning up. Plus it'll make them even more suspicious and they'll examine every detail, not just that job but everything else too. When they do, they always find something. We're a tight-run ship, Cain makes sure of that, but they only need to dig out one example of a policy not followed, one scrap of documentation not in the right file, one box not ticked anywhere, and they can throw the lot at us."

I stare at her, aghast. "This is bad, isn't it?"

Phyllis returns my gaze. "Yes. It's bad. And the worst thing, while the investigation is going on, HSE can insist that all work has to be suspended till they give us the all clear. That can take weeks. At best though, they'll pull us off the job in Rothbury, and if—when—that happens, there's a good chance A.R.T. will ditch us from the project entirely. Breach of contract, plus they have deadlines of their own to meet. So yes, Abbie, this is bad."

I flop into my chair, the awful ramifications of this only now beginning to make sense to me. We could, will, lose money. But there's our reputation to consider too, the loss of future work with A.R.T. and others like them. They're not the only ones with deadlines—we could have other clients going elsewhere. Christ, what a mess.

Something in Phyllis' remarks puzzles me though. "What did you mean, I'll have to tell him now."

Phyllis looks at me, her expression sympathetic, but there's also frustration there too. A hint of annoyance. I don't understand. What have I done? The accident was nothing to do with me, it happened before I even came here, and there's nothing I could have done as far as the investigation was concerned. She puts me out of my misery.

"Our big problem now stems from missing that interview yesterday, and not sending any reason. We could have re-scheduled, but you get fined for just doing a no show."

"Right..." I'm still not getting it.

"The letter asking us to come in arrived on Tuesday. You opened it and put it on that pile, just left it on my desk. Now, I know why you did that, I understand why you didn't, couldn't have known how important it was. But Cain won't have any idea why you didn't phone him as soon as you saw it to tell him he needed to show up in Newcastle on Wednesday. A day's notice isn't much, but it's enough."

My heart does a delicate little lurch, and not in a nice way. Not at all. *Oh. My. God. Fucking bloody hell.* All this could have been avoided if I'd been able to read even enough of that letter to know it was serious. Just showing it to Cain when he came to pick me up on Tuesday afternoon would have been enough. But no, I buried it with all the other 'junk'. Left it until now, when it's too late. When the damage has been done.

I'm just contemplating the full enormity of what's happened and my unwitting part in it when the phone on Phyllis' desk rings. It's Cain, naturally. She picks it up, speaks briefly, then hands the phone to me.

"He wants to talk to you."

I take the receiver from her, put it to my ear, as she mimes an emphatic 'tell him' at me across the desk. Rudely, I swivel my seat to face away from her.

Phyllis' manners are better than mine. She walks across the office to pick up her coat. "I'm just going for a breath of air. I'll leave you to talk."

I turn back to her, nod apologetically as she slips out of the office, closing the door softly behind her.

"Abbie, when did that letter come?" No greeting, no pleasantries, just straight in. His tone is curt, chilled. He might have been angry, at least at first, when he realized about Mrs Henderson's quote. This time, he's absolutely furious. With me.

"I-I'm not sure. Tuesday, I think."

"You think? Either it was or it wasn't. Has Phyllis got it wrong then?" He doesn't raise his voice, he has no need to. Just the clipped tone, the brusque words are enough to convey how very, very pissed off he really is.

My stomach clenches, my nerves jangling. But I can't let any of this drop on Phyllis' toes. "No. She's not wrong. It *was* Tuesday."

"Tuesday. Right. But you didn't bother to tell me? Why not, for Christ's sake?"

"I didn't realize it was important..." Even as I utter the lame excuse, I know how pathetic that sounds. Even I've heard of the Health and Safety Executive. If I'd known what I was holding in my hand, I'd have realized it was important. And I would have known, if I could read. This time next week, maybe, I would have known. But not now. And definitely not on Tuesday when it mattered. "I'm so sorry..."

"Don't, Abbie. Don't even start to say you're sorry. This goes beyond anything 'sorry' can put right. We could be out of business if I can't manage to convince the HSE to go easy on us. Was that the plan?"

What?

"What are you talking about? What plan?"

"No way was this a mistake. Another 'accident'. You saw that letter, you must have known. And you decided to keep it to yourself. That looks to me like a plan, Abbie."

I'm truly stunned. He seems to think I've done this on purpose. I might be a bit dim, but that's plain stupid. "Don't be ridiculous. Why would I...?"

"I have absolutely no fucking idea. What I do know though, is that this sort of rubbish did *not* happen before you came here. The wrong figures being given to customers, and now this. Bloody fucking hell, Abbie. I know you didn't want to come, this wasn't your first choice of job. You made it clear enough you didn't want to work in the office, and I thought we'd got past that, sorted out a compromise. But no, you go and do this."

"I didn't, really, it was…" My voice trails off, I'm lost for words. I have no idea what to say. He's right about one thing, this sort of screw-up didn't happen before, it *is* all down to me. Phyllis' advice was clear enough. Tell him. Explain. He'll still be livid, but maybe, eventually, he'll understand that it was genuinely a mistake.

But he'll also understand what a dismal failure I am, or have been up until now. I dismiss any notion of telling him the truth—opting again for an undisguised grovel.

"Please, Cain, it was an accident. I just didn't read it properly. I didn't realize." True, as far as it goes.

"Spare me that. I'm not interested in fucking apologies. I'm interested in saving this business. *My* business. James screwed it up enough just getting you involved, but I'm not letting you sink us completely. I may not be able to sack you, more's the pity, but I can sure as hell make you wish you'd never messed with me. And you can start by canceling that little jaunt of yours tomorrow. You'll be busy here all next week, helping to sort this pile of shite out."

I don't respond at first, I can't. He can't. I have to go. Everything, my entire future, all the plans I've started to make for myself, hinge on next week. If I put it off, I might as well just give up altogether. I need to go, and it has to be now. It's that simple.

"Cain, please, it's all arranged…"

"Unarrange it. I'm not bloody arguing with you. You'll be here tomorrow. And next week, and the week after and every other fucking week, like I will, until this is sorted. Get used to it."

His tone is one usually reserved for when I'm naked—then his implacable sternness is one of his finest features. Now, it just terrifies me. If I obey him, and he clearly means me to do just that, all my dreams are in tatters. Even now I suppose I could tell him the whole truth and he'd probably let me go. Hell, he'd probably insist on it, drive me to the station himself. But at what cost? His respect? His trust? It certainly seems as though I've lost those anyway, but at least I have some shreds of self-respect left. And the determination to make this right. To make *me* right. I suck in a deep breath, close my eyes. Steady myself, firm up my resolve. I know why I'm doing this. It's the right thing. It has to be.

"No. I'm not canceling. I'm going. In fact, I'm going now, today. If there's anything I can do before I leave, any way I can help, just tell me. But I'll be on a train by the end of today."

The silence at the other end is deafening. Long moments drag by before he responds, "Abbie, if you do that, if you run out on me this time, I don't want you coming back."

"I'll be back a week on Sunday, like I said..."

"No. You won't. If you disobey me and leave now, do not even think about coming back. You won't be welcome."

"Please, Cain..." I'm sobbing now, how can he be so unrelenting? And in spite of my grief, and my genuine regret at all that's happening, there's still a mutinous part of me buried not too deep. A spark of rebelliousness that he hasn't managed to spank out of me, that wonders how he came to be dictating terms. It surfaces.

"You can't stop me. This is my business too."

His tone is even icier, if that were possible. "Is it? Is it really? Stay in Bradford, Abbie, if you're so hell-bent on going. I'll send you your money, though there'll be precious little of that for a while. But if you value your hide, and if you have any shred of respect left for me, you just stay away. I never want to set eyes on you again. Are we clear? Are we absolutely fucking clear?"

I don't reply. There's nothing to say. He evidently thinks so too, because the line goes dead after a few seconds. The resounding click as he hangs up on me is as final as a coffin lid.

Chapter Nineteen

The journey to Bradford is a blur. I got on a train at Berwick station, managed to change at York a couple of hours later, eventually rolling into the tatty little station in Bradford city center some four hours or so after I clambered into a taxi outside Cain's house. My battered hold-all was once again bulging with my possessions, or at least those things I couldn't bear to leave behind — my sketchbook, my paints. A copy of a book with a gray tie on the cover — a present from Phyllis, pressed into my hand at the station where she came to wave me off. Adult reading material, she assures me. Cain's spare bedroom is still full of my other boxes. I'll work something out with him later, when I'm less vulnerable, less emotional. When I'm able to write to him asking for the return of my stuff.

I catch a bus from the station in Bradford to the estate where my flat still waits patiently for me, on the seventh floor. Tower blocks are not everyone's cup of tea, but I've never had any quarrel with it. And the view's superb. I'm glad I didn't burn my bridges entirely by giving up the tenancy. I suppose Sally would have put me up on her sofa, at least for a while. But it's good to know I have a home, my own place, security. I need that now, more than ever before.

I let myself into my flat, shivering at the chill in the unheated rooms. I flick the dial on the thermostat to kick the system into life then start to unpack my bag. It doesn't take long. By ten o'clock in the evening I've run out of things to do to keep my mind off today's catalog of disasters. As if…

I go through the motions of getting ready for bed, and slide between the chilly sheets. Just twenty-four hours ago I was in bed with Cain, warm and sated, still tingling from his spanking followed as always by his skilled and inventive fucking. I recall vividly the erotic and sensuous thrill of his cock sliding into me, slowly, inch by glorious inch. His sweet murmurs of appreciation, as well as the wickedly dirty things he likes to say to me just before he comes.

Came. Past tense. It won't be happening again. I've truly blown it. Even if I did decide to tell him the truth, all of it, he'll never forgive me for leaving when he told me not to. Not again. He made it clear enough, couldn't have been more explicit. Earlier today, it seemed worth it, seemed as though I had no alternative. Now, tonight, lying here alone and cold in my single bed, that decision looks like a big mistake. The biggest yet, and that's saying something in the circumstances.

What have I done?

* * * *

It's Friday morning and I have a whole day to kill before I can go round to Sally's to start my Grand Project. Operation Self-Betterment as I privately call it.

And before much longer, I'll be able to spell it too. Now, as I munch on some rather soggy cereal I found lurking at the back of my kitchen cupboard, the hours yawn endlessly in front of me. Sally won't be home until about four at the earliest, maybe later than that as they'll have lots of clearing up to do before the holidays. They always do.

I can't stay here, just thinking about Cain, and Phyllis, and Parrish Construction, and the total fuck-up I've made of my life. I need to get out. So I do. I end up at one of my usual haunts, this time opting for the Hockney collection at Saltaire. The gallery in Salts Mill is stunning. In fact the whole place is. I can pick out brief snippets of information from the signs around the place, but now I'm much more aware of all I can't understand, all the details I can't make sense of.

I missed the HSE letter, what else am I missing? What more have I let pass me by in a lifetime of just looking at the pictures? No more. It ends here. Today.

Late in the morning I buy a cheese sandwich in the Saltaire bakery, and phone Phyllis. I know Cain might answer, but I take the risk. I need to know what's happening, how he went on yesterday with the HSE in Newcastle.

My heart sinks as Cain's voice comes on the line. "Good morning, Parrish Construction."

My throat constricts, I consider hanging up. My finger is hovering over the little red phone.

He speaks again. "Hello? Parrish Construction."

"I... Hello. It's Abbie. Is Phyllis there?"

"What do you want, Abbie?" His tone has that chilled, deadpan quality he now cultivates especially for me I'm sure.

"I-I was wondering how things are? What's happening?"

"And you care about this because...?"

"Please, Cain, I never intended for any of this to happen. Please believe me."

"I'm done believing you, Abbie." The line goes dead again, with another resounding coffin-like click.

'I would never have walked out on you in the middle of an argument, Abbie. Not when there were things you still wanted to say to me.' Weren't those his very words to me a week ago, in my little flat above the office? I'd say hanging up the phone on me amounts to the same thing. And his actions just serve to reinforce how totally I've screwed up. Our relationship, or whatever it was, is over. Now, the rules have changed. Now, he walks away.

Half an hour later, my phone rings. I glance at the screen—*'Ofis'*. That means the office at Parrish Construction. Well, it's my phone—the spelling is my affair and no one else's. I hit the green button. "Hello?"

"Abbie, it's me."

Phyllis.

"Cain said you rang, asked for me. He's just nipped out to the bank, he wants to talk them into extending our overdraft."

"I see. Are we in trouble already then?"

"Not as much as we could have been, as it's turning out. The HSE have only suspended us on the one site, Rothbury. That's our biggest single contract, and A.R.T. are grumbling, but we were ahead of schedule. If Cain can get it sorted in days rather than weeks, they probably won't want to go to all the bother of finding a new sub-contractor for the stone masonry this far into the project. We may not be hit that bad."

I slump onto one of the long viewing seats in front of a set of landscapes, my feeling one of overwhelming relief. If anyone can make this go away, Cain can. He managed to sweet-talk Mrs Henderson, surely he can do the same with A.R.T. and the health and safety folk? And if he manages that, then surely he'll be able to forgive me. Eventually.

Except he won't. He thinks I did this all on purpose, deliberately set out to destroy his business. The fact that I failed won't be grounds for forgiveness. And even if it was, I walked out on him. Again. After he distinctly told me not to and what the consequences would be if I disobeyed him. No, there's no going back from this. I knew that, and I did it anyway.

Cain might have got over all that's happened, all that's gone wrong, eventually, if I'd stayed. But then I'd never have forgiven myself for letting this moment slip away from me, this moment when I can change my life. But however things turn out for me, I am genuinely delighted that Parrish Construction might be okay after all, and that Phyllis and the others who depend on the firm won't lose their livelihoods because of me.

"That's brilliant news, Phyllis. God, I do hope so. What happens now?"

"The HSE will be here on Monday, going through all our files with a fine tooth comb. Me and Cain are working over the weekend to make sure there's nothing at all they could pick fault with. They'll give us both a grilling too. Then on Tuesday they re-inspect at the site. After that they go off and have a think, and if they're satisfied we're safe to be let loose, they'll lift the ban. We're just hoping they won't take too long over it. Our other work is all going ahead as planned though, so we'll be fine. What about you, love? Have you started your lessons yet?"

"No. This evening I hope. I'm going over to the school where my friend works later, for when they finish. I'll help her to clear up, then go back to hers for my first lesson."

"You sound excited. Are you looking forward to it then?"

I hesitate for a moment to consider this. Then, "Yes, I think I am. I'm definitely looking forward to being able to read, read properly I mean, like everyone else can. Just to be able to look at a word and know what it says instead of having to work out every letter and then try to cobble them together into something I recognize. And getting it wrong half the time."

"It comes with practice, love. You'll soon get the hang of it. Look, I've got to go. I've a whole filing cabinet to check through."

"Oh, God, I feel so guilty. I made all this extra work for you. And Cain. Your whole weekend ruined."

"Oh, I don't know. It's not every day I get to spend the weekend with a sexy young man. My Stan has his attractions, I wouldn't swap him for the world, but Cain definitely looks better in tight jeans. Not that I'd ever say as much, and I expect you to keep that to yourself too." Her tone lowers, serious now, "And anyway, you and I both know you didn't mean any of this to happen. It was an accident. And if you'd just explain everything to Cain, he'd see that too."

"It's more complicated than that, Phyllis. I wish it wasn't…"

"I can't believe you two are finished. You've hardly got started. And you seemed so right for each other."

More than she realized, I'm sure. But as I'm now painfully aware, sexual compatibility isn't enough.

* * * *

The Three Rs

I might be relatively new to reading. Well, to serious reading. But it's pretty clear Sally's done this before. My usually fun-loving and giggly friend is an absolute demon when on duty. She really makes me work. But I'm loving it. And I'm getting somewhere.

We've been working together for three days now, though it seems less than that. Sally never lets me read for more than about twenty minutes, and always starts with something we've read earlier so I can remember and get it right, at least at first. She's been picking out the most common words, marking these in the books we read with her yellow highlighter, and getting me to recognize those on sight. The list of words I know like that is getting longer every day. Much longer.

Other words, words I don't recognize, we break down into sounds. I'm getting really good at skimming through a word on paper and picking out the sounds made by the letters, saying it in my head, or out loud. Out loud is best, it usually makes sense straight away then.

Sometimes Sally tells me what I'm about to read, what the story or magazine article is about. Then I read it for myself, knowing what to expect and finding the meanings. Sally always stresses the importance of the meaning, what the words and sentences are saying. She insists we put it all together, and makes me tell it back to her in my own words. She calls anything else just de-coding the print, and says that's easy. Anyone can do that. And she's right. De-coding print is a piece of cake — I've been doing that for years and no more. Now, for the first time almost, a paragraph of writing is starting to mean something.

Today, Monday, I had a breakthrough. A sort of light bulb moment. I started to read a paragraph from

Harry Potter and The Philosopher's Stone, got half way through then skipped most of it to read the words on the bottom line. Because I was interested, actually eager to know how it would end. I couldn't wait. I've never done that before.

We also play with plastic magnetic letters. Sally borrowed a bagful from school and we use those to make up words, moving the letters around to form new sounds. At first I felt silly, as if I were playing with kids' toys. Maybe I was, but the words we made up weren't for kids. The difference between 'dick' and 'cock' may not seem much, but just shifting those two letters around made it all so much clearer for me. Then we introduced 'prick' and I was on a roll.

If anything, Sally works harder on this than I do. Whilst I'm taking time out to sketch or catch up on trashy day-time television, she's planning our next sessions, choosing books for me, feverishly highlighting, always pushing me. Our twenty minute bursts are intensive, rapid fire. Drive-by reading. None of that pondering over hard words, which I remember being as such an ordeal at school—those endless sessions standing beside the teacher's desk stuttering over something incomprehensible. If I can't read a word pretty much straight away, Sally says it for me and makes me move on. But I know that word will be emerging out of our magnetic letters sometime soon, and I *will* learn it. And the next time, I'll read it and move straight on.

We're doing writing too. Proper handwriting. Maybe it's the artist in me, but this is the bit I enjoy the most. I love a perfectly executed aesthetic shape, who wouldn't? So forming elegant, even letters on the page is a real pleasure for me. Sometimes we read a few sentences then I choose my favorite bit to copy out in my best not-quite-joined-up handwriting.

On Tuesday we start on Phyllis' *Fifty Shades of Gray*. Sally insists it won't be unduly difficult, though she fears for my vocabulary. Words like 'nipple' and 'vanilla' quickly appear on our magnetic board, and I ache for Cain. Perhaps I could phone him. Or text. I could actually do that now. Maybe. Probably. I'll ask Sally to help.

"Are you sure? I thought you two parted on bad terms."

"We did. But I want to text him, just to ask how things are going." I pull out my phone and press the messaging button. I glance up at Sally. "I just want to ask him how he is..."

"Okay. Is he in your list of contacts?"

I click to that and find Cain's picture at the top of my list. Sally guides me through the process of putting Cain in the recipient's box, then makes me work for it, spelling out—

How are you?

She absolutely forbids me to use text speak, insists I learn the correct way to write things before I start messing with anything fancy. Sounds sensible, I don't want to be too ambitious too soon. I press 'send' and put my phone away to return to the magnetic letters. Soon I've added 'clitoris' to my repertoire.

Cain's response is curt to say the least.

Fine, busy.

It's a start.

Chapter Twenty

The week with Sally passes in a blur. Each day it seems I make some sort of breakthrough, often several breakthroughs actually, and my rate of progress speeds up as the days fly by. Reading is becoming easier, my confidence growing in leaps and bounds. A paragraph of writing, which only a few days ago might have taken me an hour to extract even the most patchy shreds of meaning from, is making perfect sense at first glance. I can open any page in my trusty Harry Potter book and be certain of following the adventures of young Mr Potter, Hermione and Ron Weasley without much effort at all. There are some odd words I can't decipher — that goes with the wizard territory — but I'm managing.

I'm also looking at other things, items I used to assiduously avoid. Magazines, newspaper headlines, written instructions on the side of food packaging. I can manage fairly simple tasks on Sally's computer, and most importantly she's shown me how to turn the thing on and off properly. No more pulling the power cable out for me, no more grumpy messages from

Windows complaining about my reckless behavior. We took a trip to a shopping mall on the outskirts of Leeds on the second Saturday afternoon, and for the first time ever I could make sense of the notices and special offer adverts plastered around the place. I even managed to choose my lunch in Pizza Hut based on the descriptions in the menu rather than the pictures—another milestone.

But now, I have a real dilemma. I should be returning to Berwick tomorrow, and there's nothing I want to do more. But Cain is clearly not having that. Since his curt response to my first text, he's ignored any further overtures from me. I've sent him messages asking how things are going with the HSE, and he pointedly ignores me. I've tried to phrase my enquiries carefully—I appreciate it's a touchy subject—but to no avail. I clearly need to be more direct. With Sally's help I send him a text outlining my immediate plans.

Hi Cain. Hope you're fine. I'll be back Monday. Train due in at 5.20pm

That works, though not quite as I'd hoped. No gushing welcome, no offer of picking me up at the station. Instead…

Your choice. Taxi rank outside station. Will ask Phyllis to insure heating in flat is turned on.

Right then, that seems clear enough, even to one with my limited reading prowess. I could go back and take up residence in the flat over the office. I daresay I'd run into Cain pretty frequently, couldn't be avoided, but frankly, I'd rather stay in Bradford. Sally has to go back to school, but we still have the evenings to further my education. And in the daytime I can prowl the art galleries, this time lingering over the displays and other information telling me all about my favorite artists. I can't keep this up long term, and in any case I need to earn a living, whether here or in Berwick. I consider asking Mr Cartwright for my old job back, but cleaning for a living is not what I want anymore. I can do better now, I *need* to do better. I owe it to myself.

* * * *

Three weeks later, I'm still passing my days soaking up the cultural delights of my home town by day, and spending every evening with Sally. Her patience and support has been nothing short of awesome, her professionalism impeccable as she's put me through my paces and released me from my self-imposed isolation. The mysteries of the written word are now unlocked for my personal delight and delectation. I'm part of the club now, included — an insider. I like to think I've been a rewarding pupil, I really have made a supreme effort, in a way that I never did before. My determination and sheer will to crack this thing have driven me forward, created the energy I needed to get past my imagined roadblocks. And Sally has built on that, used my motivation, fanned the flames of it and pulled down the barriers I allowed to prevent me from learning for all this time. She has transformed my life, nothing short of that. I'll never forget it.

I've continued to text Cain, but he rarely replies, and when he does it's with just one or two words. He made no comment on my decision to remain in Yorkshire, though I did let him know. I keep in touch

The Three Rs

with Phyllis on the phone, though not recently as she's been off work for a few days. Her Stan is ill again. When I talk to her she sounds worried. I know she wants to retire and devote her time to him properly, and her latest recruit, young Jenna, fresh from business college in Newcastle and desperate for a local job is apparently to be Phyllis' ticket to freedom. She hopes to be able to train Jenna up over the coming months then hand over the reins.

How do I feel about that? I think it's fair to say my feelings are mixed. I love that I can read now, but it's all still so new to me. My confidence is growing, and I do genuinely enjoy reading stories, newspapers, even the side of my cereal box in the morning. But I couldn't contemplate a job that consists mainly of paperwork. That's just not me and never will be. I hope Phyllis' plan works out and Jenna makes the grade. For myself, I want to draw and paint. Even if I can't make my living as an artist, I definitely want to work with my hands. I keep coming back to plumbing — I really should get in touch with Beth, find out how she got started. I daresay it'll involve some sort of college course, and for that I'll need other exams. Literacy. Numeracy. The Three Rs. But with Sally's help I really do see this as a possibility now.

Maybe I'll re-start my formal education with something a bit lighter, for me at least. An art course, that'd be nice. Interesting. Something I could excel at. Perhaps I should get a brochure.

I'm in my tiny kitchen putting the finishing touches to a home-made pizza when my door buzzer sounds. Sally's coming round here this evening, I've agreed to feed her and later we'll do some of what she calls 'guided reading'. I'm looking forward to it, I really enjoy these sessions of ours. The voyage of discovery gets better all the time. Not unlike the discoveries I started to make with Cain, although the rewards are more cerebral than physical. I think about Cain a lot. All the time, if I'm honest. Almost everything reminds me of him in some way. Still, the future stretches a long way ahead, it's full of wonderful possibilities now, and my natural optimism hasn't deserted me. I'll find a way. If nothing else, the terms of James Parrish's will mean we're bound to each other for the next five years. He can't avoid me for ever.

I press the internal door release button then open my front door, leaving it ajar as I rush back to finish dressing my culinary masterpiece before I shove it in the oven to sizzle for twenty minutes.

"I opened a bottle of wine. You can have the glass this time. I'll just be a moment..." I call out to Sally, knowing she can look after herself while I finish up in here. There's the sound of the door closing softly as she comes into the flat, footsteps, the splash of wine swirling into my one and only wine glass. Then more footsteps as she comes over to the kitchen door.

"Expecting company, Abbie? Not me, I daresay..."

I spin around at the unexpected deep tone. *Cain!* He shoots out his free hand to save my pizza from an untimely end as I fumble with it in my confusion. I was thinking about him just a moment ago. In my astonishment I could almost convince myself I conjured him here. Now that *would* be a fine trick.

"Whoah, careful." He chuckles as he rights the teetering concoction of tomato, cheese and green peppers. "Looks tasty, you've been learning some new skills while you've been away. Will there be enough for three?"

"Three?" I look at him stupidly.

"You, me and whoever's joining us. Who is that, anyway? Sally?"

I'm totally floundering. What's he doing here? How does he know about Sally? Did I mention her by name? Maybe.

I collect my wits sufficiently to crouch down and slide the pizza into the oven before my attempts at juggling with it result in disaster. And the brief respite offers me an opportunity to think, to try to sort out this new and miraculous turn of events in my head.

Cain, here! Wow!

"I—yes. Sally. She's coming round after she finishes work. She should be here by now… We were going to eat and then…" I trail off, not sure if, or how I want to tell him what Sally and I have been getting up to. But it seems there's no need for me to ponder this matter further.

"Why didn't you tell me, Abbie?"

"Tell you?" No harm in playing for a bit of time, a bit more regrouping.

Cain turns, strolls back into my living room. He picks up my copy of *Harry Potter and The Philosopher's Stone* from the arm of my sofa, turns back to me. "Good book? Been reading it long?"

I shake my head slowly.

"No. Thought not. You've not been reading anything very long, have you, Abbie?" His tone is low, gentle. Kind. Not a hint of mockery there. He tilts his head to one side, his expression just hinting at a smile. And he waits for my answer.

I shake my head again as I follow Cain into my living room, wondering how he knows. How he worked it out. And I know that only one person could have told him. Phyllis. I'm surprised, maybe even a little shocked. Phyllis promised me, and I trusted her.

My sense of disappointment that she broke her word to me is perversely keen, given that I'm actually deliriously pleased to see Cain.

"Phyllis told you." It's a statement, not a question. "I asked her not to. She wasn't happy, but she did promise."

He shrugs, glancing down at the wine swirling in his glass before he catches and holds my gaze again. "She told me under duress. I was on the point of setting my lawyers onto you for sabotaging my business."

"What?" I'm staring at him, incredulous. *Sabotage! What the fuck would that be about?*

He chuckles again. "Yeah, I know. Ridiculous. I see that now. But then, I was short on explanations. And so fucking pissed off at you. Phyllis had no choice but to fill me in."

"Why? I don't understand. I told you it was a mistake. Why would you think…?" I'm babbling and I know it, so I stop, close my mouth firmly. He *did* think I'd hidden that letter deliberately, caused all that hassle with the Health and Safety Executive. He said as much on the phone. "But why did it take you so long to get that pissed off? It's been a month since I, since…"

"Since you neglected to tell me that the HSE were on my back and I needed to go and grovel to them?"

Always helpful, that's Cain.

"Yes. Since that."

He perches himself casually on the arm of my sofa, Harry Potter now displaced to the table, next to the depleted wine bottle. He takes a sip from his glass of my finest plonk. "I was convinced you *had* dropped me in it with the HSE on purpose, though I'd no idea why. That made it all the more bitter, I suppose. I'd trusted you." He hesitates, his smile wry as he observes me.

I'm sure my bafflement is perfectly obvious.

He continues, "I more than trusted you probably, and that made the sense of betrayal sharper. But you'd gone, and I was too busy trying to dig my way out of the shit to worry overmuch about dealing with you. I was livid, certainly, but as long as you kept your distance, I'd manage to keep my hands off you. Not entirely sure how I'd have reacted if—when—you eventually came back. But then, Phyllis discovered the entire 2012-13 accounts had been deleted from the system. The whole lot. And that did it. I knew you'd been working with them, you made a start on identifying our debtors, if you recall. Not that you did anything remotely resembling a good job."

His grin softens the words, his expression warm with sardonic humor. "So, Phyllis was going to go through it again. But she couldn't, because the spreadsheet where the invoices are recorded was mysteriously missing. And when she dug a bit further, she found the whole lot was gone. I don't know how you managed it, but you did."

I'm staring at him, open-mouthed. "But, I couldn't... I wouldn't know how. I mean, I didn't..."

"Oh, you did. I'm sure you did. Not on purpose, I'm sure of that too, now. But it *was* you. The spreadsheets were fine before you used them, and they were far from fine afterwards."

My stomach drops to the floor as I remember, suddenly recalling that awful moment when the screen went blank. I did think I'd lost the invoices. But I found them again, I know I did. I went back to the desktop, and navigated my way back to the accounts.

They were there, everything was still there, I'm sure. I try to explain that to Cain.

"I don't doubt you thought it was all fine. My guess is you were looking at the previous year's spreadsheets. Would you have known the difference?"

I shake my head. I wouldn't. Not then, and probably not now either. It never occurred to me to look carefully at the dates. The spreadsheet I found looked like the one I'd been working on, and that was good enough for me.

Cain takes another sip of his wine. *I rest my case, m'Lud.*

"So, as far as I could see when Phyllis told me what had happened, you'd done it again. Yet another example of you screwing up our business, deliberately destroying records. Inexplicable, but the facts seemed to speak for themselves. Taken on top of the business with Mrs Henderson, and the HSE, this was the last straw. I wanted it stopped. I wanted *you* stopped. As long as you had any involvement with Parrish Construction I could see this stuff continuing to happen. The only way Phyllis could prevent me from starting legal proceedings was to offer some other explanation. So she told me the truth. The truth *you* should have told me at the start. So, I repeat, why didn't you, Abbie?"

I sink into one of my two little dining chairs and reach for the small porcelain cup alongside the wine bottle. Some day I'll invest in more than one long stemmed wine glass, but for now I make do. Cain leans forward, hands me his glass as he takes the cup and pours himself a splash of wine. I offer a small, nervous smile before taking a sip.

I ignore his question. I have one of my own. Several, probably. "You were going to have me prosecuted? For what crime?" I still can't quite believe all of this.

He shrugs. "I'm not sure, that would have been up to the lawyers to decide. And no, probably not prosecuted. But if I could show that you had been deliberately attacking my business interests, I reckon I could have had grounds to challenge the will and get control of the firm again. That's what was in my mind, anyway, until Phyllis put an entirely new slant on everything."

I stare at him, horrified. That does make sense. He probably could have got rid of me that way. But he hasn't. And he doesn't seem to intend that any more. Instead, he's followed me here. He's come looking for me, looking for explanations.

Sure enough, he asks me again, "Why didn't you tell me all of this from the start? You'd have saved us both a lot of hassle." He's persistent, as ever, but his tone lacks that clipped edge to it which denotes Cain in Dom mode. This is my caring lover I'm talking to right now, the man I can confide in.

"Isn't it obvious? I was embarrassed. I thought you'd think I was ridiculous. Twenty-two years old and couldn't read. I *was* ridiculous. What'll happen now? About the accounts I mean?"

"Oh, that's sorted. Phyllis got one of those data retrieval teams out to have a look. They restored the files. I'm more interested in what's happening to you? Phyllis tells me you had plans to do a crash course or something. How's that going?"

I meet his eyes confidently now, a small but significant wisp of pride forming, taking root. I have good news on this matter and I've been dying to tell someone. It's so rare I have anything to boast about.

"It's gone well. Very well, actually. Sally's a literacy teacher, she knew how to help me. She'd been on at me for ages and I should have taken her up on her offer years ago. I don't know why I didn't."

He puts his cup of wine on the table, and with both palms frames my face. His smile is sexy, sensual, and I detect there the admiration I've been craving. "Maybe the time wasn't right for you before. And now it is. Now you have a reason, a use for it. Well, I hope you do. Was it me? Us? The business? What was it that spurred you on to do this now?"

I shrug as my wisp of pride curls seductively around, growing and swelling as for the first time I can lay claim to actually having achieved something, made a plan, set myself a goal and gone out and got it. "I suppose it was. All that. And—I'd had enough. Enough of being left out, feeling excluded, enough of hiding and lying and covering up. I wanted to be like everyone else. I wanted to be someone you could be proud of, not a liability."

"I was proud of you. I'm even more proud now. Now, I'm in awe. Can you forgive me?"

I glance up, meet his steady gaze—his eyes now warm and hinting at more heat to come. But I have no idea what he can mean. "Forgive you? What do you need forgiving for?"

"For being so dim I never realized something was wrong. You had me completely fooled, love. Looking back, I can see the clues were there. That night you went to bed with a headache rather than helping me with a tender? Was that one of your coping strategies?"

I nod. "More a defense mechanism than a coping strategy, but yes. I felt so guilty, lying to you like that."

"And when we went to the site in Morpeth and you pretended to read the health and safety notice before we went in? You *were* pretending, weren't you?"

Again I nod.

He shakes his head, his grin wry. "Christ, that was so dangerous. You need to know that stuff before you go on a building site. You were an accident waiting to happen, I shudder to think what the HSE will do if they ever hear about that. Thank God I kitted you out with steel toe-caps and a hard hat. At least that bit was taken care of. And that business over the sketch of the JCB, when I asked you to draw a sign with our company name on? You were so shirty about it. Was that somehow part of this too?"

I nod again. "It was. I couldn't remember what the words looked like to draw it from memory. And back at the office, when I copied it, I was so nervous, terrified of making a silly mistake, of being found out."

"You cried, as I recall."

"I was just so relieved by then to get it right. Nervous tension, I suppose."

"And Mrs Henderson?"

"I feel so embarrassed about that. What a stupid mistake to make. And I lost us all that money."

"Not as it turned out, eventually. And I should have realized when I looked at your notes. All those bloody pictures, for Christ's sake. But the numbers were correct, and I just thought the art was sort of you — quirky. I knew how much you loved drawing so it didn't strike me as that odd at the time."

"I was so concerned with getting the numbers right I never even gave a thought to what they represented."

"I can see that now. It all makes sense now. And I was such a bastard to you. Especially over you taking that week off to come here, but before that too. Browbeating you into working in the office. You said often enough that you didn't want to…"

"You weren't to know. I made sure of that."

He steps back, widening the space between us. I see the shift, subtle but unmistakeable, from tender lover to stern Dom. They are all part of the same complex, exciting package, but it's clear which is in the ascendancy now. My stomach clenches, and already my pussy is dampening in response.

"It scares me what a good liar you are. And that has to stop. Now. Here. And it goes without saying, there's a penalty to be paid." His tone is shot through with authority. With a promise of retribution soon to be delivered, firm and sharp and painful. The rational part of my brain is telling me to be wary, to back away. But the slutty submissive in me is relishing all of this, and the wetness in my pants increases as I imagine the sharp slap of his palm against my bare bottom. Please. Soon

"Yes, I know." My cunt is now thoroughly wet in anticipation. He must know, must be able to tell.

"You're ready then? You'll bend over, now and present that sweet arse of yours for the spanking you've so richly deserved?"

"Yes. Sir."

His curt nod is the only acknowledgment he offers. It's enough though. He continues, his voice cool, the words clipped, "Then, I want you to come back with me. To Berwick, to my house. You'll live with me, as my submissive. Is that what you want too? Would you do that, Abbie?"

I don't hesitate. "Yes. I'd like that. Sir." My voice is a whisper now, a breathy sigh of acceptance, of relief.

He smiles, and despite his Dom persona which does not slip so much as a fraction, the smile is warm and reaches his eyes. "Good. I wasn't sure you'd feel able to agree, at least not at once. Particularly after everything I said to you, after everything that's happened. I thought you might require a little more — persuading."

He regards me for a few moments. "I'm going to want you naked, Abbie. Very soon. And from the way your nipples are swelling under that blouse, I suspect that's what you want too. Am I right?" By way of illustrating his point he reaches for my left nipple, rubs the pad of his thumb firmly over the hardening peak.

I close my eyes, loving the sensuous caress at the same time as I'm anticipating the sharp pain to surely come as he squeezes or twists. I see no point in denying how he makes me feel. "Yes, Sir. But — I'm expecting someone."

"I know. The someone you thought you were letting in when I arrived. I can see we'll need to be sociable but first, I have more questions. First, we talk?"

His hand drops from my breast, and I manage to bite back my groan of disappointment. I know better than to protest though. If Cain in Dom mode says we're going to talk, then that's what will be happening. He pulls out one of my dining chairs and gestures for me to sit, then takes the other chair facing me. He reaches for my hand across the table top, the wine now abandoned by both of us. His expression softens, though only slightly. It's enough though for me to glimpse the tender lover again. This is the Cain who wants to understand me, who cares and wants to help. The Cain I can tell anything to.

"I want, need to understand how this all happened. You're talented, bright. So bright you fucking dazzle me. And I'm guessing you're not dyslexic as you've made enough progress to tackle Harry Potter in the space of a month. So…?"

He raises one commanding eyebrow, then simply waits. He's silent, not pressing me. I can take my time. I draw in a deep breath, study our linked hands for a few seconds. Then I raise my eyes to meet his, and start to tell my story.

"I was ill. When I was a child. Leukaemia."

I'm aware of his slight hiss of surprise. The Big L. Serious stuff, then and now. Having started, I rush on with my explanation, "I was in and out of hospital for two years. I hardly ever went to school. I was too ill to get much out of the home tuition they tried to provide, both from my school and from Jimmy's where I spent most of my time."

"Jimmy's?"

"St James' Hospital, in Leeds. The regional center for childhood leukaemia. Getting well was the priority, the only priority. I managed to do that, with a little help from the staff at Jimmy's, obviously, but by then the damage was done. I was so far behind the rest of my class I just gave up."

"Leukaemia. Shit. It must have been a dreadful time. For you and your family."

"It was just me and my mum. And yes, she was desperately worried. I can see that now, though at the time I thought she fussed a lot. I remember she cried when I got the all clear. That confused me. But school, education, none of that ever mattered. It just wasn't on our horizon. Me being alive and healthy was all she cared about, and that sort of rubbed off on me."

He nods slowly, a slight frown on his face. "I can understand that."

"Me too, up to a point. But it wouldn't do, would it. Not forever. I had to change, had to sort myself out. And Sally was my solution. My salvation I suppose. Always there, always waiting. Once I'd confronted my demons, made arrangements with Sally, I felt the end was in sight. I could do it, I knew I could. And for the first time ever, I actually wanted to. I didn't want to put it off. I'd never been so determined, I was actually making plans to learn, setting aside the time. I had to go through with it, I just had to."

"I can see that too. You were right to do it, whatever I said. Whatever I threatened."

"I hoped you'd understand. That I could make you understand. Afterwards."

"I do. You have. But for the record, I want you to know I would have understood all along."

I squeeze his hand in acknowledgment. Phyllis was so sure he would, and I think, deep down, I knew it too. But it would have been just too humiliating to talk about back then whereas now, in retrospect, it doesn't seem so bad. Hindsight is indeed a wonderful thing, for many reasons.

"I was pissed off, so bloody mad I could have strangled you at first, but I never stopped missing you. Oscar too, though he doesn't say much."

"I've missed Oscar."

"Abbie, your bottom's already going to be very, very sore for all the lying you've been doing. You really don't want to make matters any worse."

"Oh, okay then. I've missed you too. A bit. Sir."

"I'll settle for that, on this occasion. And in due course I'll be expecting to see you naked and kneeling on the floor, ready for your spanking. But first, get over here. I think I'd like you to start playing the sexy little sub again if you don't mind."

I don't need telling twice. In moments I'm straddling his lap, and this time I frame his face with my palms. The slight roughness of his cheeks feels sensual and deliciously male against my hands as I lean in to kiss him. I run my tongue along the seam of his lips and he responds to my silent request. As his mouth opens, I slide my tongue inside to coil around his. He sucks, nibbles, and I'm no longer sure which of us is the instigator now. Not that it matters. I wrap my arms around his neck, holding on for dear life as I deepen the kiss.

"I thought we were having pizza. And in any case you seem to have started early. Will there be enough of him left over for me?"

Cain catches me as I whirl round. Sally! I'd completely forgotten about her for the moment.

"Your neighbor downstairs let me in. And the door to the flat was left off the latch. So, this would be your Mr Parrish, I assume?"

My Mr Parrish. Yes, sounds about right.

"Yes, yes it is." I scramble off his lap, keen to establish perhaps a modicum of decorum. I glance back and note with mixed feelings the bulge of his erection straining the front of his jeans. From the knowing grin on Sally's face, she's seen it too. Could hardly miss it, really. Still, I try for polite.

"Cain, this is Sally. My friend, who's been teaching me."

Cain stands, shifting a little awkwardly but managing, just about. He gets full marks for fortitude, I'll grant him that.

He extends his hand to Sally. "I'm delighted to meet you. I was hoping I would. I'm wondering if you might be able to teach me a few tricks. Abbie's coming back to Berwick with me, and she'll need to keep up the practice with her reading. I intend to help." He turns to me. "Provided that's all right with you, of course."

This is one of the things I've come to appreciate most about Cain. He's always sensitive to my deeper feelings, tuning in effortlessly to the uncertainties I find so difficult to share. Right now I can't contain my silly grin. I might just do a little tap dance on my table.

"Thank you. I'd love that."

Sally seems to think it's a decent plan too. "Good. It's important to keep at it now you've started to make real progress. Keep practicing." She turns to Cain. "I can show you a few tricks and techniques. You're not leaving straight away are you?"

She's looking from one to the other of us now, one eyebrow raised expectantly. I glance at Cain. I never asked how long he'd be staying. If he has to leave straight away, get back for the business, there's no way I'm being left behind. He seems to be in no hurry though.

"We're fine. Abbie's got a pizza in the oven which smells like it really needs to come out sometime soon. And I was hoping to stay for breakfast at least. And since we're in the area, there's a church in Leeds I seem to remember you wanted to look at, Abbie?"

Sally seems content with that. She doesn't turn a hair as I throw my arms around Cain's neck and plant a noisy kiss on his mouth. She even manages not to react as he pats my bottom — not especially gently — no doubt to remind me we have unfinished business to attend to as soon as we're alone.

Sally chuckles as she dumps a tin of alphabetti spaghetti on the table. "Great. And I brought this.

Thought it might come in useful, and it's better than the magnetic ones because we can eat it when we're done."

Cain, to his credit, doesn't even bother asking. He just gives my bottom one last firm caress before heading for the kitchen to rescue my pizza.

Chapter Twenty-One

That was almost nine months ago now. Nine months that have flown by, like they do when you're having fun. Cain and I are good, better than good. He was true to his word, helping me to get better and better at reading. His choice of reading matter might not have been to everyone's taste, but I have no serious objections. My horizons have been widened, my reading has improved in leaps and bounds now that the floodgates are opened and our collection of erotic literature is impressive by any standards, with or without pictures.

Phyllis retired three months ago, having decided that the supremely capable and efficient Jenna is fit to be left in sole charge. I agree. I do drop in occasionally, but the office was never my domain, never my comfort zone. Same goes for the flat above. Jenna needed a place to live, it made perfect sense. We let the flat to her— she moved in on the same day I handed in my keys to the housing trust in Bradford. Burning all my bridges at once. I've never regretted it.

I live at Cain's, and have no intention of moving on. My stuff is everywhere, next to his. Even when he annoys me, which I swear he does deliberately, I only storm as far as the spare room. Cain does not allow me to remain there long. And the spankings make it all so worthwhile. Oscar seems to approve, and now he's taken to shadowing me rather than Cain.

Our sex is delightful. Frequent, intense and deliciously kinky. Cain is the perfect lover for me, tender, dominant, demanding. He understands me, knows what I need and never disappoints. I adore him. And the truly wonderful thing is, he seems to love me too. He must do, he tells me often enough.

I enrolled for an art class at the high school, which takes place every Tuesday evening. From there I've graduated to weaving, textiles and pottery. I've never been especially keen on photography, but I'm beginning to think I might give that a go soon. Now that I can manage the intricacies of uploading my pictures onto the computer. My own computer that is. A funky little laptop that Cain bought me for my birthday and which is now open in front of me at the breakfast table as I nibble my toast and check out the forthcoming attractions at The Maltings, the arts center in Berwick, which offers a theater and a cinema to the local culture vultures. Of which I've become one, how amazing is that?

Cain ambles in from the hallway, today's post in his hand. He sifts through the envelopes, sorting out junk from the real stuff. He drops two envelopes in front of me, one white, one brown. Both look official. In the past, my heart would have sunk at the sight of them. I'd have debated with myself whether to open them now or later. Not anymore. I seize the brown one first. I've been expecting this. It's from the DVLA, Driver and Vehicle Licencing Authority in Swansea. My provisional license.

Cain convinced me I needed to pass my driving test if I'm to make myself properly useful to the firm. I need to be able to get around our different sites and jobs, making sketches, meeting with clients. I have a knack for charming new business out of people, whether I'm selling them a patio, an extension or a family portrait. As well as doing promotional stuff for Parrish Construction, I've also managed to sell a few pictures of my own. I feel I'm paying my way. And Cain's right, being able to drive will give me an independence I now crave. I'm not looking forward to the theory part of the test — I don't suppose anyone does, but at least now I reckon I can handle it. I open the envelope from Swansea and admire my lovely little credit card sized picture license, so symbolic of the new me and all the wonderful opportunities now opening up.

Cain grins at me as he sits back down to finish his black coffee before we leave for work. He knows full well how much being able to drive will mean to me. I smile back, no need for words. We're going to Rothbury again today, to price up a refurbishment of a school that's being converted for residential use. It's a big project — I know Cain's keen to land it if we can. I'm hoping to have a chance to call in at the converted mill while we're down that way, make some sketches of the finished item now it's fully occupied with new tenants and owners.

I look at the white envelope now. My name, and Cain's address — these days my address too — is printed neatly on the front. It's a thick, heavy envelope, expensive paper. I slide my fingers under the flap to open it and pull out two handwritten sheets. I'm surprised, I didn't expect handwriting, not in such a formal looking package. The ink is a bright blue, vivid against the creamy white of the page. I'll need to concentrate, handwriting is more difficult to read than print. I glance at Cain, but he's busy scanning our electricity bill. He's scowling, but I'm unsympathetic. He shouldn't have so many gadgets. I return my attention to my own affairs. Flattening out the sheets, slowly, carefully, I start to read.

Two lines in I stop, and flick the pages over to look at the signature. My heart lurches in disbelief. It can't be…

I gasp, drop the sheets as though they were on fire. They flutter to the floor. Cain glances up at me then does a double take.

"Abbie, are you all right? You look ashen, like you've seen a ghost."

My hands are shaking, I glare at the sheets lying innocently by my feet, make no move to retrieve them. I raise my eyes to Cain's, his expression worried now as he reaches to take my hands in his.

"I have. I have seen a ghost. Or at least, I've seen a letter written by one." I shake my head in disbelief. This has to be some sort of a hoax. A sick joke. I'm astonished that I managed to form any sort of coherent answer. I'm totally stunned by the name I saw and recognized instantly at the end of the letter.

"Abbie?" Cain is leaning down to retrieve my letter. He stiffens as he looks at it properly for the first time, as he sees the same name I saw.

Nevertheless, I state the obvious, "It's from James. Your uncle James." I'm staring at Cain, wide-eyed. "How? How could that be?"

Cain studies the first sheet, before handing the letter back to me. "I have no idea, love. It certainly looks like his handwriting though. Can I see the envelope?"

I place the letter carefully on the table now, reluctant to touch it, but mindful I should be at least respectful. However bizarre, this does seem as though it could be genuine. I pass the envelope to Cain. He studies the front, turns it over to look at the reverse. "It's franked by a firm of solicitors in Edinburgh. Looks as though they sent it."

"But, it's from James. Isn't it?" I'm looking from Cain to the handwritten letter and back again. I'm not given to fanciful notions, not even slightly, but the back of my neck is prickling and I swear if I turn my head at this moment I'll see an elderly gentleman standing behind me. I never met James Parrish, would not know him by sight, but I sense his presence now. Here in this room, in his cozy kitchen. With us.

"Do you want me to read it, love?"

Cain makes no move to take the sheets, but I can tell he's curious. Baffled, like me. But we're both desperate to know what this letter says. What it means. It must be something to do with the business, has to be. I'm on the point of shoving the letter at Cain, but I don't. James Parrish wrote to me. This came addressed to me, not Cain. He wrote to me for a reason, the least I can do is read his letter.

I shake my head, mumbling my thanks, then take a deep breath as I pick up the now slightly crumpled sheets and carefully, respectfully, smooth them out again on the table top. And I start to read James Parrish's words once more, slowly. Out loud.

"My Dearest Abigail

Firstly, I trust that my letter finds you in good health, and that you are happy. I appreciate that the last few months will not have been easy for lots of reasons. It may have been a turbulent time for you, but I know you'll cope. Have coped. I've probably caused you massive upheaval, but please be assured I meant nothing but the best for you.

Secondly, I hope that you are reading this yourself. If you are, that means my meddling just might have paid off. You're a bright girl, Abigail, lovely, vibrant. You can't spend the rest your life in the shadows. That's just a waste and I never could abide waste. Ask the lad, if you and that nephew of mine are still on speaking terms. If you're not reading this yourself, it is my fondest hope that one day soon, you will. That would make an old man very happy.

I owe you an explanation. Cain too. If you and he are in touch, please would you consider passing this letter on to him? If you'd prefer not to, though, I do understand. It was never my intention to invade your privacy. I left instructions with my solicitors that this letter was to be forwarded to you, wherever you were living, exactly one year from my death. I want you to understand my actions, and ideally I'd like Cain to understand too. You have my letter – what you do with its contents is now a matter for your judgment.

I left you a substantial inheritance in my will. I hope you've found some good use for it. I asked my lawyers to make absolutely certain that Cain couldn't bully you into giving it up. He'd try, I know he would. And he can be very forceful when he wants to be. He's determined and he usually gets his way. But not this time. I instructed my lawyers to consider every possibility, every route he might try to take to get his business back, and to block it. Time will tell if they succeeded.

You will have met Cain by now I'm sure, and I want to assure you that despite everything, he's a good lad. He looks after those he cares about. That included me, and I'm *grateful to him for all he did, shoring up the business in my later years when I was in failing health. I hope it can or has come to include you too, and forcing you into each other's orbit for a while might have had the desired effect. He's a good friend to have.*

Cain will have been angry to learn I'd left most of the business he worked so hard to build to someone else. A stranger at that, at least as far as he knew. I'm sorry I messed him about, messed both of you about, but I really felt I had no option, that ultimately this was for the best. I was meddling, but I couldn't help myself. Blame it on the vagaries of old age. And please pass on my apologies to Cain if you are in a position to.

But I'm not making myself clear, and I really should. This is not the first time I've meddled in your life. Although we've never met, we've been aware of each other for many years now. I still vividly recall the day I received a letter from the bone marrow screening trust telling me that preliminary tests suggested I might be a tissue match for a child needing a transplant. They invited me in for further tests. I went, of course. And the rest is history. You'll realize by now who I am, and perhaps why I've always taken such a keen interest in you, in your welfare. I didn't save your life, the doctors did that. But I played a part, and in return I won a sort of immortality. I'm dead now, but you're still there, my bone marrow swilling around, doing whatever it does inside you. Keeping you healthy. In time, maybe you'll have children. I love that thought.

Donors are not supposed to have any information regarding recipients of bone marrow, but I had my sources and my ways of finding out. I kept in touch, always from a distance, careful never to intrude or interfere. Until now, of course. I was so relieved, so pleased when I learnt you were free of cancer. It was my triumph, too, in a way, and made it all so worthwhile. There was a happy ending. We both came through it and in my mind from then on I was linked to you forever. I've always told myself you're not my daughter, and of course you aren't. But still, you are the closest I'll ever get. I care deeply about you, I always have. I feel a responsibility toward you. I always wanted the best for you.

As you grew up, I made it my business to keep track of you. I worried about you, first about your health, then later about your welfare. I wanted to know you were safe, doing well. And as it became clear to me that despite having beaten your illness your difficulties with reading were holding you back, I hated knowing that. It frustrated me after all you'd already been through. I wanted to help but I didn't know how. I was even more concerned about you after your mother died. You were all alone then. I wished you lived nearer. I considered moving to Yorkshire myself, but my health wouldn't stand it. I'd have been no use to you. Then I hit on my little inheritance scheme. I believed I could grab your attention. I thought if I gave you an incentive, some reason to need to read, and a way to change your life, then you'd do something about it. I knew you'd be well able to do it yourself, but I thought Cain might help, once he calmed down. As I've mentioned, he gets things done. With my lawyers' help I locked you together, at least for a while, and I hope he remembered his manners eventually.

I'm not a well man myself these days. The doctors tell me I have heart failure and need to take it easy. I do, with Cain's help, but even so I doubt I'll be around for that much longer. So I've instructed my lawyers make sure the provisions in my will are all tied up nice and tight. Now I sit back to wait, and trust that neither of you disappoints me.

I hope it worked out.
Yours, with love
James
P.S. If you do see Cain, tell him I expect him to take good care of Oscar."

About the Author

Until 2010, Ashe was a director of a regeneration company before deciding there had to be more to life and leaving to pursue a lifetime goal of self-employment.

Ashe has been an avid reader of women's fiction for many years—erotic, historical, contemporary, fantasy, romance—you name it, as long as it's written by women, for women. Now, at last in control of her own time and working from her home in rural West Yorkshire, she has been able to realise her dream of writing erotic romance herself.

She draws on settings and anecdotes from her previous and current experience to lend colour, detail and realism to her plots and characters, but her stories of love, challenge, resilience and compassion are the conjurings of her own imagination. She loves to craft strong, enigmatic men and bright, sassy women to give them a hard time—in every sense of the word.

When she's not writing, Ashe's time is divided between her role as resident taxi driver for her teenage daughter, and caring for a menagerie of dogs, cats, rabbits, tortoises and a hamster.

Ashe Barker loves to hear from readers. You can find her contact information, website details and author profile page at http://www.totallybound.com.

Totally Bound Publishing

Made in the USA
San Bernardino, CA
11 October 2017